The Stone Cypher

Tormod Cockburn

A “Mysterious Scotland” novel.

Set on Orkney

Mys.Scot

First published by Mys.Scot Media in 2022

Print ISBN: 978-1-915612-05-2

E-Book ISBN: 978-1-915612-04-5

Cover photo credit: Mark Ferguson, licensed by Canva

For updates and free books we invite you to join our Readers Syndicate. Either click the logo above in a digital copy or see details at the back of the book.

Mys.Scot

Dedication

Dedicated to the memory of CS Lewis

Also by Tormod Cockburn

The Bone Trap
The Ness Deception
The Stone Cypher

Chapter 1

Scottish Centre for Ion Beam Research.
Orkney – present day

A heavily suited figure walks deeper into the largest gun barrel in human history. Glancing sideways, he can see a compressed spaceman; his own distorted image reflected back at him from the walls of the gleaming silver tunnel. Reaching the end of the apparatus, he stands and looks at an area dense with cables, sensors and instrument panels. Squatting beside one part of the machine, he runs a gloved hand over an intricate nesting of titanium circles.

'Give me a time check, Control.'

'Tech, we're firing in twelve minutes, fourteen seconds.'

He taps this information into the keypad over his left wrist and watches the time clock start ticking down on his visor screen. Forcing his eyes to see past the display, he focuses again on the machine. 'I think I see the problem, Control. The lens cap isn't fully retracted from the targeting beam generator.' He leans closer to the instrument. 'Something small in the mechanism. Looks organic.'

After the briefest pause. 'Project leader asks if you can fix it.'

'Yeah, I'm slipping it back manually. Gimme a second.'

He reaches into a pocket for a small canister of compressed air, squirting puffs of inert gas onto the mechanism. The offending particle blows away on the third puff, and he hears the whirl of a small motor as a diamond prism slides into view.

'Meant to be a clean room down here, people. You all need to learn to wipe your boots', he says to anyone listening. 'Stand by for manual reset.'

He flips open a control panel near his right hand and presses a series of small illuminated buttons. The prism retreats into place behind a lens cover that closes with a satisfying series of tiny clicks.

'Okay, Control. That's the reset. Calibrate the beam confinement for me.'

'Tech, confirming red light has gone to green. Standing by to recalibrate the beam now. Please confirm you are clear of the apparatus.'

He is already standing but eases himself back another metre. 'I'm clear, Control.'

'Calibration running. Completion in nine minutes and thirty seconds.'

He watches the prism reappear. 'The lens mechanism is running freely, Control. We're looking good. But if calibration fails, you'll need to kill the count. I'm returning to the hatch.'

'Acknowledged, Tech.'

He has eleven minutes to walk half of one kilometre. On a beach, he'd do it in a leisurely five minutes. In the belly of the machine, encumbered by the suit, he'll have to take more care.

'Tech. Safety Leader asks if you need us to suspend the test?'

'That's a negative, Control. I'll be clear in a couple of minutes.' His mind races over the work squandered if they have to implement a full reset. It has taken a week since the last test firing to prepare the facility for another experiment. 'Control, please confirm we're not about to waste sixty hours of my life?'

The response is delayed, and he imagines the hasty conversation going on across the control room. But he knows what Harley's reaction will be. 'Tech. Countdown is still running, and we're at nine minutes, fifty-four seconds.'

'Acknowledged.' He picks up the pace now. The illuminated entrance to the access hatch grows closer with each laborious stride. All around him, the machine is starting to hum as immense batteries prepare to deliver their combined charge through the lens of the particle cannon. Up and down the mile-long corridor, the lights begin to dim as the station prepares to deliver maximum voltage to the ignition system. As he reaches the hatch, his heart rate is elevated, not because of his repressed claustrophobia but simply out of respect for the seismic amount of power that will surge down this corridor in a few minutes. He swipes a card over the exit button and waits for the hatch to unlock, then slide to one side. Nothing happens, so he swipes again.

'Control, I'm at the hatch. I'm facing a locked door down here.' He can hear the tension in his voice.

He waits a few seconds and then tries again. 'Control. I need immediate evacuation. Arm the hatch, please.' A burst of static crackles on the other end of the comm. Instead of a voice on the line, he hears a cacophony of far-away shouting.

He remembers something and fumbles in a pocket over his left breast. 'Shit.' He taps his other pockets, searching for his manual override keys. The pouch where they usually rest is empty. He leans against the door. 'Okay, I'm calling it. Safety. Kill the countdown.'

Still nothing, just distant voices falling over each other. Then a pause, a scream, a female scream, and a male voice elevated over everyone else.

'Harley, can you hear me? Kill the bloody count. I'm stuck in here.'

The shouting begins again, and he feels panic lurch inside him. His mind scans for an escape route. Without his emergency keys, this hatch has no other manual override. The door sits close to the beam generator and is flush with the walls. There's no shelter here from the energy cascade that will shortly fill the chamber.

He hears the clang of a metal door closing further down the tunnel. He remembers the emergency exit and realises someone might be trying to reach him. But it is seven hundred metres away, and he's not sure he can make it. On impulse, he decides to run.

He's a fit man and built for running but not in a suit weighing almost fifty kilos. His precious seconds ebb away as he speed-shuffles down the silver tube. Soon he is panting, labouring every breath and quite unable to speak. It seems to take forever to reach the second exit hatch, and as he runs, he sees something is missing. Just before the hatch, he pauses at a location where nozzles set into the walls push nitrogen jets to converge on a single spot. Earlier today, his team inserted a titanium probe in preparation for firing. He clearly remembers positioning the silver orb to hang suspended in the machine's gravity-defying grasp. But now it's gone. He scans the floor for it, assuming a jet has malfunctioned, allowing the tennis ball-sized sphere to fall. He can't see it and doesn't have time to look. He glances at his visor display. He only has forty-five seconds until the targeting process is complete, sending the ion pulse hurtling down the chamber. Forty-five seconds until his life is over.

Stepping up to the hatch, he grasps the jockey wheel recessed into the door. Behind this lies a short corridor, another hatch, a flight of stairs, and finally, a door leading outside. To guarantee his safety, he needs to clear all the obstacles. The wheel begins to turn, but a force resists him. He pushes back his visor and peers at the spindle of the wheel. For an instant, another man's face appears on the other side of the hatch window, then is gone. He twists the wheel again, gaining a few centimetres of movement before it snaps back to a closed position. A dense thudding sound from the far end of the tube means the first of the targeting beams has fired. He feels a gasp of anguish escape from him as the seconds tick away. A second distant thud. Leaping at the wheel again, he throws his weight against the metal. He tugs with every fibre of his strength as the sound of the third burst fires down the chamber. Moments later, he's enveloped in a brilliant flash.

The chamber fills with volleys of noise as the machine begins to wind down from its exertion. Another sound, a softer sound. That of a heavy protective suit slipping to its knees, lingering in the upright for a moment, then toppling lifelessly to the floor.

Chapter 2

Brodgar Stone Circle – Orkney.
8 weeks before present day

The fluorescent glow dances across the surface of the stone like a frenzied butterfly. Euan eases off the clamp a little so the head of the theodolite moves more freely. That's it! The beam of light picks out the small nickel coin he's glued to the stone's surface with a piece of adhesive. In a little while, he'll make sure he's removed every last scrap of the tack, because Mrs Morrison doesn't like it when he leaves marks on her stones.

Thin shafts of light leap up to illuminate the west sou' west side of the stones. These meagre beams from the headlamps of a distant car flit from stone to stone, giving the appearance of the monument itself coming to life. Euan freezes. It isn't that he resents this interruption to his work. Simply - he doesn't like cars. Besides, the whole point of working in the summer twilight is to allow him to work without interruption. So he waits as the car winds its way down the Howe road. It will be four minutes until it passes the mouth of the causeway, and he counts the seconds until the vehicle reaches its nearest point, then begins its retreat in the direction of Finstown.

With the car gone, he gets back to work. If the tack has slipped, he'll have to walk the twenty-six paces to the stone and start the whole process again. He'll need to set the striking plate on the true vertical, calibrating the beam the way Mr Robertson showed him. He gently taps the instrument, making the beam wobble just a fraction. Good.

The reflective surface blinks back at him. The plate is still in place. He crouches beneath the instrument and checks it is level. Tonight is a rare night, almost entirely still, and his plumbline hangs neatly over the web of overlapping cords at his feet. He takes care stepping between them. Each cord wraps tightly around one stone and loops back the sixty metres across the circle towards its immediate opposite neighbour. It's a simple method allowing him to identify the true centre of the stone circle. Working from that spot, he grasps the theodolite again, swinging its head to the left until he finds what he's looking for. 'The Stones of Dia', a formation several miles away. The coloured tip of the beam isn't visible at this distance across the moor, but the thin pink line it sketches across tendrils of mist is enough to secure the measurement. He fiddles a little until he has the beam centred on the stones, then takes a reading. Satisfied, he stoops to rummage in his daysack, pulling out a hardback notebook. He turns to a half-completed page at the back of the book and scribbles. *#8,351.2 degrees.* He keeps a forefinger in the book and takes the reading again. This time it's *#8,351.1 degrees.* He flicks open the book and jots down the number. Another. Back to the instrument. *#8,351.3 degrees.* He frets about the difference for a moment, then, remembering that some of the stones may have moved over the years, decides an average will suffice.

Euan had already made up his mind not to look at the vector tables; the sheets where he has calculated the distances to the far-away stones and the angle of deviation using an ordnance survey map. Terry once told him he should always delay a treat, postponing gratification until a task is complete. Even so, a slight tremor rises somewhere inside him. He knows most of those tables off by heart. An hour from now, he'd planned to sit with a calculator and factor in the orbital calculations. If he's right, and he's nearly always right, he'll have the last piece of the puzzle. Fear isn't an emotion he's used to, but his internal tremor again, more potent this time. He pauses to analyse this feeling. What is this instinct? Its cause? Its effect? Then he realises he's already done the calculation in his head. He already knows what the numbers mean. This piece of work, this piece of the puzzle, is now complete.

Immediately he starts to pack away his kit, gathering it in his arms while he lollops over the heather to the target stone. Gently he prizes off the coin, pulling out a pair of tweezers and picking at the surface until the last scrap of tack is gone. He twists his torch beam in different directions, confirming he's got it all. Then, systematically, over the course of an hour, he weaves back and forth between the stones, wrapping the cord back onto wooden jigs.

The sun's rays are strengthening again when he returns to his bike. It lies where he'd left it, chained to the information board. It's attached it to the back of the board, just in case anyone came to the stones and wanted to read about them. He stands looking at the display for several long minutes, taking each one of the long-familiar words in his mouth, articulating them soundlessly. He feels a sudden rush of annoyance. The board is all wrong. He rereads the words, tracing them with his finger to ensure he understands them. Now he knows these words are mistaken because the numbers have spoken to him.

He retrieves the padlock and chain, stowing them carefully in his bag. He's never liked words. Words online or in magazines are okay. They might tell you something. But when people use words, they might say one thing when they often mean something entirely different. He nods decisively. Numbers are better. Numbers don't lie. A number nine is always a number nine. And it isn't a number eight some days, just because it's in a bad mood. And it doesn't turn into a ten, just to annoy you. You always know where you are with numbers.

He experiences a moment of sadness as he looks at his book for what might be the last time. Brushing dust from its cover, he slides it into an envelope and seals the flap. He'd planned to send the book to Dundee, but as further evidence that history is running to some pre-determined clock, he has discovered the man from the magazine is coming to him. When the time is right, Mrs Morrison will gift this man his book, and then the next and final stage of the puzzle will begin.

His materials gathered, Euan mounts his bike. He checks left and right, then checks again, and sets off, back off along the causeway towards Stromness.

Chapter 3

Mainland Scotland - Four weeks before present day

Gill McArdle stared up at the angry face of the mountain, wondering how much further he had to go. The woman was getting away from him. Her long, brown, athletic legs powering from boulder to boulder as if this was just some giant staircase. At the bottom of the ascent, he'd told her to go first so that trailing behind her, he could act as her safety guy. But being honest with himself, he actually wanted to observe where she placed her feet. But now she'd rounded a rockface at the top of the climb and disappeared. Deflated, he paused and looked around him. The view from here over the mountains they'd already climbed was dramatic. Looking back, he could feel the bulk of *Meall Garbh* behind him, while beyond that, the peak of *Meall Greigh* swirled out of a pocket of low cloud. The looming presence of these mountains seemed to exert a gravitational force on him, making his head swim. He knew if he dropped his guard, he could slip into thin air, bouncing a few times off unforgiving grey schist with nothing to stop him until he crashed into the valley floor.

He turned his face upward and tried to decide the best route. To his irritation, his phone rang, and he glanced at the screen in case it was his walking partner checking on his progress. But it was just the office, so he cancelled the call.

Picking his way upward, a mixture of fear and exertion drained the strength from his limbs. Coming at last to the place where the woman had rounded the rock face, he clung to a handhold and studied the next obstacle ahead of him.

To the right was sheer vertical rock - the body of the mountain, tall and unforgiving. To his immediate left and straight ahead lay empty space, decorated in the distance by wispy white clouds against a blue sky. The next footsteps he needed to place were along a narrow strip of compressed mud, traversing the base of the rock and disappearing round and out of sight. Beyond that, he couldn't see what awaited him. He did know that if he missed his footing, he'd embrace a vertical drop of about forty metres. He took a deep breath and set his left foot onto the ledge. He was just in the process of swinging up his right foot when his phone rang again.

This time he just held tight and waited for the call to ring out. Both arms clinging to the rock and his face pressed against it. Wind tugged at his waterproof, and gravity whispered murderous threats in his ear. When the ringing stopped again, he took another breath and edged forward.

Finally, he emerged onto a safe platform of abundant heather that ran gradually uphill to the summit of *An Stuc*, about one hundred metres away. She was sitting waiting for him, her chest rising and falling while she recovered from her exertions.

'That wasn't too bad in the end', she said.

'The guidebook described this as a moderate scramble', gasped Gill. 'We should have had ropes.'

'You think?' She shrugged. 'The path was a mile wide.'

He filled his lungs again. 'If I wanted to die, I could probably manage to do it during office time.'

She leaned forward to kiss his cheek. 'You're making a fuss.'

‘What’s ahead of us?’ said Gill, pointing at the next mountain.

‘An easy descent of *An Stuc*, then there’s just *Ben Lawers* to go.’

‘It looks very steep and pointy from here’, said Gill. ‘The way a kid would draw a mountain.’

‘The map says there’s a clear path. If we stick to that, we’ll be fine.’

‘Good plan’, said Gill, studying the steep drops surrounding the mountain ahead of them.

Just then, it was the turn of the woman’s phone to ring. She dug it out of a zipped pocket and answered. ‘Ahmed’. She glanced at Gill while she listened to the caller. ‘Yeah, we’re together. He didn’t pick up because he was having a wee cuddle with a rock.’ She nodded. ‘Sure. I’ll put him on.’

Gill steadied his breathing and took the phone. ‘Morning, Cassy. Only you could be that persistent on a Monday morning.’

‘Hey, Gill. Really sorry to disturb you on your day off.’

‘It’s okay. We’re just risking our lives doing what Salina calls “a little, light walking”. What’s up?’

‘I’ve got a lady from Historic Scotland on the line. She’s got wind of the fact you’re on Orkney this week, and to say she’s keen to have a word would be an understatement.’

Gill rubbed his face, chasing away the trauma of the climb. ‘Yeah, I remember her. We spoke a couple of months back. Give me a couple of seconds, then put her through.’

Cassy signed off, and Gill had a moment to find his professional voice. Then he heard a click on the line as the call transferred. 'Hello. Gill McArdle.'

'Hi. Juliette Morrison here. You called me a few weeks ago asking about sea erosion around Skara Brae.'

'Sure. You're the archaeological coordinator on Orkney. How's it all going?'

'We're just wrapping up this summer's dig', she said. 'And we've uncovered something unusual.'

Gill was aware Historic Scotland used the summer months to pursue a long-running archaeological program across the Orcadian mainland. The last few years had been a Neolithic bonanza, with new settlements uncovered and a long list of significant finds. 'I like unusual', he said. 'What can you tell me about it?'

'I'd rather show it to you in-situ if that's okay. Rumour has it you're visiting this week?'

Gill rubbed his neck. 'Yes. I'm back in the office tomorrow, and then I've got an appointment at ScoCion on Wednesday. I'll check my itinerary and get back to you if that's okay.'

'I'm hoping I don't embarrass myself. The item we've found is an anomaly. But we might be missing something obvious. It would benefit from a fresh pair of eyes.'

They exchanged contact details, and Gill rang off.

He sat for a few more moments and waited while Salina studied the peak of *Ben Lawers* through her binoculars. 'You're right', she said. 'The path is really narrow.'

Gill groaned.

'Well, we either press forward or go back the way we came.'

Gill thought about this offer and shuddered. 'Then it's onward and upward. My conditions are simple. If we survive this, you buy me a couple of pints of real ale in Kenmore.'

Two days later, Gill exhaled a deep breath as his plane finally touched down on Orkney. The twin-prop aircraft eased along the taxiway and drew up to a low metal building. As the engines died and it came to a complete stop, the fuselage shook and bucked, as if the craft was tugging an invisible leash to get back in the air.

'Well! That was exciting.' The elderly lady swung a little paper bag under Gill's nose. 'Would you like another mint?'

He relaxed his grip on the armrest a fraction. 'No thanks, Muriel.' He prised one arm free from his seat and wiped his brow. 'Honestly, I'm not sure how I kept the last one down.'

Muriel gave him a heartening smile. 'It's always a bit rough coming into Kirkwall this time of year. It's because of all the mountains.'

He glanced out the cabin window at the flat, treeless landscape around him; the grass whipped so hard by the wind it almost frothed. He turned to face the sharp blue eyes beside him. 'Sure, all those peaks and the canyons. My goodness, how did we make it through?'

The spritely seventy-year-old clambered to her feet. 'I hope you have a wonderful few days on Orkney, Mr McArdle.'

'Gill, please. And Muriel, thanks for … well you know.'

She held up a hand in farewell, moving towards the exit where she immediately fell into conversation with a familiar passenger, their voices blown away in the wind as they started down the stairs. 'Did you hear the yelps outta that one?'

It only took a couple of minutes for the small aircraft to disgorge its passengers onto the windswept tarmac. Glad of a few extra moments to settle his stomach, Gill stood and stretched, before straightening his tweed waistcoat and running his fingers through his tangled thatch of copper-coloured hair. Stepping out into the brisk September morning, he was suddenly awash with fresh air. Already, the luggage was unloaded and on its way to the tiny terminal, overtaking the passengers as they snaked towards the entrance. A board announced the airport's name, in case Gill and his fellow travellers had arrived by chance at an unexpected destination. The Viking-style text looking anachronistic plastered across such a modern building.

The bags sat neatly on a long aluminium bench. A petite young woman in a dark business suit stood shadowing his battered Samsonite.

'Mr McArdle. Jenny Struan', she announced, thrusting a small hand in his direction.

He took it gently, mindful of giving it only a light squeeze in case he broke it. 'Gill, please. And thank you again for meeting me at the airport.'

'Absolutely. No problem. How was your flight?'

He gritted his teeth and formed a harmless lie. 'Fine. Thank you.'

She bent down and gave his bag a delicate tug. 'My goodness.'

‘I’ll get that.’

She flashed an embarrassed smile, warm brown eyes and a face set with fine features that matched her flawless skin. ‘Great. Then if you follow me, I’ll take you over to the facility.’

He eyed the car hire desk over her shoulder as she turned and headed for the nearest exit. ‘You’re sure it’s still okay for me to borrow a vehicle for a couple of days?’

‘No problem’, she fired back.

A few strides took them outside, where Jenny nodded in the direction of a nearly new Land Rover Defender. It was a deep shade of green, with the flash of the ScoCion logo and silver lettering, *Scottish Centre for Ion beam research*, running the length of the vehicle. She flicked the key fob to open the doors and jumped into the driver’s seat. Gill tossed his case and laptop bag in the back and climbed in beside her. The car was cleaner than any 4by4 he had ever set foot in and still smelt new. Jenny hitched up her skirt to free her legs to search for the far-away peddles. Then she kicked off her heeled pumps and started the car. ‘ScoCion is very mindful that we operate in an area of outstanding natural beauty and historical importance’, she said, following what sounded like a well-rehearsed script. ‘A big part of my media and community liaison job is to make sure we’re a good neighbour.’ She gave him another smile. ‘And that includes loaning this vehicle for visitors working with RSPB or Historic Scotland, as those bodies own most of the land we use.’

He glanced around the immaculate cabin. ‘Well, I’m glad I qualify. Certainly beats the 1.3-litre shoebox my firm would have got me.’

Jenny put the vehicle into reverse and moved off. 'Has Historic Scotland set you up with someone who can show you around?'

'Aye. I'm meeting their local coordinator tomorrow morning first thing.'

'Great. I'll point out the visitor centre on the way past.' She guided the car up through the gears as they hit the open road. 'You mentioned you've never been to Orkney before.'

'Never. Not even a school trip to Skara Brae.'

'Whoah! You're going to have a great few days then.'

The road dipped down into Kirkwall, and Gill watched the little town unfold before them. 'The big red church', he said, pointing to the town centre. 'That has to be St Magnus?'

She smiled and nodded, swinging the car around a bend into the harbour area. 'Ferries run from here to the small islands and Shetland', she said, pointing to a modest ferry manoeuvring in the cramped port. 'Are you planning to go off the mainland?'

'If I've time, I like to take a day on Hoy. Pay a visit to the Old Man.'

'Are you a climber?'

Gill shuddered as he remembered his ascent of *An Stuc* a few days before. 'Hell, no. I just want to see it, that's all. It'll offset my hard work, dropping in on archaeological sites and visiting companies that advertise in my magazine.'

'If you do go to Hoy, don't bother taking the car on the ferry', said Jenny. 'Hoy has a private taxi that will take you to all the main spots.'

'Expensive?'

Jenny laughed infectiously and shook her head. 'I can get you a special rate.'

'I don't mean to trouble you.'

She laughed again. 'No bother. He's my dad.'

They were moving out of town now, with faded red sandstone hotels to the left-hand side and a couple of newer buildings advertising themselves as jewellery workshops on the right. They fell silent for a time, Gill keeping his eyes on the far horizon to keep his nausea at bay. He relaxed a little and chided himself for his prejudice. Jenny's driving was very smooth for such a small woman driving such a large car.

'It's a beautiful island', he said eventually.

She glanced at his face while her perfect teeth flashed a smile of acknowledgement.

'Were you raised here?'

She nodded, eyes now firmly on the road as she swept around a long blind bend. 'I've been away to Uni. Had a junior marketing job in Glasgow for a while. Then this opportunity came up. I wasn't planning to come home so soon, but my dad is on his own now. It seemed right.'

'Good job?'

'Very. Brilliant experience. When the project started with seed money from the Scottish government, it committed the company to fifty per cent local hires. When I checked the fine print, I qualified, even though I wasn't living here at the time.'

'You benefited from a wee bit of affirmative action?'

She scrunched her tiny nose and grinned. 'Aye. But I would have landed the job without a hand up. I'm ace.'

Gill laughed. 'Like you already, Jenny Struan.'

They were getting closer to the ScoCion facility, and Jenny started pointing out local landmarks. The ancient burial chamber of Maeshowe lay close to the road, while below them and scattered across an isthmus between two lochs, Gill could make out multiple groups of standing stones.

Turning off the main road, one mile of narrow but immaculately laid tarmac led up a low hill to the gates of a surprisingly small complex. ScoCion was constructed with most of its facilities below ground. The only visible buildings had domed roofs covered by grass. In contrast, the fence surrounding the site formed a slim scar across the landscape.

Jenny paused at a security barrier, waiting for the CCTV operator to open the gates remotely. 'As you can see, we've done everything possible to minimize the impact on our environment.'

'Smaller than I thought', said Gill.

'The ion chamber itself runs fifteen hundred metres roughly north-south. But it's buried pretty deep. No need to throw a wall around it.'

'Can you tell me why it's a straight line rather than a circle?'

'Science question', said Jenny flicking a little wave at the CCTV as the gates slid open. 'I could tell you, but the boys hate it when I steal their thunder.'

She eased the car into a small parking area, hidden from the outside world by high earth dykes. Once Gill was out of the car, she passed him the key fob. 'All yours', she said.

Jenny led the way into the low, glass-fronted building and towards the reception area. 'I'll get you a visitor's pass. That way, if you ever want to come up to the facility, you'll be able to get through the main gates and into reception. Might be handy if you want a coffee or just to get out of the rain for a while.'

Under the unsmiling gaze of a security guard, Gill submitted himself to the signing-in procedure, then followed Jenny to a small kitchen and dining area just off the main concourse. 'I need to leave you now and make sure the presentation is ready to run', she said, pointing at a cluster of coffee machines and food chillers. 'Help yourself to anything you'd like.' She smiled again and walked smartly away.

Gill looked around. A couple of other men were already seated, nursing mugs of coffee. Gill walked towards the nearest one and introduced himself to them all. He found that most were contract writers, although the last one was a name he vaguely recognized. Arnold Broadbent was from 'Science' magazine.

'See you got the red carpet', grumbled Arnold while shaking hands. 'The rest of us came up here in taxis.'

'I'm doing a couple of pieces with Historic Scotland this week', said Gill. 'Apparently, that gives me certain privileges.'

'Do you work for them?' Arnold asked.

Gill shook his head. 'I'm the editor of *Mysterious Scotland* magazine.'

The men glanced at each other, and for a moment, Gill stood in silence.

'You're the unicorn guy?' said one of the contract writers.

'My finest hour', said Gill quietly.

'What brings you up here then?' said Arnold. 'I'd have thought this kind of pure science was a bit out of your orbit.'

Gill forced a polite smile. 'We're pretty general. If a story has a bit of mystery about it, and as long as it's in Scotland, we'll cover it.'

'Arnold, you might need to draw him a diagram afterwards', said the other man. 'No offence, pal, but you'll have to work pretty hard to make ScoCion comprehensible to your readership. I've discussed this stuff with university professors. Most experts struggle to get their heads around it.'

Gill stared at the man for a moment before bowing slightly. 'On behalf of *Mys.Scot* readers everywhere, thank you for your concern.'

An unnecessarily elevated scientific conversation broke out between the men, and Gill slipped away to pour himself a coffee. Finding a comfortable seat, he settled down with his phone and busied himself with the accumulated correspondence of the last few hours. Only once in the next thirty minutes did he stand up, visiting the toilet and casting himself around the office to see if he could find a quiet spot to call Cassy. He grasped the facility's layout as a series of adjacent glass offices that formed a circle around the public area where he stood, like petals radiating around a flower head. It was pleasantly modern but without a private corner anywhere. He had a sense of a much larger building beyond this central hub as numerous faces passed through the concourse, on their way to different sections. He got up and moved closer to the other reporters again just as Jenny emerged from a short corridor and pointed them towards a conference room.

'Gentlemen. If you'd like to join us.'

The journalists gathered their bags and devices and filed into a room designed around a single large desk with seating for about twenty people. Already seated were three men and a woman. The two groups faced each other in silence for a few moments until Jenny introduced them all in turn, concluding with Professor Jeremy K Harley, the Project Director at ScoCion.

'Well, thank you for coming', said Harley. 'We did hope for a higher turnout, but as ever, Orkney seems a long way to come for a story. 'Grab a seat, guys, and we'll make a start.'

Chapter 4

'Your taxi is here', said Jenny to two late-middle-aged men heading back to their hotel.

'Thanks', said one. 'Arnold, do you want to share a lift back into town?'

Arnold eyed Gill for a second. 'Maybe. But as the unicorn guy is staying over, I thought we might grab a couple of beers.'

'Sure', said Gill. 'Where are you staying?'

'Kirkwall. You?'

'Stromness.'

'Just to warn you', said Jenny. 'The island doesn't have masses of pubs and restaurants. There's a bistro in Stromness, but that closes early. And the hotel down on the harbourside. They're open to non-residents, but I wouldn't try getting a table any later than eight o'clock.'

'Appreciate the tip', said Gill. 'Do you want to join us?'

Jenny returned a practised smile. 'Thanks, but we've got a sponsor's seminar tomorrow afternoon, and I'm back and forward to the airport about a dozen times. Arnold, I'll see you back here tomorrow at 9 am for the technical brief and Gill, I guess I'll see you again in two days for the test firing.'

Gill nodded and shook her hand. 'Thanks for this afternoon. Very interesting. And again, for the car.'

'Ever been on Orkney before?' asked Gill as he eased the Defender out onto the main road.

Arnold shook his head. 'Never. Go to Europe a lot, Asia, USA. There's not much hard science on remote Scottish archipelagos, so this is a first. Do you travel?'

Gill smiled. 'Only around Scotland.'

'I remember your face from the Great Glen disaster. You were on TV a lot for a couple of days.'

'I was working along Loch Ness when the disaster happened.'

Arnold fell silent for a moment. 'Must have been tough.'

'I saw some things that day I'd hoped I'd never see', said Gill.

Changing the subject, he added, 'Did you understand Professor Harley's explanation for why he situated the particle cannon here?'

'Told you you'd struggle', said Arnold with a smirk. 'In layman's terms, Orkney offers a nice blank canvas. The old red sandstone he talked about is very inert, chemically speaking. It's free from metal ore deposits, background radiation is low, and they've no large power stations or factories to emit energy on the spectrum that could distort their readings.'

'They're going to fire beams of this particle they were talking about through the sandstone bedrock, right? And collect them in their detector station up in the north of the island?'

‘Yup. One mile-long cannon. Tiny subatomic particles, BAM! Fired through seventeen kilometres of solid rock. And all at the speed of light.’

Gill shook his head. ‘Didn’t even come close to understanding that bit.’

Arnold tapped the dashboard a few times. ‘I can’t explain that until we’ve had at least two pints’, he said.

The car was winding downhill now, quickly covering the few miles between the facility and the picturesque but faintly industrial village of Stromness. A passenger liner was edging into the natural harbour while vehicles scurried on the dockside, ready to service the great beast about to make landfall.

‘You staying at the hotel?’ asked Arnold.

Gill shook his head and gesticulated at a small cluster of older houses east of the port. ‘I’m a big fan of old fashioned B&B’s. And as I’m here for six days, the company wasn’t going to look kindly on a hefty hotel bill.’

Arnold sucked his teeth. ‘Must be quite tight working for a wee specialist like *Mysterious Scotland.* How many copies do you guys sell a month? Ten, twelve thousand?’

Gill bit back a smile. ‘The audited circulation for our first year was fifty-eight thousand a month. It’s looking a bit higher for year two.’

Arnold nodded slowly but said nothing.

Midway through their second pint, a barmaid came to collect their empty glasses. Her hair was a natural untreated blond, and her clear skin a shade darker than the locals. Arnold stopped talking for a moment and gave her a long admiring stare. 'Sorry, love, I'll hold on to those for a moment. Need to explain particle physics to my new friend.'

'Is not problem', said the heavily accented girl, before moving on to the next table.

Arnold took a long sip and randomly spread the four beer glasses around the circular table. 'Imagine this table represents a single atom', he said. 'The glasses represent electrons spinning around the nucleus like this.' He pulled a salt cellar to the centre of the table and slid the glasses around the table, leaving trails of condensation. 'All very safe and predictable. Then, if the atom is a conductor, add a little energy like electricity or a chemical reaction of some kind, and you can dislodge the electrons. In effect, moving our pint glasses onto another table while some other glasses come to our table from somewhere else. Got it?'

Gill nodded. This was high school physics.

'Now zoom inside our atom', said Arnold. 'Imagine the table is now one of those electrons, and the beer glasses are the subatomic particles within it.' He glanced up. 'You with me?' Gill didn't complain, so Arnold continued. 'And repeat this zooming idea. Keep going down deeper and deeper into the layers of the atom, and eventually, you get to the elementary particles Harley was banging on about.'

'So-called because they cannot be subdivided? They are the lowest level of subatomic particle that we can even theorise about', said Gill, keeping up.

'Exactly. And this "graviton" - that's the interesting little fellow. Theorised by Einstein in 1916 but not conclusively confirmed for over a hundred years. This chappie doesn't flow, or react or stay put. He can disappear into nothing only to reappear somewhere else in the universe.'

'Unhindered by time and space', remembered Gill.

'Exactly. And that's where Harley hopes to make his money. When he and his team of string theorists formally identified the graviton a couple of years back, they also pinpointed it leaving the host atom and detected it arriving in a new host at exactly the same moment.'

'This is where I lose it', said Gill. 'How's that even possible? How can it be measured?'

Arnold smiled. 'That bit eluded scientists for a century. And it's the part of the story Harley hasn't shared. Maybe he's saving it for the public test on Friday. I only know a fraction from reading Harley's technical papers and then taking a little leap all of my own.'

'Go on.'

'Think about it. If you can generate a particle that is unlimited by time and space, and with a cunning bit of physics, get it to disappear, then reappear in a place of your choosing in the same moment ...' Arnold paused and held up his arms in an act of intellectual generosity.

Gill stared at him. 'Sorry. I'm lost.'

Arnold's arms flopped back to his sides. 'Well, do you understand the essence of digital communication?'

'Do you mean binary code? A gate on a processor being open represents a bit. A gate closed is another bit, and if you gather a million of those, you have a megabyte of data.'

'That's it. You have enough information to send a small picture if you have a megabyte. Scale that up another thousand times, and you send a short movie. Scale up again, and you have enough data to get a 3D printer to produce a complex physical object.'

Gill nodded.

'Now, apply Harley's work on the graviton to digital communication. Make the appearance or disappearance of a graviton imply the same transfer of information as a "bit" of data.'

'You're saying this could be a new way to transmit data?

'Yes, Gill. But transmit it in a way that is unlimited by time and space.'

Gill nodded and stared at the table for a few moments. 'You're saying it would be faster than fibre optic broadband?'

'Give me strength', said Arnold to no one in particular as he stood up and walked the few short steps to the bar. He ordered two more beers and stood to face Gill with his back to the bar. 'Unlimited by time and space, Gill. Think space. Think distance.'

'Okay. You're talking about faster-than-light communication', said Gill borrowing back his glass to knock back the rest of his pint.

'Not just faster. Imagine communication on an intergalactic scale. Speaker and sender, talking in real-time, anywhere in the galaxy.'

Gill paused with his glass still at his mouth before letting it sink back to the table in a slow, involuntary motion. 'Oh my goodness.'

Arnold paid for the drinks and returned to the table. 'You're getting it?'

Gill felt a flood of understanding brightening his face. 'So a mission to Mars could have real-time communication without the time delay caused by the huge distance.'

'Or imagine a mission to a more distant body, like one of the Jupiter moons. As technology develops back on Earth, we could beam updated components to a 3D printer on the mission ship. Perhaps even use the technique to resupply them on the way. I know it sounds far-fetched, but from where I'm sitting, it might be possible.'

'Now that is awesome', said Gill.

The two sat in silence for a long moment, comprehending the significance of Harley's discovery.

Arnold cocked his head in a pessimistic expression. 'Of course, lots of hurdles before we get into that world. The test on Friday, for starters.'

'What does Harley need to achieve to get proof of concept?' asked Gill.

'At very least, he needs to generate the graviton in public and get it to recognise its pairing with the receptors on the north side of the island. I'm assuming he's done it already, or he wouldn't risk a public test.'

'How does that work?'

'Harley has been completely silent on that topic. It will be the basis for a big fat patent one of these days. Make him a zillionaire even if it's decades before the application is commercialised.'

Gill tilted his head but said nothing.

'Harley's early experiments were in a confined lab. The ion generator and receptor had a clear line of sight over a short distance. But, the theory is that distance shouldn't matter, and no physical obstacle should block the connection, not even if he puts a planet in the way.'

Gill nodded. 'So for the sake of the experiment, Harley's facility generates the graviton from the particle cannon and projects it through seventeen kilometres of inert Orkney sandstone substituting as the planet?'

'Exactly', said Arnold. 'These guys have parallel atomic clocks at both sites. If they detect a signal at the same moment it is generated, then it's game on.'

Gill laid down his glass and sat back in his chair. 'This is huge.' His mind spun with the magnitude of Dr Harley's technological ambitions. 'Jenny said you're going back in tomorrow morning?'

'Aye. I'm meeting Harley's technical engineer, a guy who wasn't at today's meet and greet. He's going to explain the basis of Friday's test run. By understanding their success criteria, I'm hoping I might get some clues to the underlying science.'

'Any chance I could tag along?'

Arnold pulled a mock wince. 'Science for the big boys, Gill. We won't have time to track back over the basics to keep you up to speed.'

'Fair point. But how about you listen to the science, and I'll watch the body language? See if I can get a feel for how confident they are.'

Arnold thought for a second. 'You can give me a lift then. Pick up from Kirkwall at 8.45, please.' He raised his pint towards Gill in a modest salute. 'Welcome to the exciting world of quantum physics.'

Chapter 5

Gill had spoken to Juliette Morrison on the phone on a couple of occasions. She had a husky voice, laughed easily and was more than a little prone to innuendo. When he saw her for the first time, bustling towards him across the empty car park at Tormiston Mill, he wasn't sure if he was disappointed or relieved.

'Juliette', he called out to the large, late middle-aged woman as she half sprinted, half shuffled the last few yards to grasp his outstretched hand.

'Gill. Wonderful to meet you at last. What time did you get in yesterday?'

'Mid-morning. One of the ScoCion folk met me at the airport and took me straight over to their facility.'

'Did they make good on their promise of a vehicle?'

Gill nodded and tipped a thumb at the gleaming car.

'Nice! Glad to see they're taking care of you.'

Gill nodded and rubbed his hands together. For mid-September, the early mornings were already very cool. 'Shall we?' he said, nodding at the well-made path leading south from the car park.

She smiled, and they started walking.

'Do you always start work this early?' asked Gill. It had just gone 7 am, and he was trying not to resent the disruption to his regular schedule.

Juliette shook her head. 'I normally work office hours. But if we were down at here at 9 am, we'd be surrounded by curious tourists.'

Gill thought for a moment. 'Would that be a bad thing?'

Juliette glanced at him before facing forward again as the path got rougher. 'We're still trying to figure out what we've got here. In the meantime, I hope you'll respect our preference for no publicity at this stage.'

'Of course', said Gill. 'Nothing will appear in our media unless you sign off on it.'

They walked in silence for a few moments while Gill adjusted to Juliette's sobriety. 'You were very coy on the phone', he said eventually. 'Now I'm here, can you tell me what it is you've found?'

Juliette looked ahead, glancing at him only briefly with the faintest of smiles. 'I'll show you in a second. Let's just say, we have what Hutton would have described as an "unconformity".'

The path narrowed, and Gill shrugged to himself as Juliette went ahead. To their left, they were passing Orkney's greatest monument, the *Ring of Brodgar.* Behind them, but only now visible in the lie of the land, lay a smaller artefact, the *Stenness Stone Circle.* For now, Juliette was making for a single large stone, standing separate from the others in a small area of mown grass. She was panting when they arrived at the spot. Leaning up against the stone, she stood coughing for a few moments. When she'd recovered, she slapped the face of the stone a few times. 'This big boy is the *Comet Stone.*'

Gill walked around the lichen-covered semi-rectangular block, stopping to gently rub at the rock's sedimentary layers visible on its narrow edge. 'It's a beauty. Any idea what it was for?'

Juliette shrugged. 'What was any of it for? It's a pity the people who built all this didn't leave us a manual.'

Gill acknowledged the truth of her words with a smile. 'Anyway, so good it's survived this long.'

'You're right', Juliette wheezed. 'We have historical references to half a dozen others quite like it that have either been ploughed under or robbed for their stone. But this fella. He's twice the size and sunk three times as deep. He isn't gonna move until the end of the world.'

Below them, through a gap in a simple fence, lay a little hollow, only a short distance from the sea. Within this, Gill could see a large blue tarpaulin covering the dig site. Juliette led the way downhill, ducking under some temporary barrier tape and beckoned Gill to follow her.

'Give me a hand, would you.'

They worked together to push stones off the tarp's edge, then rolled back the cover to reveal excavations. Then, with a gentle groan, she sat heavily on a small stack of pallets and lit a cigarette. Gill surveyed the scene while she caught her breath. An area of roughly twenty square metres had been cut into the turf, taking the surface area down half a metre at its shallowest point, but almost two metres depth where the excavation cut deep into the edge of a mound.

'We were just wrapping up our annual dig', said Juliette, expelling a lungful of smoke. 'We had a little bit of budget left, so long story short, we picked this place for future exploration. We planned to have a poke about and cover it all up again before the winter arrived.'

Gill walked over to the vertical face of the excavated bank. He found it richly laced with shells. 'And you've found a midden.'

'Which isn't unusual. Ancient Orcadia built a lot of dwellings in middens. No idea why. They must have stunk.'

'What did you find?'

'Oh, we got lots of interesting stuff. Plenty of data on the Neolithic diet, a few pottery shards, tiny pieces of organics. And finally, our mystery stone.' She leaned over and pointed at the deepest part of the mound. 'Take a look under the hessian sacks.'

Gill knelt and rolled back the covering to reveal a single flagstone, lying at a slight angle and still partially embedded in the mound. He stretched to brush soil grains from the surface. To his surprise, he saw the outline of a neatly carved symbol. The letter "X" over stamped with the capital letter "P". 'Interesting', he said quietly.

'Exactly', said Juliette. 'We think it's a grave covering. We stopped digging as soon as we found it. And before you ask, our ground survey suggests the area hasn't been disturbed since the midden was abandoned,'

'What about the shell debris? You've dated it?'

'Between four to four and a half thousand years old. Just as we'd expect', Juliette replied.

Gill shook his head. 'Well, something isn't right. You obviously recognise this symbol. It's the Chi Rho. It's still in use today, but it mainly crops up before the common era …'

Juliette interrupted. 'Mainly a marker on early Christian buildings or gravestones. I've done my research. I found two examples from the pre-Christian era, but even those are 250 BC at the very earliest.'

'Christian expressions of this design normally incorporate symbols for Alpha and Omega', said Gill, dropping his forefingers left and right of the centre point.

'If the stone is as old as it should be, given where it's lying, then it's definitely pre-Christian.'

'And based on what we can see, the stone slab is hexagonal. Ever seen that before on Orkney?'

Juliette shook her head. 'The fact that the top surface and the edges are all milled smooth makes it extremely rare. And the hexagonal configuration has never been seen here before.'

'You have a two-thousand-year-old symbol decorating a four-thousand-year-old grave covering', Gill summarised. 'Thinking about it, why have a grave covering at all? Neolithic Orcadians buried their dead in ossuaries like Maeshowe.'

Juliette gave a husky laugh. 'That, my friend, is the mystery. And it's the reason I called you.'

They arrived back at the visitor centre just after 8 am. Juliette made coffee for the other staff members as they readied the centre for the day, then carried a cafetiere through to a cramped staff room while Gill followed with two mugs.

'Apologies for the lack of legroom. Our main offices are up at Skara Brae. This is just my hidey-hole for when I'm down on the isthmus.' She picked up an intricately carved stone about the size of a tennis ball and passed it to Gill. 'What do you make of this?'

He examined the object's symmetrical detail. The carvings seemed Pictish, although he knew this object was from an older era. 'I've heard of these. Orcadian stone spheres. Any idea what they were for?'

'We turn up a few every year, so they must have been ten a penny back in the day. The carvings are too fragile for use as tools. My guess is they were either currency, or the neolithic equivalent of I.D. cards. These days they make excellent paper weights', she said, accepting the stone back from Gill.

'Incredible craftsmanship.'

'And that's my reason for showing you one. A reminder that our Chi Rho stone isn't the only mystery the Neoliths left us.'

'Agreed', said Gill, repositioning the mugs so they wouldn't get knocked over while they both got settled. 'But the discovery of a relatively modern hallmark in a location this old means your site must be contaminated. Personally, I've found Roman remains on the Isle of Lewis. Maybe they've been here too.'

'I've thought about that', said Juliette. 'Even if Romans touched Orkney, I've seen no evidence of infrastructure, no sign they had even a transitory base. We know from their writings they circumnavigated the islands around the time of Claudius. But even if we assume they landed briefly for supplies, and let's suppose an officer died in the field, would they have taken the time to cut a grave? And then go to the trouble of moving an old midden on top of it? Surely any fatalities in the field would have been buried in haste before the unit moved on.'

Gill nodded slowly. 'But the fact that the stone has a carved symbol is strange. The neoliths didn't have any written language, so it just looks odd.'

Juliette leaned over and poured the coffee. 'The inscription is interesting. We took a microscope into the field to prove the carving was etched using flint rather than a metal tool. That at least is consistent with the date of the midden.'

Gill sipped his coffee but said nothing.

'My only working hypothesis is that it's pure coincidence. Someone cut a symbol on a rock and just happened to create a Chi Rho', she said.

'The Vikings liked to doodle on ancient monuments. Have you discounted them?'

Juliette sighed. 'Nothing like the Chi Rho in their lexicon.'

'Can we get any clues from the context here? I mean, what was the purpose of the Orcadian monuments?'

'The unwritten consensus is that Brodgar and the other standing stones in the surrounding area were used for astrological observations. I've never bought that idea myself.'

'Why not?'

Juliette grunted and bent down to rub one of her legs. 'There are monuments around the world that we can be confident had some application in astronomical measurement. They exhibit features like aligning with the sun during a solstice, or with the moon when it sets behind a prominent local feature like a mountain. Other sites have distant cairns that correspond with the movement of the sun or moon across the sky during a seasonal cycle.'

'I'm guessing Brodgar has none of these?'

'No, and I assure you, people have spent many a cold night out there trying to prove otherwise. There are a few theories, but nothing that convinces me.'

'And there's no demonstrable link between the various Orcadian monuments?'

'None. It's all random, as far as I can see. The whole thing might have been an open-air market, or a temple, or if you're an optimist, some form of parliament.'

'Maybe the Chi Rho stone will offer us a clue?'

Juliette sat up straight again and gave a theatrical shrug. 'That would be grand.'

'The obvious thing to do', said Gill. 'Is carry on with the dig. Finish excavating the midden, go through it with a fine comb, then lift the stone to reveal what's underneath.'

Juliette shook her head. 'I'm out of money for this year. And pretty much out of time. The days are about to get very short around here.'

Gill replied quickly. 'Could the magazine help?'

Juliette looked at him for a long moment, clicking her biro open and closed a few times. 'Possibly. But just so you know, that's not the reason I asked you to come up here.'

'It wouldn't matter if it was the reason. The magazine sponsors several digs a year. Without question, this looks interesting. And pretty straightforward compared to some of our recent stuff.'

'Thank you', said Juliette. 'But I'm nervous. In all likelihood, we'll find a perfectly logical explanation for this. You might spend money on a duff story.'

'Maybe. But it's up to my publisher and me to take the risk', said Gill. 'We don't always solve the puzzle, but sometimes just having a go is what makes the story.'

'I'll need to clear it with my management too. Make sure we don't fall foul of some local regulations.'

'Why don't we make a couple of calls; see what buy-in we can get? Meanwhile, with your permission, I'll sniff around the site. Get a feel for the wider context.'

'No problem. But is it okay if I set you up with a minder? Someone who can answer your questions and get you around the site unchallenged.'

'That's fine. I could use a little help to navigate the place. I was aware the Neolithic remains on Orkney were huge, but the scale here …'

'I'll set you up with Jim Robertson if he's available', Juliette interrupted. 'Jim's retired, a volunteer of many years standing. Outside of the paid staff, no one knows the Brodgar area better than him. I'll give him a shout now if you like.'

'Thanks. I'm due in Kirkwall in half an hour to pick up a colleague, and then I'll be at ScoCion for the rest of the morning. Could I meet him after lunch?'

'Sure, I'll set that up. I'll text you if Jim can't make it.'

'One last favour. Before we think about more digging, could you provide me with a site plan showing where any previous excavations have taken place?'

'No problem. And there've been plenty. Our oldest record is from the early sixteenth century, but it wasn't until the nineteenth century we had any formalised digs.'

Gill thanked her and stood up to leave.

'Oh, and I almost forgot. Someone left this for you', she said, passing him a flat brown package. Gill took it and studied the small neat letters printed on an address label. 'To the man from *Mysterious Scotland*', he read aloud.

'And before you ask, I've no idea who left it for you. It was just dropped through the letterbox over the last few days.'

Gill smiled. 'Don't worry. We get a lot of stuff sent in by readers. Someone's just saving themselves a few quid on postage.' He lifted the package in a brief salute. 'Thanks for the tour this morning. Very interesting.'

Chapter 6

An hour later, Gill lingered impatiently outside Arnold's Kirkwall hotel before his tentative colleague finally appeared, looking less than fresh. He explained that after he got out of his taxi the night before, he'd gone to a kebab shop and, as he put it, "fallen amongst thieves." The crew of an industrial trawler had just offloaded after two weeks at sea and were eager for a drink. Someone made some calls, and doors opened for them. Arnold had got to bed around 4 am. 'Just so long as you can do your science thing', grumbled Gill. 'The only thing I'm qualified to analyse here is the punctuation in their brochure.'

'I'm gonna be fine', said Arnold, suppressing a belch.

After arriving at ScoCion, they were detained in the reception area for twenty-five minutes, which Gill reckoned was justifiable retaliation for their lateness. When a team came out to meet them, Arnold seemed disappointed to see Professor Harley leading the group.

Jenny Struan stepped in to make the introductions. 'On the ScoCion side, we have Professor Harley, who you met yesterday, David Trevelyan, our Technical Director and Lisa Fairbank, our data specialist. And from the media, we have Arnold Broadbent of Science magazine and ...'

But David Trevelyan was already crossing the room and grabbing Gill in a brief embrace. 'Gillan McArdle! How are you?'

'Awesome, man! Great to see you.'

Jenny looked between them. 'And two people who already know each other.'

'Gill and I were undergrads at St Andrews together', David explained. 'Shared a flat for a couple of years.'

Gill smiled. 'Aye, I could tell you some stories about this guy. So where've you been? Last time we spoke, we were at a wedding, and you were moving to America.'

David nodded. 'I was at MIT for a few years. Eventually, I did a doctorate in particle physics. Then this job came up. Been back here since this place started fitting out.'

'David is the senior engineer in charge of all our hardware', added Harley. 'His team have the challenge of fine-tuning the machinery that allows us to test the various hypotheses we're working on.'

'He means I'm a glorified instrument technician', David whispered. 'But it's fascinating work. I'm enjoying it.'

'And you and Alice ...?' probed Gill.

'We married eight years ago when we were still in the States. Over the years, we've added a son and twin girls.'

'Secretly, that's why he loves working late', said Jenny, giving David a sly smile.

David stepped forward and gave Gill another embrace. 'Look, we'll get our heads together after the meet, see if I can get you over for dinner. Today's pretty manic, but maybe tomorrow, after the test?'

Later that morning, Professor Harley stood up and moved to the conference room window. It was one of the few rooms in the building with natural light, and the facility's hilltop location gave everyone a decent view across the island's entire central basin. Harley used a laser pointer on the glass to highlight the location of the receptor array at Sleet Moss, just visible on the north mainland. 'With all this complexity, you'll appreciate we're not guaranteed an easy run on Friday. We're aiming a beam from an entirely new form of laser at a receptor the size of a pinhead. If we're off by even a fraction, we'll get a dud result.'

'But you've tested your targeting array before?' broke in Arnold.

'Aye', said David. 'But this will be the first public access test where we factor in the graviton transmission. The power upscale will be enormous.'

'And we have the rock, air and water mediums to contend with', said Harley. 'While our theory suggests the particles will transmit regardless of the distance, whether through a vacuum or a planetary body, Friday's test is the day we demonstrate it's possible.'

'Can you confirm the rumours that a satellite is being readied for a space test next year?' asked Arnold.

'We're looking at …' began David.

'No, not at this stage', Harley interjected. 'To move the theoretical work forward, that would be the logical next step. But it wouldn't be a near-earth satellite. We'd need a high-speed probe sent on an elliptical orbit through the solar system. This station would fire basic data packages at the probe, which would report back to earth using conventional technology. As you can imagine, all that is very expensive, so we need to secure a robust investment package. It's some years in the future.'

Arnold furiously tapped his iPad. 'Based on yesterday's brief tour, the particle cannon runs south to north, with its beam tilted just above the horizontal. How will you use it to target a moving off-earth object?'

'I'm sorry, Mr Broadbent. That technology is ...'

But Arnold spoke over him. 'Subject to an international patent application. Like most everything else we've talked about this morning.'

Professor Harley forced a generous smile onto his face. 'The economics of this process are quite simple. To secure funding for our continuing work, we must ensure we don't undermine the downstream commercial payback.'

An uneasy silence settled onto the room. Gill, who had stayed quiet through the technical exchanges, did his best to summarise. 'So, although you can't tell us much detail about the science behind Friday's test, the essence is that if it is successful, you will have sufficient proof of concept to secure your next round of funding.'

Harley dropped his smile and nodded vigorously. 'Exactly. When you pull out your smartphone and connect a video call to a friend in Sydney, you don't care how it works. You just want a clear, reliable call in real-time. It's the same with our test on Friday. Either we have a workable technology, or we haven't. This test will be the latest of many, but it's the next step in the journey for us.'

Gill glanced at the other faces around the room. 'Thank you, Professor Harley. And I think I speak for us all when I wish you the best of luck.'

A brief lunch with David and Arnold in the ScoCion canteen was all Gill had time for before his next appointment. As Gill walked into the Historic Scotland visitor centre, the man he presumed was Jim Robertson was standing by himself. Dressed in a weathered brown Barbour jacket, he was slightly built, of average height, with a shock of untamed snow-white hair. He was standing with his arms folded, leaning against the receptionist's counter. As Gill approached, the man offered him his hand.

'Mr McArdle?'

'Hi, Jim. Call me Gill.'

Jim pushed his hair back over his forehead and studied Gill with watery blue eyes. 'Juliette says you want to spend a few hours amongst the stones.'

'Yes. I'm working on a feature.'

'Well, the tourists go to Stenness, then to Brodgar. A dedicated few make it out to the more distant monuments.'

'Thanks', said Gill. If it's okay with you, I'd like to do it the other way around.'

'That's a lot of walking on damp ground.' Jim glanced down at Gill's walking boots.

'No problem. I'm up for it.'

'We'll take your car if that's okay.'

During the ten-minute drive to the hamlet of Voy, Gill tried to make conversation with his host. Jim Robertson ran a mixed croft that had been in his family for generations. And his professional life had been part-time as a local Presbyterian minister from which he was now retired. His knowledge of the Orcadian monuments was that of a layman. But this was his backyard, and the stones had always interested him. Gill didn't doubt the man held opinions on many subjects, but the walls around his personal life were raised so high their conversation was limited to Jim bluntly answering Gill's questions.

Parking in a layby, Jim indicated a low hill in a nearby field. 'We'll start up here. Best vantage spot for miles around.' They walked in silence, with Jim keeping some metres ahead of Gill until they reached the top. Surrounded by a landscape he clearly loved, Jim became more animated. 'We have tumuli to the south, east and north of us here.'

'I presume those are all burial sites?' Gill asked.

Jim nodded. 'The big one you can see to the east is typical. It would have functioned as an ossuary during Neolithic times. During the Pictish period, the custom was to lay entire bodies to rest, so I daresay they quickly filled up. In later periods, lack of space meant they only preserved a few bones from each corpse. Most of these bone pits were sealed and abandoned when the Norsemen came.'

'What about that circle?' said Gill pointing to a small feature of raised stones about a mile distant.

'Ring of Bookan', said Jim. 'It's the first significant feature on the isthmus between the two lochs. As you look southeast, you can see a string of monuments, large and small, including Brodgar and then Stenness. Finally, beyond that is Maeshowe, which I'm sure you know is the biggest tomb complex on the island.'

Gill took a moment to survey the lochs dominating the Orkney central mainland. 'In geological terms, these patches of water will be quite new. Do you know if they've ever been surveyed for Neolithic remains?'

Jim glanced sideways at him. 'Are you thinking of going swimming, Mr McArdle?'

Gill shook his head. 'Just that if no one's tried it, I know a girl who can.'

'Sea levels rose after the last ice age and inundated all the coastal sites used by the earliest hunter-gatherers. The sea swept in and created these lochs. But the neoliths who built the Orkney monuments came later. To them, this land would have looked much as it does today.' He shook a finger at the landscape. 'Minus all these wee farms.'

'Breath-taking', said Gill. 'So much history crammed into one small area. I can't think of anywhere in Scotland quite like it.'

'We'll see how small you think it is when we've walked its length a couple of times. Shall we make a start?' Without waiting for an answer, Jim set off down the hill toward the nearest cairn.

Four hours later, Gill arrived at the centre of the Brodgar circle and wheeled slowly through 360 degrees. He shivered as the sweat he'd worked up now cooled in the persistent wind. Amid these standing stones, he couldn't help feel vulnerable, a throwback perhaps to a life-changing morning at the Callanish stone circle less than two years before. Behind him, Jim Robertson prowled, his steps weaving between the individual standing stones like a disgruntled cat. This dour man had become increasingly melancholic as the day progressed. Conversation had been thin at first and deteriorated further so that by mid-morning, they communicated only by nods and gestures. He did know the monuments, even the stumps and fallen rocks, remnants of once-mighty megaliths, so he saved Gill a great deal of time. But it would have been easier to share the experience with a more cheerful face. But now, it was time to break the silence and Gill strode to where Jim had paused.

'During my morning walk with Juliette, she mentioned that there has been a lot of digging here over the years.'

Jim shrugged. 'Aye, plenty. Apart from the Brodgar circle.'

'Interesting. Why not?'

'It's been subject to technological scans of various types. There's no sign it's ever been disturbed.' He stomped the ground with his right foot a few times. 'And you can see why. It's bedrock with just a skim of soil and a wee bit of heather.'

'What about the ditch and dyke?'

'A cross-section was dug out many years ago. These days, Historic Scotland rightly prefers to leave these landmark sites well alone.'

Gill walked out to the edge of the raised dyke to where he could see the edge of the blue tarpaulin covering the dig. 'Juliette tells me you identified the Chi Rho dig site. I must say, you've got an impressive instinct for where to excavate. I've been in this game for fifteen years, and nothing about that mound would have caught my attention.'

The nod of Jim's head was barely perceptible. 'Ach, some animal had dug a wee scrape. I could see the shells straight away. Round here, a midden is always worth a poke about.'

'Interesting choice. Juliette said she originally planned to dig amongst the existing monuments.'

Jim stared at his feet for a few moments. 'I think you could sink a spade anywhere around here and have a chance of finding something.'

'If only it were that easy.' Gill turned to face him. 'Now they have found the grave covering; you must be very curious?'

At this, Jim looked away, focusing on the far-away stones at Stenness. 'If it's someone's final resting place, I think they should be left in peace.'

'But you've seen the marking on the stone? I sense a real mystery here.'

'When you're dead and gone, Mr McArdle, do you fancy the thought of another creature handling your bones?'

Gill had thought about this question, and it didn't bother him in the slightest. But in a conciliatory gesture, he forced a smile. 'I take your point.'

Jim looked up again and stared at a distant headland. 'Now, sir. Is there anything else I can help you with before we head back to the cars?'

Weary after a long afternoon on the moors with Jim Robertson, Gill elected to drive to the high end of Stromness. Abandoning the car and its uncertain satnav, he got out and looked down at the village. Even though it was late in the season, a huge passenger liner was getting ready to leave while another immense vessel lingered on the horizon, awaiting its turn to dock. From his jacket, Gill felt the weight of the brown paper packet Juliette had given him. He reached into his pocket and pulled open the package to find a small hardback notebook. As he flicked through it, he could see every page was dense with hand-written numbers. Without notation or punctuation, the thing seemed quite meaningless. He returned to the car and tossed it on the back seat. Then he retrieved his phone and dialled Salina.

Chapter 7

A small viewing gallery overlooked the ScoCion control room. It was raised to chest height above floor level and reached by steps along the back wall. It was Friday morning – the day of the test. Gill took up his allocated position in the second row and tried to grasp what was happening. The voices of the technical team had no amplification, so from this position, he could barely hear what was being said. One row back, he was aware of Arnold Broadbent twisting and stretching, struggling to get a view of the instruments. Gill could see the gallery had been a late addition to the room and wasn't entirely fit for purpose. The grunts and mutterings from Arnold suggested he felt the same. Brass rails separating the viewing area from the workstations felt garish in a scientific setting. At the front, in a row of roomy, comfortable seats, the representatives of sponsoring companies and organisations murmured together.

Gill tuned out the people around him and glanced at a digital display, counting down the seconds until the test. David Trevelyan sat midway along a row of technicians, staring impassively at a bank of screens. Professor Harley prowled behind the technical team, pausing now and then to focus on a data stream. Glancing at his watch, he nodded to Doug Featherwell and introduced him as *Test Controller*. Wearing a mic so he could be heard, Doug was the master of ceremonies.

Doug glanced around and cleared his throat. 'Ladies, gentlemen, the clock stands at two minutes and forty-five seconds, and we're making final preparations for the thirty-sixth test firing of the ScoCion Particle Cannon. All quiet in the gallery now, please.'

The room immediately settled, and the lights dimmed a little, adding to the sense of theatre.

Doug spoke again. 'Sleet Moss, this is Control. Please confirm your green light for the test.'

Somewhere in the room, a radio link crackled back. 'Control, this is Sleet Moss Receptor array. We are go for test.'

'Thank you, Sleet Moss. Tech, please confirm clock alignment.'

David reached forward and stroked the keyboard in front of him. Two identical digital clocks filled his central screen. To a dizzying number of decimal places, the screen displayed readouts from the atomic clock at ScoCion station and the second at Sleet Moss. David looked across at Doug. 'Clocks aligned, Control.'

'Safety officer. Are we set?'

'My board is green, Control.'

'Power?'

'Capacitors are primed and ready to charge.'

'Thank you, team. This is Control. Test thirty-six is green for go. Please charge the ion chamber.'

Lights in the room dimmed momentarily. And a background hum started to build with such intensity Gill began to wonder if Harley had added it for dramatic effect. After more than a minute, one of the technicians looked up. 'All batteries functioning normally. Cannon fully charged.'

‘Team, we are at T minus sixty seconds’, said Doug. ‘Ignite targeting beam.’

David tapped his keyboard. ‘Targeting beam is up.’

‘Thank you, Tech. Sleet Moss, please confirm target is illuminated.’

The room sat in silence for a few seconds. ‘Control, the target area is blank. We don’t have your beam.’

Doug turned sharply to David. ‘Tech?’

David ignored him for a few moments while he tapped on his keyboard. ‘Control, misalignment confirmed. I can’t see the target. I’m resetting the targeting system. Reboot will take forty-five seconds.’

The room stayed silent other than the gentle footfall of David and Harley as they moved between workstations and tapped monitors. In the gallery, someone coughed. And Gill could hear a hushed conversation in Italian somewhere in the room.

David broke the silence. ‘Control, targeting system reboot is complete. Diagnostics confirm a clear beam.’

Doug shifted uneasily in his chair. ‘Sleet Moss. Please confirm targeting alignment.’

Another brief pause. ‘Negative, Control. Still can’t see your targeting beam.’

Professor Harley moved quickly across the room. He and Doug leaned closely together to have an intense whispered conversation no one else could hear. In the background, the clock moved past zero and continued to roll beyond the planned time.

David pointed at his screen. 'Control, we need to drop the charge, or we'll damage the batteries.'

Harley glared across at David before picking up his conversation with Doug again. The last comment of which was audible to all. 'We can't bloody well shoot in the dark.' Then he turned on his heels and walked over to where Jenny shepherded the gallery.

Doug gave a long exhale. 'All sections, this is Control. Stand down, please. Test thirty-six is a scrub. Repeat – test thirty-six is abandoned.'

Gill tried to listen to Harley's explanation to the investors but was distracted by Arnold leaning over his right shoulder. 'This puts a bollocks on it.'

Gill half turned to face him. 'Do you understand what just happened?'

'Ya bloody tech lightweight.'

'Thanks, Arnie. Just put it in terms this humble journo will understand.'

'Simply put, the particle cannon is a mile-long tube that points a few degrees off horizontal. It doesn't point at the Sleet Moss observatory any more than it points at a spaceship rushing away from the earth. Okay so far?'

'Yep.'

'The targeting mechanism to steer the beam must be very complex. Harley might have a wonderful piece of kit here, but if he can't steer it, then, for the time being, it's useless.'

Harley's voice rose in the background as he worked to deflect criticism. 'As I've said already, a test is just that, a test. In a couple of weeks, we'll try again … it takes time to reset this machine … a lot of data to go through … yes, essential to diagnose what didn't work today.'

Arnold tapped Gill's shoulder. 'I've had enough thrills for one day. Fancy a beer later?'

'Sorry. I can't. Got a dinner date.'

'That wee Jenny? Wouldn't mind a piece of that action myself.'

'Arnie, you're so bloody twentieth century. Look, I'll catch up with you tomorrow.'

'Hope so, matey-boy. Last day on the island for me. I'm heading off tomorrow lunchtime to write my big piece on the marvel that isn't ScoCion.'

'You're not overwhelmed then?'

Arnold shrugged. 'Perplexed more like.' He glanced around to make sure no one could overhear them. 'I still don't understand why this place is so sodding huge. Sure, CERN was gigantic, but that was primary research. This place should be about application physics. The Chinese have been commercialising quantum communication using a satellite and a couple of labs. There's a mystery for you, Gill. Why does this place need the power output of a small town? Why is it a cannon and not a rifle?'

Gill nodded solemnly.

'If you find out, you'll definitely let me know?' pressed Arnold.

'Look, I'm not sure I've got the expertise to ask those kinds of questions', Gill confessed.

'You're the investigator. Sniff around; turn over some damp stones.'

‘And if I don’t understand the answers?’

‘Reach out to me. Even if you allow for the complexity of gravitons and all that shit, the only facility Harley really needs is a well-equipped lab. Not all this ...’, he waved his right arm around him.

‘Okay. Maybe I’ll solve that and then put it in my magazine.’

Arnold laughed. ‘Of course. All fifty-eight thousand copies.’

‘Plus one’, said Gill. ‘I’m hoping to pull you in.’

Arnold stood, ready to walk away. Then he turned and shook Gill’s hand. ‘Just in case I don’t see you tomorrow.’

‘Been a pleasure, Arnie.’

Across the control room, two technicians lingered at their positions, monitoring the machines as they gradually wound down from the test. The rest stood in clusters, leaning wearily against their desks or standing, hands thrust deep in pockets. Gill slipped in amongst them until he found David.

‘Look, David. If it’s a nuisance this evening, we can always reschedule.’

David excused himself from his conversation and slapped Gill on his upper left arm. ‘No problem. I’ll need to get out of here for a few hours. I should be clear by 6 pm.’

‘Won’t Harley want to debrief the team?’

David glanced at his boss, stuck in an earnest phone conversation in what sounded like Mandarin. ‘He’s too damn furious to speak to me right now. Besides, we won’t have the first diagnostics until Monday morning.’

'Big problem?'

David shook his head. 'Probably not. But it's one unanticipated problem after another at the moment.'

They were distracted by Harley shouting on his phone to one of the investors. 'The targeting beam worked perfectly in half a dozen preliminary tests we did this month. The only thing that's different this time is that we gave the ion chamber a full charge. I'll bet when we review the numbers, we'll find we under or over-compensated for the magnetic pull of all those batteries getting ready to fire.'

'You see', said David, winking at Gill. 'No big problems.'

Gill mustered a sympathetic smile. 'I'll go and be a tourist for a few hours. Meet you outside later.'

With a few hours to kill until his evening appointment, Gill would happily have walked amongst the monuments and found an atmospheric spot to call Salina. But the weather-front bringing driven rain made a stroll on the moors less attractive, so he returned to his car and pulled out his laptop to check his emails. Back in Dundee, the team was starting work on issue sixteen, so for now, little was happening that demanded his attention. Putting his laptop away, he came across the book of numbers he'd discarded in the car the day before. Opening the book's inside cover, he scanned the first page for an address. He didn't see it immediately, but eventually, a name; Euan Mearns. The number 81 and a postcode, KW16 3FX. At some point, the text in the bottom left-hand corner might have been the only writing on the page. Later the author had swept back through the sheets, filling the empty spaces with many rows of sparsely punctuated numbers. This backfilling was common throughout the book, making the neat writing even denser and destroying any hope a causal reader had of grasping any meaning. Tempted to dump the book, Gill felt a tug on his conscience. Stromness wasn't far-away, and he had time, so he'd try and return the book.

Fifteen minutes later, and confident he was on the right street, Gill walked the length of an unremarkable stone-built terrace until he came to number eighty-one. A weathered wooden sign proclaimed *David Street Hostel.* Unable to find a doorbell, he resorted to a couple of swings against a corroded brass knocker.

Thirty seconds later, a man in his early sixties opened the door to Gill, acknowledging him with a brief nod.

'I'm looking for Euan Mearns', said Gill.

The unshaven face bore a puzzled expression. 'Euan? What do you want with him?'

'I have his book. I was passing through and thought I'd return it.'

The man glanced at the black notebook and held out his hand. Gill released it and half turned to go. 'Just a second, pal.' The man leafed through a few pages and nodded. 'Aye, it's definitely Euan's. He's got handwriting tighter than a laser printer, that fella.'

Gill raised a hand in farewell. 'Tell him, thanks for the loan of it.'

'Hang on a mo. When did you say Euan sent you this?'

Gill shrugged. 'He left it for me in the safekeeping of Tormiston Mill, sometime last weekend.'

The man stepped towards Gill and thrust the book back into his hands. 'Thing is, Euan's not about just now. I've been told not to touch anything in his room, so you'll need to keep hold of this.'

Gill tried to keep the frustration out of his voice. 'Well, do you know where I could find him?'

'Not likely. He's been missing for a month. So it's weird his book should turn up.' The man turned and then muttered over his shoulder. 'Come in a second. Gettin' a bit cold out here.'

Reluctantly, Gill followed the man into the house, pushing the door behind him as he followed his host into a threadbare kitchen.'

'I'm Terry, by the way. I run this hostel. Cuppa?'

'No thanks. I'm good.'

'Do you know Euan then?' said Terry putting a little water in a kettle.

'I've never met him.'

'Honestly, mate. I'm surprised he sent you that book. The whole two years he's lived here, I never saw him without it.'

'I work on a magazine', said Gill. 'As I say, Euan left it for me. Maybe he had in mind I could publish part of it. I dunno. He didn't include a covering letter.'

Terry grunted a laugh while popping a tea bag into a stained mug. 'Euan isn't a great conversationalist.'

'I can imagine', said Gill thumbing through a few pages, 'He hasn't explained any of his work.'

'It'll have meaning', said Terry. 'I'm told Euan is very bright. Autistic, something like that. But everything he does is very deliberate.'

‘How did he come to live here?’

‘The hostel provides temporary accommodation paid for by the council. One or two boys who’ve lived here have done time; short custodial sentences. Others, like Euan, have been in the care system. Eventually, they get too old to stay with foster parents or such like, so they end up here.’

‘He doesn’t have any family on the island?’

‘None I’m aware of.’

‘Maybe he’s left for the mainland?’

‘That’s possible. Most of the lads I cater for head to the cities eventually. They wake up one morning, watch the ferry coming in and think, “Sod it, I’m off”.’ Terry shook his head. ‘But for Euan to do that, I’m surprised. And it worries me.’

‘How so?’

‘Routine is everything to Euan. He has a wee job dishwashing at the bistro. Spends the rest of his time crawling over the stones.’

‘Do you mean the monuments?’

‘Aye. Brodgar, Stenness. All of that.’

‘I take it the police are looking for him?’

Terry shrugged. ‘I guess so. They did come and see me after I called them for the third time. Had a poke around his room. Told me the council would likely keep payin’ for a while. As I say, Euan’s not the first lad from here to scarper without telling anyone. I don’t think his disappearance is a big deal for them.’ He poured water on his tea bag. ‘It’s a pity. Eventually, the council will stop the money for his room. I'll have to re-let it. If Euan ever comes back, he'll be gutted.'

Gill sat for a second, uncertain what to say. 'If he has belongings here, maybe I could leave the book?'

Terry was already shaking his head. 'Police asked me to lock the door and leave it undisturbed.' He glanced around the kitchen. 'I suppose I could leave it in here, but it's a fair bet it would end up as fag paper.'

Gill felt the burden of responsibility. 'Okay. Maybe I'll hold on to it for a little while.' He fished in his pocket for a business card. 'If he ever comes back, tell Euan I still have his book.'

Terry surveyed the card and nodded. 'I've seen Euan reading your magazine.'

'And you've no idea what he was working on?'

Terry took a long draw on his mug of tea. 'I'm sorry. Absolutely none.'

Chapter 8

Gill hovered in the car park at Tormiston Mill while he waited for David's car to arrive. The plan was to travel in convoy to David's house on the far side of Kirkwall. But the latest text from David said he would be another twenty minutes, so Gill had time to kill. On the off chance Juliette was still at her desk, he called at her office.

'I was passing, and I saw your car. Are you pulling a late one?'

'Daylight is about to become a rare commodity around here. I'm trying to wrap up a few things.' She pointed at a chair. 'How can I help you?'

'Just to say, I spoke to my publisher this afternoon, and we're happy to sponsor the recovery of the Chi Rho stone.'

'Great. I'm getting positive noises from my management too. Do you think we'll be able to get on with it while you're still on the island?'

'Definitely. If you can firm up your volunteers for a start on Tuesday, I'll run the dig and pick up any expenses.' Gill got up to leave but found himself lingering in the doorway. 'Tell me, have you ever heard of a young man called Euan Mearns?'

'Of course. Euan is a regular fixture around here.' She checked herself. 'Why do you ask?'

'The packet you gave me. The one left for me here at the Mill. It was a notebook. Apparently, it belongs to Euan.'

Juliette frowned. 'You're aware he's missing?'

'Aye. I met the chap who runs the hostel where he lives. I'm curious. What can you tell me about Euan?'

Juliette's gaze lowered. 'When he first appeared a couple of years back, I was worried he might be a bit of a nuisance, wandering around the stones day and night. He's got some social issues, but he's respectful. I'd say he's harmless.'

'Does he volunteer with you?'

She smiled. 'No. He's too caught up in his own head to cope with the instructions I'd have to give him.'

'Interesting. I gather Euan has a dishwashing job at the bistro in Stromness. I spoke to the owner about him after I visited his bedsit. He said Euan was as regular as clockwork. Inflexible, but never missed a day, never a minute late.'

'He is fascinated by the stones', said Juliette. 'He spends all his free time hanging around them. Not that you could ever draw him to talk about it. I couldn't get him to talk about anything much. Always walking, always measuring. Jim took him in hand for a while. Tried to teach him some useful skills. Even lent him some equipment, I believe.'

Gill dug into his rucksack and produced Euan's book of numbers. 'This is his book. It's a total enigma. Have you ever seen it?'

Juliette waved a hand at him. 'My relationship with Euan stopped and started with ensuring he didn't make a nuisance of himself. You could ask Jim.'

'What's the story about Euan's disappearance?'

'I only know what went out in the local news. He disappeared about four weeks ago, and his landlord raised the alarm. The police looked for him. Even raised a few volunteers to comb the area around the monuments where he spent most of his time. But no one has seen him.'

'Any theories?'

'I'd concur with the local gossip. Euan wasn't from the island. He'd been brought here by foster parents. Most likely, one of his blood family got in touch, and he went to live with them. It wouldn't occur to Euan to tell anybody he was going. But that's gossip. Best to talk to the police if you want to know more.'

'Och, I'm not so keen to get involved. Just curious.'

'Makes me realise, though', she said. 'Someone dropped off his book a couple of weeks after Euan disappeared. And come to think of it, how would anyone even know you'd be here?'

Gill shrugged. 'Maybe a friend of his? Someone who thought I might be interested.'

'Well, I hope he's alright wherever he is', said Juliette. 'It's too cold these nights for him to be sleeping rough.'

'I'll keep an eye out for him. Maybe he'll come looking for his book.'

Juliette pursed her lips into a sad face, then nodded. 'Let's hope. So, what are you at this evening?'

'Dinner with a friend. You?'

Juliette shrugged. 'I'll phone potential volunteers for our wee dig, and then I'm off to fill the rest of my weekend with alcohol and cigarettes.'

In thinning sunlight, Gill followed David's car through the outskirts of Kirkwall to a small newly built estate of good-sized family houses. Coming across an old friend on Orkney had been such a pleasant surprise. But now, standing on the threshold of David's home while the man grappled with his keys, Gill realised how nervous he'd become. Catching up with David felt like grabbing an impulsive beer with a pal. But seeing David at home meant seeing Alice, and that was an entirely different barrel of emotions.

David led the way through a porch lined with small shoes and boots into a wide hallway floored with polished pine. The din of a cartoon spilt from the living room where a boy of about four was watching TV. He smiled and waved at David, then turned back to his viewing.

'Good evening, Noah. Aren't you coming to say hello?'

David was mid-way peeling off his jacket when two little girls, barely more than toddlers, appeared from nowhere and secured themselves to each of his legs. 'Aaargh! Twin attack', he laughed before bending down to scoop up both girls.

David smiled at Gill, leaning forward with his left arm. 'This is Esther'. Then with his right. 'And this is Grace.'

Gill smiled at the two girls, sweetly dressed in black leggings and bright-coloured cardigans, and tried his best not to appear intimidating. 'Beautiful. How on earth do you tell them apart?'

'That's easy', said David, bumping the twins up and down in his arms. 'One is always cheeky, and the other is always nice.' He looked between them for a few seconds. 'Now, I forget? Which one is the cheeky one?'

In a well-rehearsed game, the girls flung out an arm and pointed at each other.

'Gillan!' A woman appeared from the far end of the hall, strode over and hugged him.

'Alice. Great to see you. You look fantastic.' She did look good. A little older, her figure a little fuller, but still the pretty, smiling woman he'd known at university.

Alice turned to her husband. 'How was the test?'

David grimaced. 'Fault with the targeting array. Had to scrub it.'

Alice pulled a pained face and reached to brush David's cheek with a kiss, slipping her arm around one of the girls. 'More problems! The professor won't be pleased.'

David said nothing, just flicked his face heavenward in a gesture of resignation. He released Grace to her mother while Esther slid out of his arms to the floor, attracted by her brother laughing at the TV. 'The kids have already eaten', said Alice, so if you can bear with us for a while, we can sit down and properly catch up.

'Of course', said Gill, moving into a doorway to lean against the architrave while the family slipped efficiently into their evening routine. Noah quickly abandoned the TV to his sisters and started busily telling David about some detail from his day. Gill watched for a few minutes, marvelling, as he had in the house of other friends, at the ability of the partially formed creatures of his university years to morph into parents. Becoming sudden and unforeseen masters of domestic bliss.

At Alice's insistence, he took himself off to the kitchen to make himself a drink. As the kettle boiled, he tracked down tea bags and milk, enjoying a moment by himself. A kitchen, he always thought, was a window into a family's life, and perhaps even its soul. Pictures by the children. Bulletins and letters lying in a pile by the mug rack. A Sunday School rota stuck on the fridge. There was something in David's choice of words and the kids' names. He rebuked his internal detective, who was already filing clues.

At the start of dinner later, David spoke aloud a short prayer of thanks, causing Gill a twinge of anxiety which only diminished when Alice placed a bottle of red wine on the table. They talked for a while about where they'd been and what they'd done. When the food was finished, and enough chat had passed to warm up their old friendship, Gill asked, 'So, you guys do church these days?'

Alice laughed. She didn't look embarrassed, but maybe she'd anticipated his question. 'Aye, you wouldn't have predicted that back in St Andrews.'

'You guys knew how to party.'

'Yes, we did.'

'A bad habit you picked up in the States?' Gill asked, making sure they both caught some warmth from his face.

David shook his head and threw Gill a half-smile. 'Since we came here. Since the kids arrived.'

Gill sat smiling, waiting for David to elaborate. Alice, he noticed, was slowly twisting her wine glass, rotating it between her thumb and forefinger, in a gesture he remembered well. When no further explanation seemed forthcoming, he tried to defuse the situation. 'Well, having kids. It changes most people.' He nodded to himself, then added, 'for the better, generally.'

Alice rose from the table. 'Excuse me a sec. I want to check on the girls. Can I bring you coffee when I come back?' David gave her a thumbs-up, and Gill watched until she left the room. When he turned back, David was staring at him intensely. Gill checked his posture and stared back.

David threw a nod in the direction Alice had just left. 'Still no hard feelings?'

Gill raised both hands. 'David, absolutely none. You guys were made for each other.'

They both allowed a few moments of silence to heal the threatened rift. Then David settled back in his chair. 'Aye, I honestly believe we were.'

'And the kids', said Gill. 'And this house; your job. It's all great.'

David put warmth back in his smile, then pointed at Gill's ringless left hand. 'You're not going to tell me you're still single?'

Gill felt his face flush. 'I've met somebody. What's the dreadful phrase? Somebody special.' He started to talk about Salina, but David held up a hand. 'Hold on a minute. Alice is going to want to hear all about her.'

'Okay', said Gill as the conversation slipped into another silence. 'Tell me one thing while Alice is upstairs', he paused. 'You guys and religion … I mean, what happened there?'

David laughed and turned away. 'It's not a simple thing to explain.'

'You were the most ardent humanist I ever met. I mean, I'm not criticising your lifestyle choice, just trying to get my head around it.'

David stretched out his right arm and tapped his fingertips on the table. 'We were all scientists first, Gill. You remember?'

'Sure, we accepted nothing as proven unless we have the data to back it up.'

'Right.' David paused again, looking for words. Eventually, he pulled back his arm and let it rest freely by his side. 'I got new data, that's all. I had to re-evaluate.' David's eyes searched Gill's to see if he understood.

Gill nodded once, urging him to go on.

David opened up the palm of his right hand. 'I don't want you to make fun of this. I mean, you can rip the shit out of me all you want, and I'll take it. But this stuff …' he shook his head again, uncertain how to proceed.

Gill leaned into the table. 'No, it's okay. I've seen some things over the last couple of years that I can't explain. I'm cool with it.'

David smiled and rose to his feet. 'You haven't changed, Gill. Always searching, always trying to figure things out.' He walked over to a cabinet and returned with a solid oak box. He opened it and spread the contents on the table. 'Do you still play?'

Gill picked up an ornately carved chess piece and smiled. 'Sure. While my dad was fighting the early stages of dementia, we used to play quite a bit.'

'Was he any good?'

'Dogged rather than brilliant', said Gill. 'Some of the games lasted weeks. He had the master set at home, and I followed on my phone.'

'Fancy a game?' said David, already setting up the pieces.

'Sure. But I can't help feeling you're changing the subject.'

David paused, a black rook held in mid-air. 'Actually, no. It's a representation of my life these last few years.'

Gill tilted his head with the slightest of nods. 'You're becoming metaphorical in your old age.'

'Oh yes. Outsmarted at every turn by a higher intelligence. Come on. Set up your side, and I'll tell you what happened.'

Chapter 9

Gill pulled the Land Rover to a standstill, touching the electric handbrake for a second time as the car settled forwards a little in the loose gravel. Beside him, Alice was already extracting one of the twins from her car seat. Meanwhile, David ran after Noah, who had slipped his father's grasp and scampered into the building. Gill inhaled deeply and got out of the car. He stood self-consciously beside Alice for a few moments and wondered why he was here.

It was Sunday morning. When he'd left them on Friday evening, he'd only agreed to join David and Alice for church because it was the path of least resistance. Now he found himself regretting his cowardice. He'd spent the intervening Saturday walking on the Orcadian island of Hoy. Only a short distance from the mainland, the rugged isle was scarcely populated. Gill was beginning to wish he'd stayed a second day.

An older lady broke away from another family group, arriving to take Grace from Alice while she dived back into the car to retrieve Esther. Immediately the two women fell to chatting, and Gill felt like a spare part as the two friends spoke in such abbreviated sentences that even the gist of the conversation passed him by. As a diversion, he busied himself looking at the building, the spread-eagled and patched remains of an old fish processing factory, with a plywood board over the door declaring *The Fish Shed.* Most people were streaming into the main building, while others carried plastic crates towards run-down prefab huts. In the distance, a group of teenage and older boys improvised an energetic football game on a high-sided court. David reappeared, minus Noah, and chatted momentarily with an older man in a high-viz jacket who was directing a steady stream of cars towards a diminishing selection of parking places. Gill felt his shoulders sag as he realised he would soon be parked in.

David gathered Grace from Alice's friend and re-joined Gill. 'Normally, the kids go straight into their own groups, but we're doing an all-age thing this week.' He grinned at Gill. 'Which is great because it means I can pass you a small child to hold. Save you having to think about what to do with your hands.' David turned down a small corridor and passed an open space full of pool tables, table tennis and arcade games. Gill turned to watch young people spread across the room, chatting, bragging, waging the battle of the sexes with the relish only teenagers can muster. Ahead of them, a rock band was already striking up so that by the time Gill's group entered the hall, most people were on their feet. Hands raised, eyes closed, most folk oblivious to the people around them. Any hope he had of finding anonymity in the formality of religion seeped away.

He nodded politely to Alice as she indicated a row of chairs the family could file down, and he came to a halt somewhere towards the middle. He glanced around. David and Alice were already lost in whatever this communal activity was, and for a second, he wondered if he could escape without anyone noticing. Just then, he felt a tug on his right hand. A little girl in a pretty purple dress peered up at him. He was grateful he'd taken a moment to decode the twin's dress sense on his earlier visit. Grace nearly always wore red or pink. Esther had a fondness for purple. He knelt down and offered his arms to her. She accepted, and together they rose again amidst the squeeze of bodies. Esther slipped an arm behind his neck and twisted a little so she could see what was going on at the front. Gill shifted his body position a little to make it easier for the child to see. She didn't say anything but met his gaze for a moment to acknowledge this little act of kindness. Gill couldn't recall ever holding a small child in his arms before. She didn't smell. She didn't wriggle, and altogether, he found the moment surprisingly intimate. The noise of the band escalated, and he found in Esther, he had camouflage after all. He didn't know the song, but the tune was catchy, and the bass beat made it easy to follow. He checked Esther was still happy and did his best to hum along.

The next song was more accessible. An old hymn he knew from his youth but updated to a modern tune with a sparkling guitar riff. Eventually, Esther slipped wordlessly from his arms, eager to follow her siblings towards some kid's activity at the front. The adults took their seats, and David asked if he was okay.

'Great. Thanks.'

A young woman came to the front and delivered a short talk. The application in the kid's story followed seamlessly into an adult version. While, in the background, Gill could still hear unrestrained teen voices in the games room, and from further afield, the shouts of the football match reaching its crescendo. Gill only realised he had relaxed when he suddenly found himself worrying that someone might go out and shout at them.

The service finished with the same ambiguity with which it had started. He didn't see a signal that the formalities were over, but about half the people got up from their seats and started to chat or move around. Meanwhile, the band struck up again, and many people slipped back into a devotional posture.

Alice excused herself and took the kids to the toilet. David let them pass, then nudged Gill and pointed at a coffee bar in a small adjoining room.

'Well, what did you make of it?' David asked as Gill took a sip of quite reasonable coffee.

'Good. I've not been to anything like it before.'

David looked at him intently for a few moments as if parsing Gill's limited feedback into something more substantial. 'Took me a while to get used to the informality.'

'It's not quite Church of Scotland', said Gill. He'd noticed a large information board and moved a few paces to take a closer look. A mass of local and some international activities spread across the board. 'No one telling you when to stand up and when to sit down. That was confusing.'

'It's kinda the ethos of the church', said David. 'Keep the structure to a minimum. Makes it accessible.'

A little way off, the older man Gill had seen earlier directing traffic was finishing a conversation. As he did so, he turned to face them. 'Morning, David. Good to see you. How was the system test this week?'

David grimaced. 'Another washout, Mack. We're just struggling to get everything to work on the same day.'

'It was assembled so quickly', said Mack. 'You have to expect teething troubles.' He stopped and offered Gill an outstretched hand.

David leaned forward. 'Sorry, Gill. This is Mack. Our pastor.'

Gill returned the gesture but couldn't suppress a puzzled look from passing over his face. 'Sorry. I didn't see you up the front. Perhaps I missed that bit of the service?'

Mack smiled. 'No. That's just the art of delegation.' His sharp blue eyes darted between the men. 'Do you guys work together?'

'Old friends, recently reacquainted', said David. 'Gill's a journalist. He's doing a piece on ScoCion this week, amongst other things.'

'That's great. I'm glad you've had the chance to visit', said Mack, waving to a couple walking past.

David looked distracted for a few seconds. 'Sorry, Noah is wandering too close to the games tables again. Excuse me while I see what he's up to.'

'Well, it was nice to meet you', said Gill, edging after David.

'I'll walk with you', Mack replied. 'Technically, I should be out in the car park. Not a job I relish. Easier to pack them in than get them out.'

Gill pointed to the games area as they walked. The teens had been supplanted. A tide of smaller children forcing their older siblings to retreat to the back of the room, where they stood in small groups, hunched over their phones and capitalising on any excuse to brush against each other. 'Nothing like this in church when I was growing up.'

Mack shrugged happily. 'It was an experiment. We've tried to open the building to local people as much as possible. It gave us some benefit by way of relationship building, and it's been good to offer young folks a safe place to meet.'

Mack exchanged a few brief conversations with his parishioners while they made their way to the car park. To Gill's relief, the car that had parked him in was already loading up. To make conversation, he nodded towards the

"For Sale" sign on the old building. 'Are you buying or selling?'

'Selling', said Mack.

Gill nodded. The church was filling the old factory to bursting. 'Where's the new venue?'

Mack smiled a little wistfully. 'We don't have one.' He looked at Gill. 'We're winding up the church.'

Again Gill was perplexed. 'I'm sorry to hear that. You seem to have a good thing going here … Money issues?' he said after a gap.

Mack shook his head. 'Quite the contrary. We struggled financially for decades, but not these days.'

'Why then?'

Mack stared into the far distance for a moment. 'Churches are like any other organisation. They tend to peak.'

'Okay. A little disharmony in the ranks?'

Mack shrugged. 'A few folks are opposed to us closing the church, but even in our sense of community, we're in better shape than we've been for years.'

Gill's confusion bubbled to the surface. 'But surely, all these families, all the activities you run. Won't you be missed?'

Mack turned fully to face Gill. 'If you've not been around churches, you won't know what I mean. Don't get me wrong, most start well, with real passion and great intentions. But eventually, they become moribund, or fiefdoms, or worse.' He stopped to look around the car park, where a dozen conversations flowed. 'We're selling a building, Gill.' He jagged a thumb back over his shoulder. 'That's the church. It's them, all those people and relationships.'

At that moment, David and Alice appeared behind them with a hungry brood in tow. 'Gill! Lunch?'

'I've got to spend a couple of hours over at Skara Brae this afternoon, and I'm not sure this good light will last.'

'Come on. A quick sandwich, then I'll drive you over. I need some beach time with Noah.'

Gill thought for a moment. 'Okay. Thank you.'

Mack grasped Gill's upper arm and squeezed it. 'Good to meet you, Gill.' Then he slipped off to join another cluster of people.

'Your pastor was telling me he's winding up your church', said Gill as they left the Skara Brae visitor centre car park and walked towards the dunes.

'Well, it's a group decision', said David. 'When Mack and his wife and a few others formed the trust that ultimately became the church, they decided right at the start to allow it a limited life. The constitution they established said when the church was forty years old, we would wind it up and divide its assets amongst successor groups.'

'At least something continues', said Gill. 'This isn't really the end?'

'Not at all. At the last count, we have fourteen separate projects that will either continue as separate entities after the church has closed, or will launch as new ventures.'

'Such as?'

'At the moment, we pull in people from all over the island. In a few months, half a dozen smaller outfits will work in their local communities, including one here in Kirkwall.'

'But without the backing of a larger organisation', said Gill. 'Why didn't the mother church just plant out a lot of little churches?'

David smiled and stared at his feet as he walked. 'It was one potential model. But you end up with a hierarchy, pressure on finances, and other potential problems. It's painful, but I'd imagine it's better this way.'

Noah ran ahead and diverted off the main path onto the beach. The men followed behind with Gill's photographic equipment split between them. 'Must be tough for you and Alice, seeing the end of something you care about.'

'Yes, and tough for the kids as they won't see all of their friends every week. But we both believe church should be organic. Stop it getting formal.'

Gill laughed. 'I wouldn't have called it a formal.'

'No, but this way, we all get to put our energies into something new; see what happens.'

Gill felt his eyebrows arch, and he hoped David hadn't seen. 'What if nothing happens and the whole thing fizzles out?'

'Every church fizzles out eventually', said David. 'We're choosing to explode rather than fade away.'

Gill shrugged. 'Well, it seems crazy to me.' He stopped and stared up at a patch of the dunes. It wasn't evident from where they stood, but Skara Brae, Britain's finest Neolithic settlement, lay nestled behind crumbling rock armour. The whole site was fighting a losing battle against the sea.

'Doesn't look like much from here', said David as he dropped to his knees and started to assemble a small kite.

Gill sighed. 'Not exactly the pyramids. But I suppose, when you look at how the rest of Britain lived four thousand years ago, it must have seemed pretty advanced.'

David securely fastened the kite to its line. 'No rush, but roughly how long do you need?'

'Couple of hours max', said Gill, shouldering the tripod David passed him. 'I'll get a bunch of close-up shots while the light is strong, then drop back into the dunes to get some context.'

'Great. We'll come and find you later.' David started to walk off but turned and waved his phone at Gill. 'If you get bored, I've sent you my next move. Knight to B2'

Gill refused Alice's offer of yet another meal and left the family to their Sunday evening and to prepare for the week ahead. The children were so at ease around him that Noah insisted on walking him to his car while Esther waved from her father's arms.

'Will you come back and see us before you fly away?' said Noah solemnly.

Gill gave the boy's hair a tiny ruffle. 'I'll come back and see you all again soon', he said.

He drove through the outskirts of Kirkwall and out onto the Finstown Road, suppressing the instinct to find a bar.

Instead, he went on a few miles and pulled up in the deserted car park at Tormiston Mill. He pulled out his phone and dialled Salina.

Half an hour later, lifted by the sight of her face and the energy in their conversation, he stepped onto the tarmac and started a few warm-up stretches. He'd had the foresight to throw in his running gear before he left that morning. He surveyed the landscape around him and selected a point on the lower ground, some four miles distant beyond the Ring of Brodgar. Then he checked his watch and started to run.

Jim parked his car in Brough and walked the half-mile along a fisherman's track on the fringe of the loch. Some distance out, he stopped and studied the landscape for any sign of threat. The land around him was a mix of browns, and greys, and muted greens. It looked autumnal. Though it saddened him to realise it, everything looked autumnal through Jim's eyes these days. The world itself looked smeared with the washed-out colours of a season past its best.

Approaching Harray Church via this overland route, he noted with satisfaction the gravelled car park sheltered only a single car. Annie Sinclair, a caretaker for the church and the oldest member of "The Vigil", wasn't as sound on her legs as she used to be. Glancing about, he entered the church via a side door, closing it carefully before making his way through the main building and into the vestry.

'Ah. Our merry band is further reduced', he said, nodding in turn to the faces of the three already seated.

'Evening to you too', said Annie, tilting her head at an empty chair.

'No sign of Brian?' he said, sitting down.

Annie shook her head. 'It's hit him pretty hard. I don't think we'll see him back again anytime soon.'

Jim forced a business-like smile. 'Well, locusts and honey. What we do isn't for the faint-hearted.'

'And just what are we doing?' said Ivor Flett. None of the usual warmth lighting his eyes.

Jim stared at Ivor before reaching across and grasping his shoulder. 'We keep doing what we've always done. Protect the stones. Wait until *he* comes.'

Ivor didn't look reassured. 'I thought we'd agreed *he'd* be here by now. Unless someone's done the numbers wrong.'

Jim sat back in his chair. 'The numbers aren't wrong. We've had one hundred and seventy years to make sure of that.'

'But what if they are wrong?'

'Jim's right. We need to stay the course', said Annie.

'I hear Morrison's started another dig.' Thomas Muir this time. Self-styled gentleman farmer and the most militant of the group.

Jim nodded. 'Aye, she took a notion right at the end of the season.'

'Any threat to the stones?'

'None. I managed to deflect her towards a midden well away from the monument.'

'I hear she has an archaeologist from off-island. Do we need to worry about him?'

Jim shook his head. 'One of these, here today, gone tomorrow types. He thinks he's very grand. I took him for a long walk a couple of days ago. By the time he's had the excitement of digging up a few shells, he'll have had enough fresh air to send him happily back to Dundee.'

'Not sure we need to bother protecting the stones anymore', said Ivor.

'I disagree', snapped Annie. 'Until we know what's happening, orders are orders.'

'And in the meantime, none of us are getting any younger. This isn't sustainable as things stand.'

Annie glared at Ivor before swinging her attention to Jim. 'Any news on your erstwhile protégée?'

Jim looked away. 'He's still missing.'

'And are we certain he's not, you know; *him*?'

'Twitch!' roared Thomas. 'Annie, give us a break!'

A debate exploded, and Jim had to stand to quieten them down. 'We don't know what Twitch's role is in all this. But we all saw him that night. Whether he was just an observer of our search or if he has a deeper role, time will tell.'

'Twitch is a distraction', said Ivor quietly. 'It's ScoCion we should be worried about.'

Jim was trying to remain patient. 'We've no evidence ScoCion is any threat.'

Thomas again. 'They're on the bloody map. Of course, they're a threat.'

'Twitch will show up. He always does. And then we'll sit him down and ask him what he knows.'

‘And ScoCion?’

‘ScoCion, Thomas. What would you have me do?’

Thomas rearranged himself on a chair that was too small for him. ‘As long as we’re ready to move against them if the time comes.’

Jim kept his face expressionless as he considered the weight of what his oldest friend was asking of him. ‘Aye, Thomas’, he said after a pause. ‘Whatever it takes.’

Chapter 10

Gill stood in the centre of the Brodgar circle and studied the landscape. It was Monday morning, and he was trying to grasp the context of the Neolithic remains before Juliette's dig commenced the following day. He'd done a lot of reading over the weekend. She had emailed him digitised site plans of various excavations over the years. Usually, he'd have this kind of information printed on large sheets, but today he only had the scans and his iPad to work with. Nevertheless, he managed to identify the locations of past major excavations, walking the turf and setting his upcoming dig within the perspective of what had gone before. Crucially, he confirmed no one had ever dug in the location of Juliette's Chi Rho stone.

One thing did perplex him - that no record existed of an excavation in the centre of the circle. Jim had mentioned this and Juliette's data was confirmation. Over the years, various digs had intersected the ditch and dyke to investigate its construction. And the Victorian era had seen several fallen stones restored to standing. Ancient pits cut in the bedrock had revealed their original locations, guiding the gentlemen archaeologists to slot the standing stones back into place. But nothing in the centre.

Gill began his morning by sweeping the area with a magnetometer he'd borrowed from Juliette. Then he revisited data gathered by a team surveying the circle several years before. Everything pointed to the same conclusion: the ground at the centre of the circle was a skim of earth over bedrock and had never been disturbed. And yet every fibre of Gill's instinct told him something was there. As he stood contemplating this, he saw a man walking beyond the stones. He looked faintly familiar, so Gill lifted a hand in greeting. The man reciprocated and started to stroll towards him. When Gill reached the perimeter of the circle, he waited on firm ground until the older man made his way through the heather.

'Pastor Mack. Good morning.'

Mack approached and shook Gill's hand. 'Good to see you again. I thought you were working up at ScoCion?'

'I've attended a couple of meetings. It's far too technical for me. Archaeology is my sweet spot.'

'Plenty of that around here', said Mack, waving vaguely towards the stones. They stood in silence for a few moments until Mack spoke again. 'I'm constantly drawn to this place. It's fascinating.'

'Are you local?'

Mack shook his head. 'A Shetlander, originally. When my wife and I moved here four decades ago, I still worked in the oil industry. Stayed at that until the church started to grow.'

'My brother worked in oil', said Gill, hoping this part of the conversation didn't go any further.

Perhaps sensing his discomfort, Mack waved at the stones. 'You must be an expert. What do you make of it all?'

Gill glanced around and suppressed a shrug. 'No one knows for sure. Maybe astronomical measurement. Or perhaps a place of worship. Either way, it must have been an attempt to understand our world and its place in the universe.'

Mack smiled. 'That's interesting. What makes you think that?'

Gill glanced around the stones. 'An ancient society invested a great effort to build the monuments on this isthmus. In my experience, the most durable buildings were either fortresses or places of worship. And this place wasn't a fort.'

Mack considered this. 'It certainly doesn't look like a castle.'

'A long time ago, the ditch and dyke were much larger than we see today, meaning it could have been a defensible position. But we have no signs of construction inside the circle, so that pretty much rules it out.'

'So by process of elimination, it must be some form of temple', said Mack.

Gill's head dipped to his chest. 'A temple. An observatory. People with a purpose and in search of meaning.'

'From a time long ago.' Mack shook his head. 'I'm amazed they had the time.'

'And clearly, they were working to a technical model we haven't fully understood.'

Mack seemed interested. 'In what sense?'

'It's messy. Usually, the stones would synchronise with various alignments of the moon or the visible planets.'

'To what end?'

Gill shrugged. 'Who knows. It would help tell the time of year and the passing of the years to some degree. But the alignments here are a bit off. Makes me wonder what they were trying to achieve.'

'Not a giant sundial then?'

'More likely paganism and bowing down to heavenly bodies.' He glanced at Mack. 'I doubt they practised a form of worship you would have approved of, Pastor.'

Mack shrugged. 'It was a different time.'

'Different religions, but folk still asking the same old questions?'

Mack smiled. 'If you have the courage to ask your big questions, you can travel towards faith.'

'So there might still be a place for naked nymphs dancing under a solstice moon?'

Mack laughed. 'Definitely! In fact, find me some and I'll invite them to *The Fish Shed's* closing party.'

Gill smiled, realising he had relaxed in the older man's company. 'Are you looking forward to a bit more spare time? Retirement even?'

'Ah, I think just a little bit of me is', said Mack, brightening.

'I'm sorry, but I'm intrigued', said Gill, picking his words carefully. 'Do you regret writing a forty-year lifespan into your church's constitution?'

Mack shook his head. 'I don't regret it. "For forty years, I'll bless you. Then you must scatter your inheritance across the islands." That was the deal.'

Gill was puzzled. 'Deal with whom?'

'God, of course', said Mack, shifting his balance to lean against an upright stone. 'He kept his side of the bargain. Now we're keeping ours.'

Gill said nothing.

Mack glanced at him. 'What makes you uncomfortable? The thought of us closing a reasonably successful church or the idea of God speaking?'

Gill thought for a second. 'Both, I suppose. Especially the latter. Bit outside my experience.'

'That's why I love coming to these stones', said Mack. 'Somehow, the voice of God is just a little easier to hear.'

'I thought the Bible was the voice of God?' said Gill.

'Yes. And I believe it is. But sometimes we need a wee nudge to help us focus on the bits that are especially relevant to us.'

'What kind of nudge?'

'To remember a promise or receive encouragement. It could be many things.'

Gill stood silently for a few moments. 'I met a girl a while back. She was a prophet. She heard some scarily accurate things in her consciousness that she ascribed to God.'

Mack nodded. 'Which brings me back to our forty-year conviction. That began with three honest people who all quite separately heard from God. Faced with that amount of confirmation, we've never doubted it.'

'Still, it must be tough', said Gill, momentarily distracted by a text coming in.

'Aye, but we're committed to it.' Mack pushed back from the stone and stood upright. 'I'm sorry, you came out here to muse on stones, and you're on the brink of getting a sermon.'

'No, it's fine, Mack. It's nice to bump into folk and ...' He paused, losing his train of thought.

'Are you okay? You suddenly look quite pale.'

Gill lifted his phone and gave it a jiggle. 'Just stuff. Life can be complicated.'

Mack smiled and lifted a hand in farewell. 'It can indeed. I'll leave you to it. Have a good day.'

'You too', Gill murmured. He wasn't sure he meant it. Glancing at his phone again, he didn't think the omens for today looked all that good at all.

Gill waited for an hour before responding to Alice's text. 'Do you think this is a good idea?' he said in reply.

Her response came back in moments. 'I only want to talk.'

He took a long, slow breath. 'Okay. Where?'

'Has to be the house. Children. Remember? By 1 pm if possible.'

He looked at his watch. 'Dammit, Alice', he said quietly, though there was no one there to hear him. 'Let's not do this.'

Against his better judgement, he confirmed he'd be with her shortly, then began the short drive over to Kirkwall.

Alice was smiling as she opened the door, though Gill thought she looked nervous.

'Thanks for coming. Have you had any lunch?'

He shook his head. 'I'm fine, thanks. Breakfast and dinner at the B&B. Even at two meals a day, I'm putting on weight.'

She stood back and held the door open for him.

He hesitated, studying her face. 'Alice. What are we doing here?'

She looked puzzled for a few moments. 'You and David got so into it the other evening, and I had a few things I didn't get to say.'

He nodded, weighing her intentions. 'Look, David is a friend. If my presence is an issue for you guys, maybe I should make myself scarce.'

Her face switched from puzzled to utterly confused. 'I'm not sure what you mean. All I wanted to say …' She stopped, and a hand flew to her mouth. 'You're worried I'm propositioning you!'

'No, I. Well …'

Alice stepped out of the house and flung her arms around his neck. 'You lovely, lovely guy. As ever, you're emotionally about a lap behind the rest of us.'

She released his neck and held him at arm's length. 'Amazing as this might sound, even though you're still gorgeous, I'm not scouting for some kind of emotional encounter.'

He glanced left and right, checking Alice's neighbours weren't within earshot. 'Okay … Coffee?'

'That was kinda the plan. Follow me.'

Gill trailed sheepishly behind her into a kitchen still strewn with the remains of breakfast, lunch, or both. 'You said you wanted to talk.'

'Yes. If it's okay with you, I'd like to talk about the Great Glen disaster. Especially Fort William.'

Gill paused, staring at the floor. 'It's a bomb site. What do you want to know?'

'They're rebuilding, yes?'

Gill nodded. 'They will in due course. Chance for a clean sheet.'

'What about you?'

'How do you mean?'

'Are you rebuilding? Are you working off a clean sheet?'

'Alice, a lap behind, remember? Drive slower.'

She pointed him to a seat and popped the kettle on. 'We saw you a few months ago on TV. The day of the disaster. Someone interviewed you in Fort William.'

'Yes. I'd figured out what was happening. Too late to help everyone, unfortunately.'

She shook her head. 'The emergency alert that went out. That was you?'

'No. That was a retired navy engineer.'

'But you had something to do with it?'

Gill shrugged.

'I knew it! And it's typical of the Gill McArdle I knew; he never tried to bag the glory.'

Gill released a deep breath he'd been holding, remembering some terrible things he'd seen that day. 'There wasn't much glory to be bagged.'

She nodded again. 'I understand. Just a shedload of pain. And in a moment, I'd like to pray with you about that.'

'Beg your pardon?'

'You were on a battlefield, Gill. You are carrying emotional scars. For David and me, prayer is a bit like medicine. If you're willing, of course.'

Gill shrugged. 'I guess.'

'First, there's something else'. She poured water over the coffee grains and then buried her fingers in a rack full of notes. Finding what she was looking for, she presented him with a newspaper cutting. Pointing to a cluster of people in the foreground, she said, 'This is you, right?'

Gill nodded. 'It's the wild cat interview Salina and I did with a freelance news team. The majors picked it up.'

Alice moved her finger towards the back of the picture. 'What about these guys?'

Gill strained to see who she was highlighting. His eyesight wasn't up to the job, so he reached into his pocket for his illuminated magnification. Looking closely, he made out three burly men standing among a group of people, watching the news interview. Two men with muscular arms flanked a third, wearing a short ponytail.

'Rescuers', he said. 'Everybody was mucking in.'

'Yes, but who are they?' she protested.

He flicked the photo with his index finger. 'You tell me. You started this conversation.'

'I haven't a clue. For some reason, these guys stuck out to me. Their presence is significant.'

'Why?'

She shook her head and shoulders. 'Never mind. Squirrelly Christian stuff that would take too long to explain. Just look at them again. Any idea who they are?'

Gill sighed and studied the image. The big guy on the left he didn't recognise. The guy on the right had his back to the photographer. That left the man in the middle. The man with two swords nonchalantly slung behind his back.

'Oh', he said quietly.

'Yes! I was afraid you might say that. Who is he?'

Gill studied Alice's face for any sign he was being manipulated. He found her expression was deadly serious. 'I believe his name is Raphael. As crazy as it sounds, my friend Salina thinks he's her guardian angel.'

Alice took a step back from him, then a second, slumping heavily into a kitchen chair. She rubbed her face, then asked, 'The writing on the other guy's jacket, can you make it out?'

Gill had to dig deep with his lens to overcome the blurring effect of the pixels. Eventually, he confirmed enough letters to make an educated guess. 'It has the words "Rex Gladio" around the motif of a lion's head.'

She nodded. 'And does that mean anything to you?'

'Probably just coincidence.'

Alice vigorously shook her head. 'Don't think so. I can see the look on your face. This means something to you.'

'I saw it before. At Callanish, but I don't know what it means.'

Alice leaned forwards and joined both forefingers to point at him. 'Can I suggest that, at your earliest convenience, you make it a priority to find out?'

The growing chatter of young voices over a baby monitor was what it took for Alice to release her grip on him. For twenty minutes, she had prayed to her God for Gill's healing from trauma, for his relationship with Salina, and most ambiguously, for his enquiries into the three men in the photo. She cried freely throughout, and towards the end, he did too. She prayed for his forgiveness that she had drifted away from him and into the arms of David Trevelyan. And she thanked her God for both these men and for her children. When they prised themselves apart, they were both sticky with sweat and tears.

He held her at arm's length, not knowing exactly what it was she'd done but certain she'd poured her heart and soul into it. 'Thank you', was all he could say.

She smiled a teary smile. 'Better than sex, eh?'

He laughed. 'Maybe! We must be getting old.'

She followed him to the door. 'Love you, Gill McArdle.'

He hugged her one last time. 'Love you too, Alice Trevelyan.'

Chapter 11

Thanks for the legacy site drawings', said Gill as Juliette walked up to him in the car park the following morning. 'I walked the old dig sites yesterday afternoon and confirmed there's no overlap with today's activities.'

'Great. Sorry I couldn't get you paper originals.' She reached into her kit bag. 'I do have one other source document for you. It's a bit of a personal treasure, so I'd like it back.'

Gill took the book she offered and surveyed the cover. '*An Account of the Celtic Antiquities of Orkney, including the Stones of Brodgar, Stenness, Tumuli, Picts-houses, etc.*' he read aloud. 'By Lieutenant Wilson, Commanding officer of HM Surveying Vessel, *Curlew*, writing in 1851.'

He flicked through the pages, darkened by time and the passing of many hands. 'It's beautiful', he said. 'Before science, there was only art.'

Juliette scowled at him. 'Don't get all farty on me. And it's a bloody good read. Technically sound but without any academic pretence. No offence.'

He smiled. 'None taken. I'll pop it in the car for later. Keep it out of the rain.'

A faint but persistent drizzle hung over the dig site as Juliette poked flags in the ground to set the limit around where they had permission to dig. Jim had set up an outer perimeter of red tape and was already fending off the curiosity of the first passers-by. The four volunteer diggers stood in a semi-circle around Gill as he gave them directions.

'You're going to find lots of shells. When everything you're handling looks the same, it's easy to miss something significant, so we need to stay alert.'

'Apart from recovering the stone', said one middle-aged woman, 'What are we looking for?'

Gill stared at his feet for a few seconds. 'The key finding today will be to confirm if someone dumped the stone while the shell midden was accumulating or if a con artist, most likely from the Victorian era, is trying to bluff us. I'll be looking for any evidence the ground has been disturbed in the last four and a half millennia.'

The group nodded and exchanged tips on what they might observe if someone had inserted the stone during the centuries since the midden had formed.

'You're not expecting any unicorn bones', smirked one of the team.

Gill sighed. 'Unicorns, dragons, fairies. Anything's possible. Keep your wits about you.'

The group laughed, and Gill wrapped up the briefing. He stood watching the diggers as they headed back to the car park to fetch more tools. He was searching in his psyche for his "tell". That weird, undetermined sense of expectation, hinting he was on the trail of something important. At this moment in time, he felt nothing of the sort.

Juliette walked up behind him an hour later and patted him between the shoulder blades. 'Relax. These guys have worked with us for several seasons. You'll find they're quite good.'

Gill nodded stiffly and forced a smile. 'Can see that.'

'Gosh, you're really keyed up', said Juliette. 'Are you always this stressed at the start of a dig?'

Gill looked at her. 'Probably, yeah.'

Juliette withdrew her hand. 'It's just history.'

'Aye', said Gill. 'Completely harmless.' He walked away from her and prowled along the perimeter established by Jim. He glanced to make sure she wasn't watching him, then stalked the route again, facing away from the dig, his eyes scanning the low ground around them, and senses alert for any kind of threat.

A few hours later, Gill and the rest of the team stood caked in the rich peaty mud that permeated everything. The exception was Jim Robertson, who had declared his discomfort with disturbing a potential grave. He'd delivered a short lecture on what he saw as the sacred nature of human remains and withdrawn outside the barrier tape. From there, he watched the proceedings with his arms folded and a scowl on his face.

Gill ignored him and focused on his task as he guided the low lifter to edge forward until its tangs overhung the exposed slab. He ordered it to stop, and they all breathed relief as the diesel engine switched off again. Gill slipped the first of several leather straps under the Chi Rho stone and walked back to check the wooden pallets were level enough to support the entire length of the stone once it was free. Then the process of strip, grade, sort and tipping the spoil continued for another hour. The first straps gradually tightened, indicating that the half-formed cradle supported the stone's weight. Then Gill called another halt, slipping more straps under the other end of the stone.

'Are you ready?' he asked the team.

Juliette, red-faced and sweating, gave an urgent nod. Gill repeated his instructions to the driver of the low lifter, then stepped in amongst the straps to make sure nothing was about to slip. The engine fired up, and Gill's forefinger tapped skyward as the stone gradually began to lift. Once it was a foot clear of the ground, he called a halt, then called the team to help guide the stone through 180 degrees until they could lower it onto the pallets. The machine eased back a few yards from the dig until the driver cut the engine.

'Hold on a second', cried Gill as the others clambered back into the midden. He had to restrain himself. Instead of leaping into the shallow pit uncovered by the stone, he crawled along the edge, studying the hole from different angles. Eventually, he stood up and walked back to the crew.

'Anything?' Juliette asked.

Gill shook his head. 'Just shells. We're back to strip and sort. Let's take this area down forty centimetres, and then we'll review.

Juliette swore under her breath and then turned to shout at Jim. 'Happy now, Mr Robertson? No human bones.'

Robertson just nodded and walked away.

Gill watched him go. 'What's his beef?'

Juliette glanced over her shoulders. 'As well as being a devoted conservationist of this entire area, Jim has a wee side-line in something called "The Vigil".'

'Never heard of it', said Gill.

'Hang around here long enough, and he'll try to recruit you. It's a bad habit he learnt when he led the kirk.'

'I'm not following.'

Juliette glanced skywards. 'It's a wee sect or some local splinter within the Presbyterians. They believe the second coming will be on Orkney. Or something whacky like that. I don't sufficiently give a shit to know the full details.'

Gill just looked at her, open-mouthed.

'They believe the date of the second coming is written in the stones', said Juliette. 'I guess it makes them fussy if we move anything.' She shook her head at Jim's diminishing figure. 'Because the stones are his passion, he knows them better than anyone. Doesn't stop him being a right pain in the ass.'

As the working day waned, Juliette waited until the volunteers were safely out of earshot, then leaned deep inside Gill's personal space. 'Well, that was crap.'

'You never strike gold on the first day', said Gill, closing his eyes and turning his face to the ebbing sun.

'And we broke the bloody stone', she said, turning away from him so she could cough violently into the crook of her arm.

'Just a piece. Don't beat yourself up. The rock flaw wasn't visible until we'd committed to the lift. It was probably broken before we arrived.'

'Well, I'm bricking it until we stow it safely at Tormiston.' They both turned to watch the low loader inching its way across the heather towards the main road, with the precious stone resting in a sling hung between its tangs. It was on level ground, but it would take another hour before the stone arrived at the car park, where Juliette could safely stow it in a workshop.

Juliette nodded at the excavation. 'You think we'll find anything?'

'Apart from shells?' Gill forced some warmth into his smile. 'We'll have to dig all day tomorrow if we want certainty. But no. I see zero evidence the ground has ever been disturbed. And I'm sure the midden isn't faked.'

'But is it a burial site?'

Gill shook his head. 'It's not looking that way. You wouldn't use a decorated stone to bury a low-status person. And you're not likely to bury a high-status person in a midden.'

Frustrated, Juliette took six long strides until she stood in the middle of the works. 'So, what's your theory? We have an anomalous stone with a carving that couldn't possibly exist, covering ... what, nothing?'

'Thinking about this', said Gill slowly. 'Maybe there's no big mystery. Given this is a Neolithic rubbish heap, maybe the stone was simply dumped.'

'What? They did all that work and just tossed it away?'

Gill shrugged. 'There are natural flaws in the stone. And by the looks of things, it wasn't quite finished.'

‘Bloody brilliant’, said Juliette, stepping back out of the hole. ‘Massive sodding leap forward for human knowledge.’ She turned on her heels. ‘I’m going to supervise the loader, just in case he knackers the one artefact we can bank from today.’

Gill watched her for just long enough to return her farewell wave if it came. When it didn’t, he drew a deep breath and dropped wearily onto a clump of heather. He pulled out his phone and called up the images he had taken of the stone from multiple angles. Then he zoomed in on the Chi Rho, sitting to the left of the centre in the hexagonal stone block. He passed through the images twice and then put away his phone. Then he stared out to sea and started to think.

Chapter 12

The foul mood Juliette brought with her the following day lasted until Gill brought her a coffee and enthused about the book she'd lent him.

'I read until midnight, then finished it this morning. Wonderful.'

'It's his hand-drawn illustrations', said Juliette. 'They must have taken Wilson a day each. An absolute passion for detail.'

Gill nodded. 'It's the way he sticks to facts as he sees them. He never speculates what the stones were for.'

'Ah, I think he does that in a later book.'

Gill felt his face brighten. 'Really?'

'He wrote the first book while employed by HM Government, where the brief was purely to study and record. I gather he didn't write his second volume until after he retired.'

'I googled him', said Gill. 'He was quite an expert on Persian antiquities. I saw references to the 1851 volume but didn't read about any other books.'

'Might have been privately published.'

'Do you have a copy?'

Juliette shook her head. 'Only heard of it by reputation. Jim Robertson told me about it. He might have one on his shelf.'

'I'll ask him.'

'Oh, I'm sure it will be his pleasure to assist a modern-day graverobber like yourself.'

'I can ask.'

'Right. Shall we get to work?

'Aye. Are you okay to supervise the Chi Rho site? I want to follow up on something in Mr Wilson's book.'

Gill sensed her resentment as he left her to manage the tail end of the unpromising dig while he turned his attention back to the ring of Brodgar. He'd had some extra equipment flown in and busied himself criss-crossing the circle with ground-penetrating radar. During the mid-afternoon, Juliette strolled over to see him. 'I think we've wasted enough time. I'd like you to give our excavations the once over. Then we'll do a quick backfill and let the volunteers go home. If that's alright with you?'

Gill nodded. 'Definitely.' He greeted her deflated scowl with a steadying smile. 'Can I show you something?'

She wiped her brow, smudging mud across her forehead. 'As long as it doesn't involve me wasting two days of my life digging a meaningless hole.'

'No promises.'

'Piss off then.'

Juliette lingered to enjoy the shock on his face before she added, 'Sorry, bad joke. What have you got?'

'Wilson claims in 1851 that no one ever attempted an excavation in the circle's centre. And based on contemporary records, I recall you said the same.'

Juliette nodded.

'Well, I think it's intriguing.'

Shrugging, she said. 'It's bedrock under a skim of heather. What do you expect?'

Gill pulled out a digital pad from his waistcoat pocket. 'The Chi Rho stone; it's this shape, right?' He sketched the uneven shape with a few finger strokes. 'And if we add back the piece that fell off, it gives us this hexagonal shape.'

'Unfinished, but yeah, basically hexagonal.'

'And the logical assumption is the Chi Rho symbol was originally in the centre of the stone.'

Juliette shrugged. 'Okay, a hexagon. And I can see how the shape of the slab is an extension of the six arms of the Chi Rho. But you don't see this anywhere in Neolithic art, so I'm bound to ask you, where does that get us?'

'Why they chose this symbol is still unknown, but it does help us in one subtle way.'

'How?'

'This', said Gill. He tabbed to a screen criss-crossed in multiple faint lines. 'I scanned the centre of the Brodgar circle and built up this image of crack lines in the bedrock.'

'It's a mess.'

'That's because I've scanned at different depths and overlaid every discernible rock fissure on the same screen. Watch what happens when I pick out the cracks at eighty centimetres.'

Juliette took his pad in her hands. 'Hmm, looks hexagonal. The dimensions …'

'Match the Chi Rho stone quite snuggly.'

Juliette considered this, then shook her head. 'Eighty centimetres, Gill. That's well below the surface. I see the shape you're pointing at, but it's wishful thinking.'

'Bang in the centre of the circle? No coincidence.' He tabbed to a different screen. 'Look what happens when I pull back a little and drop to sixty-centimetre depth.'

'Okay. Looks like a thin horizontal cavity.'

'You can see it?'

'Aye. So, you think there's a hexagonal stone with a much larger slab placed over it?'

'Yes. And this is the spot where every other survey in the past one hundred years has interpreted as bedrock.'

'The Chi Rho stone we took out of the midden ...' said Juliette, pointing vaguely in the direction of Tormiston. 'What's the link?'

'I think the manufacturer's goal was to place it in the centre of the circle, but my guess is a piece broke off, and they scrapped it before making a new one. But to prove that, we need to lift the cover slab they've placed on top of the buried hexagonal stone.'

Juliette blinked at him a few times. 'Gill, that's a massive task. And in the middle of the stone circle! You've no idea how long it would take to get permission to dig in here.'

'All I need is just a peek. If we find nothing, then fair enough. But my educated guess is if you lift off the capstone cover, you'll reveal the second hexagonal with a Chi Rho etched right smack in the centre. And if you investigate that, you'll find the cause of this mystery.'

When Gill arrived at David and Alice's on Wednesday evening, they were clearing up and getting the kids ready for bed.

'Do you want to come in?'

Gill thought David looked sincere but very tired. 'No, I won't, thanks. I need to get back to Stromness to write up today's dig.'

'How did it go?' asked Alice, arriving behind David and slipping an arm around his waist.

Gill shrugged. 'Solved one little mystery, I think. Posed another.'

'Worthwhile then?'

'Yes. And the good news is I'll be back for a piece of follow-up work.'

'When?'

'We might get it done this season, but more likely in the spring.'

'Historic Scotland won't be in any hurry', said Alice.

'Me neither', Gill replied. 'If Brodgar holds any secrets, they're not going anywhere.'

Alice smiled wearily and said nothing.

'And how are you guys?'

David pulled Alice a little closer to him. 'Morale at ScoCion has been pretty low since Friday. It's one technical niggle after another. The good news is we've found some coding weaknesses in the software running the targeting array. We'll run some simulations next week, and if they go well, we'll be ready for another full test in about ten days.'

'Come back and see it', said Alice. 'You can stay here and let us be your chauffeur.'

Gill shook his head. 'I've blown the budget on this one. But I'd appreciate it if you could let me know how it goes. I want to put ScoCion in the magazine soon, so an update would be useful.'

'We'll see you again.' Alice leaned forward and gave Gill a fleeting kiss on his cheek, then excused herself to go and sort the kids.

Gill nodded after her. 'I assume Alice told you we spoke?'

David smiled. 'You had quite a session, I gather.'

'We did.'

'I hope it helped. Trauma can be debilitating.'

'You know, until Alice mentioned it, I hadn't realised how raw the memories are.'

'You must have seen terrible things.'

Gill shrugged. 'In the moment, I was just another survivor doing what they could to help. What I hadn't anticipated was the guilt I feel.'

'What do you mean?'

Gill turned and stared at a far-away object until he steadied himself. 'That I couldn't save more.'

‘When you come back, let’s talk about it again.’

‘Definitely’, said Gill. He gave his head a tiny shake. ‘It has been so good to link up with you guys again.’

‘It’s been a pleasure’, said David, grasping Gill’s outstretched hand.

‘It has’, said Gill. ‘Beautiful family. You’re a lucky man.’

David laughed. ‘I don’t believe in luck.’

Gill smiled, taking his meaning. ‘Okay. Let’s see if you get divine inspiration for this one.’ He lifted his phone and keyed a move into his chess app.

David’s phone buzzed, and he opened the app to see Gill’s move. It was several seconds before he spoke. ‘Queen to D4. You bugger.’

‘Took me two days to come up with that’, said Gill, leaning into the doorway to embrace his friend. ‘Just a little something to remember me by.’

Gill’s flight on Thursday morning was first thing, so it was late morning when he rolled into the Dundee office of *Mysterious Scotland.* The team was busy, so it took the sound of his laptop bag hitting his desk to alert Cassy to his arrival.

‘Welcome back, stranger. How was it?’

Gill tilted his head from side to side. ‘A mixed bag. ScoCion thing was interesting, but they haven’t got it working yet. Loads of pictures of Skara Brae and other sites. The Brodgar dig was useful. Got more work on that in the future.’

Cassy glanced back at her screen and continued typing. 'I didn't see your face on the news. That was positive.'

'My face on the news sells magazines', said Gill with mock offence.

Cassy nodded across the office to another cluster of desks. 'The other editors have started to call you "The Angel of Death".'

Gill surveyed the room for a second, avoiding eye contact with anyone who lifted their head. 'No one dies in a hobby mag', he whispered indignantly. 'We're different because we cover real news.'

'And the news is …' said Cassy theatrically, 'there's loads of work to do.' She nodded at the heap of post on his desk. 'I'll let you get on with that. And I've taken the liberty of organising a team meeting for 2.30.'

Gill gave her a sloppy salute, then wandered off to make himself a coffee.

Chapter 13

Right. That's issue sixteen coming together', he began. 'Let's get some planning done for issues seventeen through twenty.'

'Where are you placing your Orkney material?' Cassy asked.

Gill turned over several pages in his notebook and thought for a second. 'ScoCion needs to go in nineteen as they're gonna make a real break-through one of these days, and I don't want to be behind the game on that.'

'Thanks for taking time to call on all those Jewellery manufacturers', said Tracy. 'I've had confirmation of three more full-page ads this week.'

Gill nodded gratefully. The potential advertising revenue from Orcadian manufacturers had helped to justify his trip.

'Geeze your notes on ScoCion', said Larry. 'I'll start drafting it.'

Gill shook his head. 'No, it's horribly technical. I'll draft, then you sense check. Craig, I'll need a bunch of technical diagrams. And Larry, I'm giving you Skara Brae and a provisional slot in seventeen. I took a lot of wide angles shots, so work with Craig to get the right effect.'

'You got any particular storyboard in mind?' asked Craig, scribbling on his pad.

'Two articles. One factual; the significance of the site, etc. I'll mail you my ideas. Then a second on coastal erosion.

Skara is just one of a whole bunch of sites in Scotland we will lose in the next two decades if we're not careful. Can you knock up illustrations demonstrating the retreating shoreline over the last few hundred years?'

'And the Brodgar dig?' Cassy asked.

'Incomplete', said Gill. 'I'm working with the local rep for Historic Scotland to see if we can do some follow-up work. Pencil that in for issue twenty, but it might go later.'

'What's with Johnny's school jotter?' said Cassy leaning across and tapping the book of numbers.

'Aah, another mystery that surfaced during my time on Orkney.' Briefly, Gill outlined the book and how he had come across it.

'Hardly the big story', said Cassy rubbing her eyes. 'How come you've still got it?

Gill held out his hands. 'I tracked the guy down to where he lives. Just a young lad. He has a few mental health issues. Unfortunately, he's been missing for weeks.'

'Probably dead', muttered Craig.

Larry sat back heavily in his chair. 'Shite, man. That means the Cat mag wins the bloody sweepstake again.'

'No one's dead', said Gill, trying to keep an edge of protest out of his voice. 'In fact, no one has died on a story since issue eleven.'

Larry shrugged. 'Yeah, but tha' was Fort William. It wuz carnage, man.'

'My efforts saved thousands of lives', Gill protested.

'Back on track, please', Cassy demanded. 'Gill, the book of numbers. What's it to be?' An action plan or bin?'

‘I went to chuck it a couple of times. I can’t quite shake off the feeling it might be significant.’

Cassy picked up the book and skimmed it across the conference room table. ‘Larry. You’re a numbers guy. Make a change from Sudoku.’

Larry picked it up and flicked through a few pages. ‘Aw cum-mon, boss. Wha’ am I meant to dae wi’ this?’

‘Take an hour’, said Gill evenly. ‘See if you can find anything of significance. And if I hear you mention the Cat mag’s sweepstake again, take two hours.’

Gill turned in his chair to scan the rest of their cluster. ‘Craig, can you give me a second?’

‘Aye, Gill. Lemme save this. You got a couple of changes for me on issue sixteen?’

‘I do. And I’d like to see anything you’ve done so far on Loch Lomond.’

Craig walked over to Gill’s desk, and together they hunched over the proof copies. It was Friday morning and was Gill’s last chance to influence a couple of articles for the upcoming issue. Gill’s pen flashed across several minor changes while Craig took notes. As the layout artist, Craig kept the magazine’s master file and implemented all the edits.

‘Cassy has seen these’, said Gill. ‘So you’ve got her inputs already.’

'Great', said Craig, noticing Euan Mearns book of numbers on Gill's desk and picking it up. 'Larry made any progress with this?'

Gill shook his head while he finished typing an email. 'Can't make head nor tail of it. Begged to be the one who got to drop it in a shredder.'

Gill looked up nervously as Craig settled his backside against Gill's desk and started to flick through the pages. 'Tell me again who wrote it?'

'A kid on Orkney', Gill replied. 'He's been missing for a month but managed to leave it with someone I was due to meet, before disappearing again.'

'Poor lad', said Craig, pausing over a page of densely packed numbers before moving on. 'You say the kid's got issues?'

'Aye. He's somewhere on the spectrum', said Gill looking up. 'He been in the care system and now lives in a hostel.'

'Travelled that way myself', said Craig. 'Then I got lucky and was adopted by the finest human beings on the planet.'

Gill pushed back in his chair. 'I didn't know that about you.'

'Sounds like your wee pal on Orkney hasn't been so fortunate.'

'I think he has his troubles. But that said, his book is meaningless. I'm trying to work up the courage to just bin it.'

'No. I want to help him. It looks like he was trying to work something out', said Craig. 'The pages are dated, but they don't follow in order.'

'I didn't see any dates', said Gill looking up.

'Top right-hand corner of every section. Day, month, year, hour and minute. Just digits, like a computer clock.'

'Right. I wonder why he would dart around like that?'

Craig shrugged. 'Lists and lists of numbers. With calculations spiralling off the data.'

'But he's not explained what he's doing', said Gill. 'Zero notation and not even a *QED* at the end. Just lists and lists of numbers.'

Craig looked blankly at him.

'*QED*. As in "Quite Easily Done". Like saying, "Here is the solution", written in red ink.'

'That's magic, Gill. Wish I'd gone to a posh Uni, then I could have been a clever twat too.'

'Sorry. Didn't mean to patronise.'

'I detect a wee bit of emphasis', said Craig, pulling the book towards him. 'Now and again, a number is underlined.'

'We're wasting time', said Gill. 'I'm going to toss it in recycling and then get some proper work done.' He reached for the book, but Craig pulled it out of his reach.

'Gimme a second, boss. I'd like to have a longer look at this.'

'And the Lomond set will prep itself?' said Gill, glancing at his watch. 'Remember, we'll need to pull in some aerial photography to base your illustrations.'

'Ach, no problem. Stuff like that's available off the shelf.' Craig snapped the book shut and pointed it at Gill. 'Julie is taking the kids to her mother's this weekend. I could cry off.

Claim pressure of work and all that. I've a sneaky scheme to bag a couple of munros on Saturday, but I could take a few hours on Sunday. See if I can work out what was so important to this guy he couldn't explain with words.'

Gill swept a hand in front of him. 'Be my guest. In the meantime …'

'Aye, The bonnie, bonnie banks. I'm on it.'

Gill's phone pinged, and he picked it up to see his chess app had received a new move from David. He smiled. David had blocked Gill's attacking move. He'd already anticipated this and tapped in his response, Bishop to D2, adding the note, 'You can run, but you can't hide.'

He turned back to the current issue of the magazine. Cassy's organisational skills, coupled with his own growing experience, made them a competent team. The next edition would be off to the printer in a couple of weeks, and the cycle would begin again. The focus for his weekend would be Salina. In the meantime, he squared off against another puzzle. Flicking towards the back of issue fifteen, he found the simple advert he was looking for. He'd not seen it during the final scans before the magazine went to press. But he remembered it from issue one. It had simply said, "Rex Gladio" followed by a mobile number. The same phrase had been on the back of Biker-man's jacket the morning they faced the Waterhorses. And in the newspaper cutting Alice had shown him, the "Rex Gladio" icon had appeared again. He'd googled the phrase. It translated as "The King's Sword".

A year ago, he'd done nothing with it. It caught his curiosity, but Raphael, aka Biker-man, was intimidating, so he'd let it go. He'd assumed he would never see the man again, but he'd been wrong. A few months ago, in a moment when he and Salina had fought for their lives, the man appeared again and steered them to safety. They'd assumed he'd died in the deluge that hit the Great Glen, but a few days later, they'd both seen him alive. Salina recognised him and, for a time, had suffered nightmares about drowning. In each dream, Raphael had come to her rescue, and she had come to believe he had supernatural powers. And now the advert had appeared again, only days since Alice had urged him to take the matter seriously. His uncomfortable curiosity was fermenting into compulsion. He resolved to fire an arrow and see where it landed. He entered the number and toyed with addressing the text to Raphael, but in the end, he'd simply said, "Can we meet?" Having pressed send, he immediately got back to work.

Chapter 14

It was Friday lunchtime before anybody replied to Gill's text. 'DD 6 pm', was the enigmatic reply.

He stared at the message and tried to fathom it. "DD". Was it a reference to location? Dundee perhaps? That suited him. But where? The words "Desperate Dan" dropped into his head. He smiled to himself. It couldn't be, could it? He put his phone away and carried on with his work. He didn't think about it again until 5.40 pm when he was closing his laptop for the day.

'DD 6 pm'. The statue was pretty much on his way to the bus station. He decided it wouldn't hurt to swing by. So he grabbed his jacket and left, walking away from the office along Crichton Street in a slight deviation from his usual route.

The bronze figure of *Desperate Dan* sat in the centre of Dundee's main pedestrian thoroughfare. While other cities raised cast brass to city fathers, slave traders and other once-upon-a-time heroes, Dundee celebrated its native Scottish comic book characters. If Edinburgh thought of itself as rather grand, Gill figured Dundee's fault was tilting too far the other way. Arriving at the statue, Gill saw the young man immediately. A skinhead with a prominent barcode tattoo on his neck, the man was dressed simply in a white T-shirt over blue jeans and steel-capped boots. His clothes were dirty, and his body was lean and muscular. A hard hat clipped to a tool belt hung lazily from his waist as he leaned against the statue, a weary scowl completing his challenging appearance. He was the kind of guy Gill usually chose to detour around. Eye contact would be out of the question, never mind a conversation. Something in Gill's posture must have signalled recognition because the man flexed his chin at him, acknowledging his presence.

Gill took a step backwards, but the man just smiled and made a show of looking at his watch. Gill thought about taking another step backwards and just mingling into the crowd. But he'd got nowhere the past year and a half, trying to walk backwards. Good things only happened to him when he leaned into the wind. So he strode up to the statue and lifted his phone close to the man's face.

'DD 6 pm', said Gill. 'Are you the guy?'

The man stepped beyond Gill, invading his space to brush his shoulder on the way past. 'Aye, pal. 'Am the guy.' He turned to make sure Gill was following. ''This way. Ah ken a place.'

Gill followed him down Reform Street, pushing away the distracting thought that this experience felt like a Tinder date sliding towards some dangerous encounter. Every once and a while, the man turned to check he hadn't lost Gill in the evening crush. By picking up his pace, Gill managed to get alongside him.

'Enigmatic text', said Gill. 'How did you know I'd find you?'

The man shrugged. 'Solomon's idea. Old Soly kens this dis'nae work wi'oot a bittae divine inspiration.'

'Solomon?' repeated Gill.

'Aye. You'll meet in time. Mebbe.'

They stopped outside an all-hours snack bar, and the man said. ''Y'awright if we gang an here?' He tilted his head at a bar across the street. 'We kid gang an there, but 'am on the coffee either way.'

Gill thought for a second. A beer did appeal. Maybe two, but the man had already ducked into the snack bar.

The two men sat with steaming mugs in front of them.

'Charlie's the name', said the man, leaning across the table and offering Gill a dusty, calloused hand.

'I'm Gill.'

'Nice tae meet ya, Gill.' He looked away, with an amused smile spreading across his face. 'Tae be honest, when A git the text frae Solomon, A thocht A wis bein' set up wie a lassie.'

'Common mistake', said Gill, impatiently. 'Are you the person who put the "Rex Gladio" advert in my magazine?'

'Naw. Tha' wis Solomon.'

'Why isn't he here himself?'

Charlie dipped his head left and right. 'A'm here. Whit can A dae for ye?'

Gill wasn't sure what to say. He hadn't expected to be the one answering questions. '"Rex Gladio." What is it for a start? I mean, is it a gang? Is it a movement?'

Charlie licked his forefinger and used the wet skin to lift sugar grains spilt on the tabletop. 'They're the vanguard o' the biggest power the warld haes iver seen.'

'Okay, what power?'

'The wan tha's gaun'ae mak things aw richt.'

'Things, Charlie? What things?'

Charlie looked away, giving himself time to think. His shoulders dipped a little, and then he spread out his hands. 'Everythin', he said at last.

Gill said nothing and tried to keep his face from screaming.

Seeing his frustration, Charlie leaned across and tapped the table. 'Dae ye iver tak a daunder in the hills and wunner whaur it all cam frae?'

'I did geography at school. I know about mountains.'

Charlie scowled. 'No the muntains, ye eijit. Mair than tha'. The rocks, ken. The sky, the air. The hale planet?'

Gill nodded, even though he wasn't any clearer.

'Tha's whaur A started. Whaur'd it aw cam frae?'

Gill shrugged politely. 'Big Bang. Cosmic dust?'

'An before aw tha'?'

'I dunno. I guess it's always existed.'

Charlie pulled back his hand and opened his palm. 'Yon's a huge lowp o' feth, pal. Intell-leck-tual apathy. An' it disna mak sense.'

'Maybe. I'm not sure I'm qualified to comment.'

'Whaur did ye see yon "Gladio"?'

'I met a man with it written on his back. I say he was a man. I'm not so sure now.'

'Whit kind o' man?'

'Big. Olive skinned. Wearing a black jacket. I know him as, Raphael.'

Charlie rocked back in his chair and stared at Gill. 'Ye actually met yon fella?'

'Yes.'

'In the flesh, like?'

'Yes.'

Charlie emitted a long, low whistle. 'A telt Solomon this wis gaun'ae happen.'

'Raphael. Who is he?' Gill pressed.

Charlie laughed and shook his head slowly. 'Shite, man. If ye dinnae ken that, A cannae be the wan tae break the bad news.'

'Bad news?'

'Aye, weel, it's guid news and aw. It's just, yer gaun'ae be in the firin' line.'

'Not sure I like the sound of that.'

'Whit did yon big fella say to ye?'

Gill thought back to the misty morning at Callanish. He wasn't sure that mixing that mysterious conversation with the one he and Charlie were having now would make much sense. After a moment's thought, he cleared his throat and said, 'Not much. We were in a … challenging situation. He offered me a sword.'

Charlie's mug was midway to his mouth, but he set it down abruptly. 'Nae shite.'

Gill shrugged. 'That's what he did.'

Charlie leaned forward. 'Did ye tak it? Man, tell me ye teuk it.'

Gill shook his head.

Charlie sank back into his chair and thought for a second. 'Man, ye should hae taen the swuird.'

'I didn't understand what he was asking me to do.'

'Okay, lemme gie ye a haund', said Charlie. 'Ye got a wirried leuk aboot ye, pal. Next time ye gotta grab the swuird.'

'I don't get it', said Gill. 'What so important about a sword?'

Charlie smiled and closed his eyes and murmured;

'Dinnae worry aboot yer life, claethes or fid.

Ken the birds, they're aricht.

Weirrying daes nae gud, dinnae gang to yon place.

If ye has belief, the Big Man will mind ye.

Day at a time, pal. Taemorra's for anither day'

He opened his eyes and met Gill's gaze. 'Tha's the swuird. Pure genius for any situation. I ken it's a bit mental at first. But I tell ye, the mair ye ken it, the mair it grows on ye.'

Exasperated, Gill leaned forward and let his fingers slide into his hair. 'The sword is poetry?'

'Poetry. War stories. Cries' o the heart, man.'

'Sorry, Charlie. I don't "ken".'

Staring at the floor, Charlie nodded. 'Aye. In a while, A think ye will.' He looked up brightly. 'Chaunces are, he'll gie ye a second try. Teuk yon big fella three goes tae brak ma hert.'

'But that's what I've been trying to ask you. Who is the guy? What is "Rex Gladio"?'

Charlie smiled and took a deep swig of his coffee. 'Gladio is the swuird, ken? Now aw ye need is tae gie yer fuzzy wee heid aroond "Rex".'

'Rex? Is that Raphael? Is he some kind of king?'

Charlie shook his head. 'Raphael is mair 'o a despatch rider. Tha's why he rides a bike, an' that.'

Gill threw his hands out to Charlie. 'So you must have an insight into Raphael's objective.'

'No personally, pal. But he keeps poppin' up. Like there's stuff aboot tae happen.'

'Okay, so he's not "Rex". Let me ask you this; is he human?'

Charlie stood and pushed his chair against the table. He cautiously glanced around the room then back to Gill. 'Aw I can say is, aungels are ivreywhaur.'

'What? I don't understand!' Gill retorted.

Charlie winked at Gill, 'After ye see him agin, ye hae oor nummer.' Then he tapped the table twice and walked to the door. At the last moment, he paused and turned. 'Neist time, man. Tak the swuird.'

Chapter 15

With the swish of flowing fabric, Cassy approached his desk and laid down the morning's post. Gill noticed again how her trademark baggy shirts drowned her figure and made her appear shorter than her true height. Her glossy hair was pulled back in a tight bun and as usual, her flawless skin carried no makeup. 'Good weekend?' she asked brightly.

Gill shrugged. 'Weird drink before I left town on Friday. Then a lovely Saturday. Salina was home between jobs so we went for a long walk; had a bite and caught a movie. Then she was off early Sunday morning on another trip. How about you?'

'Had a gig Saturday night. Sunday was domestic chores followed by a long swim. Did you see your dad?'

'Aye. Went up to Montrose on Sunday afternoon.'

She left a few seconds of silence. 'Not easy, is it?'

Gill sighed, his arms slumping onto his desk. 'It was tough when he stopped recognising me. The folk in the care home warned me that would happen. But now he doesn't even register I'm in the room. He just stares out the window.'

Cassy's shoulders dipped, and she leaned against his desk. 'That's tough.'

'Och, I just blether on. Tell him all my news. Talk about Stonehaven; everything I can think of. Eventually, I run out of things to say. Just sit and wonder if I'll be like that in thirty years.'

Cassy squeezed his shoulder. 'You're doing your best. Stick at it. Someday you'll be glad you did.'

Gill blew out a breath and pulled himself upright in his chair so Cassy's hand fell away. 'Aye, I doubt he's got long.'

'Does Salina ever come with you?'

'Once or twice. But she barely knew Dad before this mist closed in on him. Mostly she leaves me to it.'

'How are you getting on with Salina's folks?'

Gill snorted a laugh. 'Glasgow's Pakistanis are a canny lot. Sal's dad is a real live wire. Keeps trying to get me to join his golf club or invest in one of his schemes.'

'I thought he was a surgeon or a consultant or something?'

'He is. But he's also got a property portfolio. Always buying and selling. Restaurants are his thing at the moment.'

Cassy looked up as Craig approached. 'Got a second, boss?' he asked.

Gill turned to see Craig holding the book of numbers. 'Sure. I trust the book was a useful "get out of jail" card.'

'Spent most of Sunday on this. Really got into it.'

Cassy let out a deep sigh. 'Honestly, Craig. You could have been with your kids. Or gardening. Helping old folks with their shopping, painting your nails.' She tapped Gill on the shoulder. 'I'll leave you to it.'

Craig stared after her for a few moments before ignoring her jabs. 'I'd love to know what this guy was measuring.'

Gill turned to give Craig his full attention. 'All I know is he was obsessed with the Orcadian monuments. Anyway, how do you know he was measuring anything?'

Craig shrugged. 'Just the way he lays out some of the numbers. I've done a bit of coding so I know how people tabulate data. Though most would add a bit of notation.'

'Can you give me an example?'

Craig flicked towards the start of the book. 'Aye. Here's one. This table is just one of thirty-four. Each list starts with a single datum point. I think they're measurements in relation to the other thirty-three points.'

'Okay. And this means?'

'I tried plotting the data. Funny thing is, when I added the data together in each table, I got pretty much the same total each time.'

Craig stood, waiting for Gill to catch the inference. When Gill's face didn't light up, he continued.

'Sorry, I thought the next bit would be obvious. It means each one of the points sits in a circle. No matter where you start in the circle, the circumference will always be the same.'

Gill nodded, confirming he was on track.

'After that, it goes whacky for a while. Our boy went back to every datum point and repeated the exercise with slightly different variables. He must have been factoring in some other data. Then he's recorded a whole bunch of other measurements he starts to play about with …'

'Okay, Craig, sorry to cut in on you. You're saying the lad was measuring stuff in a slightly intense way. Do you see anything meaningful?'

'Ah', said Craig, laying the book flat on the table and thumbing to a page just past the mid-point. 'He gets to a kind of breakthrough here. You see this big number 40,075. He underlines it twice. That's significant.'

Gill glanced up at Craig. He was trying to think of a way to tell Craig it wasn't significant to him.

'You don't recognise that number?'

Gills eyes flicked towards the office ceiling, then back to Craig. Then he shook his head.

'It's the circumference of the Earth. In kilometres.'

Gill studied Craig's face for a moment, assessing if he was the victim of a joke. 'So this kid is clever enough to take measurements from the Orcadian landscape and out pops the size of the planet?'

'No need to be sarky, boss. And there's more', said Craig flicking forward a few pages to another number faintly underlined twice.

Gill shrugged. 'Another big number. What is it?'

'The mean distance of Earth's orbit around the sun', said Craig. 'In kilometres.'

'Wait. Back up a second. He's getting this from the stones?'

'I can see mathematically how he's done it', said Craig, taking back the book. 'But I don't know what base data he used. You said it's Orkney, but we've no information about where he took his measurements. Could have been Timbuctoo for all I know.'

Gill's curiosity rose. 'Gimme a second. I want to check something.' He lifted his laptop and opened Google. A few seconds later, he tapped an image on the screen. 'The Ring of Brodgar; it's where I was last week.'

Craig nodded. 'And?'

'It's got thirty-four stones left standing. And I know this kid was obsessed with it.' He gesticulated for Craig to pull up a chair and sit. 'Is it possible Euan derived these astronomically significant numbers from measurements he took around Brodgar?'

Craig scratched his beard. 'I see so many problems with that I don't even know where to start.'

'But suppose he did', said Gill, opening the book at its first page. 'What's his goal?'

'You taking this to Tony?' said Cassy as she strode in from her lunch break. Gill could tell she was frustrated with him. Since talking to Craig, he'd been distracted all morning, making him less than productive. He shook his head. 'At the start of the book, I've got what looks like the Ring of Brodgar. And at the end, I've got what might be a significant dimension in the solar system. And I've got nothing but mush in between. So far, I've got no story.'

Cassy sighed. 'But I know you. You haven't tossed that book away, and now it's got its hooks into you. Gill, it's just a big number puzzle with no cypher.'

'I'm not planning to spend any more time on it.'

'And Craig? Where was he off to this afternoon with a big smile on his face?'

Gill held up his hands. 'I told him to take tomorrow in the Mitchell Library. See if he can nail any cause and effect in the book. If he can't do that with one day's work, we'll drop it.' He could see he hadn't entirely convinced her. 'Editor's instinct, Cassy.'

'You're the boss', she said, gripping the hem of her shirt and walking away.

Chapter 16

With a bit of advanced planning, the last part of Gill's working day took him to Glasgow, which suited him as he had to make a social call afterwards. He drove to the city's west end, where an old hospital was being demolished for redevelopment by the university. Before they lost the site to a fresh tide of concrete, *Mysterious Scotland* had accepted the invitation to excavate. Having been in the offing for months, a solid start date for the dig had been a long time coming. When it finally kicked off, he'd struggled to pull together a team. Then he was saved by a call from an old friend returning from a three-month contract in London.

Arriving at the building site, he was challenged by security. Accepting a hard hat, he flashed his credentials and waited for permission to enter the archaeological cordon. He listened while security explained the route they wanted him to take, then set off, noticing evidence of new buildings all around him. Towers of fresh concrete rising with hands on their hips, chasing his team towards their finishing line. He sighed. Doing archaeology in these circumstances was like trying to excavate a beach in front of a rising tide.

After a five-minute walk, he stepped into an area the size of two squash courts. Surrounded by temporary wooden hoardings the barriers offered some protection from the noise and dust of the building work. Here and there, the stone foundations of the old hospital lay exposed at ground level like the stumps of once-mighty teeth. Gingerly he stepped onto boards laid across the gaps in the earth where

Fiona's team had pressed far below the footings of the old building.

He stepped into the portacabin and found her prepping the job rota for the following day. 'Afternoon, beautiful', he said, knowing how Fiona resented cheerfulness of any description in her workspace.

'Twenty-first century, Gill. Show a bit of sodding professionalism.'

He leaned over the desk and waited for her to offer him her cheek. 'We're related', he said, planting a single kiss. 'And I see it as part of my familial duty to encourage you.'

She looked at his clean, smart-casual office wear, then down at her grubby blue boiler suit. 'Aye, fair enough. Give us a hug, then.'

After the briefest of hesitations, he moved to do just that, but she brushed him off. 'Ach, away. If any of the crew see you.'

He slumped into a dirty orange chair that looked like something salvaged from a skip. 'One week to go. You got anything for me?'

Fiona jabbed her pen in the direction of a pile of labelled crates. 'Urban digs are always fascinating. I've got lots of bits and pieces, but nothing that's quite *Equis pictus*.'

Gill smiled. Their first dig together had delivered astonishing results, including the classification of a hitherto unknown species of horse. It had also healed the distance between them following the death of Davey, Gill's brother and Fiona's husband. 'Great. Maybe you could email me a list when you get a moment.' He stood and wandered over to a whiteboard covered with a site plan. 'What's left on your wish list?'

Fiona dropped her clipboard and came over to join him. 'This section here is pretty much untouched. But it's brutal. If we go in, we'll be doing ninety per cent demolition, ten per cent archaeology.'

'What did the radar show?'

'Plenty of big cavities. But it might be rubble rather than anything useful. But we only have four more days before I have to start securing the site. If we decide we're not going in, we'll be left picking at the margins of what we've already done.'

'Let's nip out and take a look', said Gill. He took the Hi-Viz jacket Fiona offered him, then followed her out onto boardwalks and across the part of the site closest to the road. Around them, Fiona's team were finishing up for the day, storing tools and making sure they covered the spoil heaps in case of rain. The feature Fiona had identified represented a quarter of the ground they'd been allocated but lay under piles of tumbled red brick.'

'Take a day even to scratch the surface', said Fiona, kicking at the loose debris.

Gill nodded and gingerly stepped along the perimeter of the area. 'I remember the building that used to stand here. Six storeys. Been derelict for a decade.' He stooped to examine one spot and managed to drag out a solid block of fused bricks. 'I see a course of dressed stone below the old brickwork. That could be the old coaching inn.' He stood and tried to imagine a lone stone building standing in thin woodland, two miles outside the heart of the old city.

'Maybe. Or it might be recycled masonry. You reckon it's worth a look?'

'Rather than try to clear the whole site, I'd follow this stonework. Try to get below it in one spot and see what comes up. At the very least, we should get something to carbon date.'

'Okay. But we're only five people, so don't get your hopes up.'

'Fi, you always come up with the goods.' He glanced at his watch. 'Look, gotta dash. I'm staying in the Southside tonight, so I'll be here first thing tomorrow to put in a day's labour.'

She grunted a goodbye but had already turned to focus on the job at hand.

Gill left the site and walked back towards Hillhead Underground. He was a couple of minutes late for his next appointment. Almost at the station, he ducked down Ashton Lane. Scanning the tables, he spotted Salina's father nursing a hot drink at an outside table.

'Hey, Waquar. Sorry I'm late.'

'Not a problem, Gill. Would you like a cup of tea?'

Gill seized the back of a stool and sat down. 'Yeah, let's do that.'

'Excellent. While we're waiting, let me tell you about some new property I've seen.'

The following day, Gill arrived at the Glasgow dig a little after 8 am. Fiona was there, although she didn't expect her crew until 8.30.

'You look bright-eyed and bushy-tailed', she murmured after the briefest of glances.

'Always sleep well at Salina's folk's place.'

'Nice cooking?'

'Excellent. And the absence of alcohol helps on a work night.'

'Set a wedding date yet?'

'Not even asked her.'

'Gill!'

'I've still to pass final vetting. Her dad and I get along like a house on fire, but her mum is still testing me.'

'Doesn't like the look of you? I can imagine that.'

'Something to do with me not being a millionaire.'

'Has she checked your fingernails?'

Gill suddenly realised that, yes, in a subtle way, she had.

Fiona had a good look at him now. 'Nice new boiler suit. Let's see if we can get some dirt on it.'

Gill grabbed a pair of heavy protective gloves. 'Yes, boss.'

Fiona was right about the demolition work. By mid-morning, his back ached, and Gill was looking forward to escaping back to the office. He'd inserted himself at a spot loosely known as "the end of the line". Practically, that meant as Fiona and her team stripped back bricks from the building, he collected the rubble in a barrow and carted it off to the designated dump. It was physically numbing and required him to wear a mask. It did, however, give him time to think. As he shovelled and barrowed, his mind wandered back to Alice's prayer for him and how she'd tried to chase away the brutal images locked in his mind. He'd realised, up to that point, he'd not even been conscious of living with trauma. Instead, Alice had known him well enough to see that part of him was numb. And she cared enough to do something about it. He had no idea what prayer was meant to achieve. A shout-out to a higher power? That felt primitive. Maybe it was a psychological benefit brought about by sharing your pain with another human being? Either way, their little session together had achieved some positive effects. In recent days, when he thought about the victims of the Great Glen disaster, his overriding emotion was compassion rather than guilt.

'You okay?' Fiona asked when she finally called a snack break.

'Yeah. Why shouldn't I be?'

She flicked her chin at him. 'Your eyes. You have tear stains through the brick dust.'

'Hay fever', he shot back, pulling off his gloves and rubbing his face.

She snorted. 'Worked with you for ten years. Never known you allergic to anything other than hard work.'

'Maybe that's what it is.'

She patted him on the chest and walked past him to pour two teas. 'I popped in with Gordon last weekend.'

'How did you find him?'

She shrugged. 'Hasn't recognised me for a while. I think that distressed him. Not sure I should go again.'

Gill sighed. 'In his right mind, he'd be so appreciative of all you've done.'

'Just trying to do right by Davey.' She took a long sip from the mug. 'How are you coping with it all?'

He had to consider his response. 'Okay, I think. Kinda resigned to the inevitable. Life goes on and all that.'

She nodded, sucking again on the mug before laying it down. 'We'll miss him when the time comes.'

Gill reached to stroke dust from his eyes. 'Already do.'

They drank in silence for a minute until Fiona finished her mug and set it in the washbasin.

'Back to work', said Gill.

She brushed against him as she strode outside. 'Walk with me a moment.'

She led him to where the team had been digging and pointed at the seam of old stonework. 'Place your hand by that little hole.'

Gill did as she told him, reaching into the small gap in the wall. 'I can feel a draft.'

Fiona gave a curt nod. 'Which means what?'

'A significant enclosed space rather than an air pocket.' He looked up at her. 'Promising!'

'We can push on for a day or two more. I'll focus our firepower right here.'

Chapter 17

He'd enjoyed a day in the field helping Fiona on the Glasgow dig, even if his body hated him for it. "Pressure of work" came to his rescue, calling him back to Dundee for Wednesday morning. He caught up with Tony before meeting Cassy to discuss potential lead articles for issue seventeen. This rolled over to include lunch at their desks. As they were finishing, Craig requested a moment. Gill had a couple of urgent tasks at his desk, so it was almost 4 pm when he and Craig finally closed the conference room door and sat down. Gill saw the right side of Craig's mouth curve up in a half-smile while he spread a slew of papers across the table.

'What've you got?'

'You're not going to believe me, boss.'

Gill rubbed his forehead. 'This is *Mysterious Scotland,* Craig. If a bizarre idea can be trussed up and draped in the saltire, I'm pretty much up for anything.'

'Okay, let's start with the data.'

'The thirty-four stones?'

'No, we're beyond that now. I found a slew of tables with datum points from nine through to three-five-one. The key thing is; no number goes above three-sixty.'

'Meaning you're talking degrees in a circle?'

‘Yes, somehow an extension of the Brodgar circle. Let me show you.’ Craig slid an ordnance survey map out of his pile and opened it on the table. ‘Show me north.’

Gill was uncertain if this was a trick question. ‘It’ll be straight up the page. All these maps run north-south.’

Craig took a ruler out and laid it on the map. ‘That’s where I started. Then I looked at the data tables and the increments our man was working with. He’s reporting the numbers nine, thirteen, seventy-eight, one hundred and eighteen and so on. Assuming these were degrees, I laid them against true north and looked where they pointed.’

‘Which was where?’

‘Farmland mainly, open hillside and a couple of lakes.’

‘In other words, they’re meaningless.’

‘They are’, said Craig smiling, until you rotate north.

‘I’m sorry, Craig, but north is north.’

Craig hunched his shoulders for a moment, then relaxed again. ‘Yes and no. I mean, in the context of a four-and-a-half thousand-year-old monument, magnetic north has moved around a wee bit in that time. But maybe magnetic north isn’t what the book's author had in mind.’ Craig overlaid the map with a sheet of transparent cellophane, on which he'd drawn a circle, plus several lines coming out from the centre at seemingly random angles. ‘Imagine the markings on a compass. You know, the knob you have to twist to make the compass face line up with the map.’

Gill nodded. ‘Yep, I can picture that.’

‘What I did was to plot the degrees on my cellophane here, like the hands on a clock. Then I overlaid it in the Ordnance Survey, with the centre on the Ring of Brodgar.

Then I gradually spun it around to see what turned up. Look at this.'

Gill watched as Craig laid the cellophane to true north, centred on Brodgar. Then slowly turned the dial back a few degrees until north now faced north-west on the map. Then he paused and held the cellophane in place so that Gill could trace each one of the lines out across the map.

'Oh, I see', said Gill. 'Each hand of the clock points to a significant ancient monument. Cairns, tumuli, stone circles. And the author's north passes from Brodgar directly through the Ring of Bookan.'

The two sat silently for a few minutes while Gill's forefinger traced each line from the Brodgar epicentre. Each intersected a monument, apart from one spanning south across an empty hillside and then out to sea.

'Well done', said Gill eventually. 'You've worked out where our man was taking his base measurements from.' He paused. 'The big question is still, what does all this mean?'

Craig pulled his chair closer to the table and spoke in a hushed tone. 'Well, you know how I spotted the Earth's circumference underlined in the numbers? Here's a list of others I found.'

Gill looked at a list of immense numbers. Beside each one was the name of a planet. 'Okay, I'm still interested. What's with the planetary bodies?'

Craig gave himself a little shake, then spread out his hands. 'I worked out these huge numbers using the map and thought my maths had just exploded, but then I noticed this one here. It's representative of Earth's orbit around the sun.'

'And these others?'

'All the numbers represent the approximate orbit of a planet in our solar system.'

'Approximately?'

'The planets run on elliptical orbits', said Craig. 'The variation between the minimum and maximum distance from each planet to the sun is quite small. The numbers in Euan's book are calculated from eight of these clock hands out of Brodgar, and each of them represents a point between the various maximum and minimum orbits.'

'But planetary distances, expressed on a Neolithic monument', said Gill eventually. 'What do you reckon? I bet our man had to jump through a few hoops to make that happen.'

Slowly and without smiling, Craig shook his head. 'No, the maths are complex, and the book records he had a fair number of false starts. But once he hit a cypher that worked, he applied the same method to each one of these clock hands I showed you. Having cracked the code, he applied it to each piece of data in turn.'

Gill didn't feel convinced. 'Can you run me through some of the maths?'

'Okay, here's the data off the Ordnance Survey, plus the more precise measurements I found in Euan's book. First of all, we have the monuments, being intersected by angles off north. That's Brodgar north to you and me. Those are expressed in degrees, nought to three-sixty. Then we have the distance from the centre of Brodgar to each of the monuments, measured in kilometres. Multiply the degrees by the distance, and you get this list of numbers here.'

Gill leaned over long enough to confirm his agreement between Craig's calculations and a corresponding table in the book of numbers.

'So far, so meaningless', Craig continued. 'But then I noticed Euan had picked out one of the stones and given it a factor of one.'

'One?'

'Yes. It means he's scaling all the other data points off this key relationship. Let's call it his "Neolithic mile". He doesn't spell it out anywhere, but if you imagine Brodgar represents the sun, then a monument, known as the *Comet Stone*, represents planet Earth.'

'Okay, but …'

'It kinda screams at you in the end. The *Comet Stone* is the third closest object to Brodgar and Earth is the third closest planet to the sun. If you scale up the data, multiply the degree of angle by the distance from Brodgar times the distance of Earth from the sun, you get this list of numbers.'

Gill looked to where Craig was pointing. 'But these figures are enormous.'

Craig nodded. 'They are. And Gill, get this. They're accurate representations of the orbit of each planet in the solar system.'

Gill blinked. 'But humanity didn't know all the planets until the twentieth century. And you're deriving them from the position of monuments built four thousand years ago ...' Gill staggered to a halt as his brain ran out of road.

Craig pointed at each of the monuments on the map in turn. 'The only logical conclusion is this. The builders selected the locations of the monuments to articulate the constants, as derived by the position of the planets.'

Gill's arms fell heavily onto the table. 'Craig, it's possible whoever built those monuments wanted to observe the movements of the sun and the moon. But the planets were only like bright stars to the Neoliths. I really doubt they would have known this information.'

Craig splayed his hands in front of him. 'You gave me the numbers to decode. All I'm telling you is what they say.'

Gill stood up and started to pace the room. 'Okay, let's get some objectivity into this. The Neolithic landscape on Orkney evolved over a couple of thousand years. Most likely the work of several different clans.'

Craig got up and leaned against the back wall. 'Maybe the entire culture was more sophisticated than we've realised up until now.'

'But these people didn't even write. How could they have expressed Earth's orbit to a few million kilometres? And that's another thing, Craig. The Neoliths didn't use kilometres.'

'They didn't need to.'

Gill said nothing but nodded to Craig to carry on. He produced an expanded copy of the area between Brodgar and the Ring of Bookan a mile to the northwest. The base measurement derives from the distance between Brodgar and Bookan. Here, I'll show you.'

Gill followed Craig's explanation until, on the third attempt, he finally understood. 'Okay, take this Neolithic mile you have derived ...'

'Not me. It's in the book', said Craig.

'But if you translate this distance into twenty-first-century kilometres, you get the planets, just like that.'

Craig thought for a second, then nodded.

'I mean, it's amazing, but the big question is why? What does it mean?'

Craig shrugged. 'No idea, boss.'

'We could be talking about a lost civilisation', said Gill. 'One with technological powers beyond the rest of humanity.' He rubbed the back of his head with his right hand and spun round to face Craig again. 'Or we could be looking at some form of base intelligence where unknowable facts become discernible in the natural environment via complex arithmetic. Bloody hell, Craig, this is great work.'

'I have a theory', said Craig quietly.

Gill studied his face for a few moments, searching for any hint that he was the victim of an elaborate joke. 'Go on.'

'I think you need to consider the possibility the ancient Orcadians had some kind of contact with species more advanced than our own.'

Gill studied Craig's expression again, then pulled his hands up to cover his eyes.

'You okay, boss?'

'Imagine the next publisher's meeting. If you're right, I'll have to convince Tony we've potentially found evidence of extra-terrestrial life.'

Craig thought for a moment. 'When you say it like that, it sounds pretty weird.'

Gill clapped him on the shoulder as his mobile started ringing. 'Keep on it. Until we know more, let's keep this within the team.' After glancing at the caller display, he sat at the conference room table and picked up the call. 'Fi. How's it going?'

'You know how I never call you from a dig', said Fiona slowly. 'Except under exceptional circumstances.'

'Shit', said Gill under his breath, subconsciously catching the eye of the layout artist on *Love your Cat* magazine. 'I'll get back as quick as I can.'

Chapter 18

Gill parked his car and picked his way against the tide of students walking down Byres Road. He crossed into University Place and stopped outside the security hut to sign the visitor's book.

'Your instincts were spot on about the inn', said Fi tipping back her hard hat to sweep dirty blond hair out of her eyes.

'Glad to hear the old maps were correct for once', said Gill, accepting her offer of a hand as he stepped down into the operational trench he had helped excavate the previous day. It had deepened considerably since then, and now bare earth stretched beneath the foundations of the demolished hospital.

'But I don't think I would have made this place my local pub', said Fiona. She dropped to her knees, squeezed into the dark cavity, shuffled slightly, and then disappeared. Gill berated himself for leaving his new boiler suit in the car. Sighing, he got down on his knees and peered after her.

Emerging into a low-ceilinged room, Fiona flicked on a torch and shone it around. 'It's a basement room from the old hospital. And over here, we spotted this blocked doorway.'

Gill looked around. 'Literally the bowels of the old building.'

'As we're on a tight schedule, we just banged in a few roof supports and pressed on.' She pointed at a low arch bricked up centuries before. Sliding through the gap her team had knocked in the wall, she led Gill into a stone-built cavity. 'Mind your feet', she said, indicating the rubble-strewn floor.

After five metres, the narrow stone passage opened into a more expansive space allowing Gill to manoeuvre beside Fiona. The noise of west-end Glasgow was diminished here, replaced by the low rumble of traffic passing somewhere above their heads. 'I'm just thinking', she said, turning to face him so that her head torch dazzled him for a few moments. 'You never met my mum.'

'No, don't think I have', said Gill deflecting her head with his hand. 'Did she live around here?'

'Naw. Barr-heed.'

Gill peered at her for a few seconds then gesticulated into the darkness. 'Can we keep going?'

'There's a tight wee crawl space and then a flight of steps', she said, leading the way. 'We're heading for a chamber below.'

'Very Indiana Jones', he mumbled to her backside. A minute later, he saw her reach the steps and descend ahead of him. As he caught up with her, they entered a small room with a low vaulted ceiling.

'Incredible preservation', he said. 'You're sure you don't need joists?'

'Nope. It's solid for now. Until one of those cranes buggers the whole place.' She pointed to a wooden crate standing in a corner. 'This is what I want to show you.'

Gill stepped over and used his phone light to examine the box. It was approximately two metres long and one in width and height. The wood was dry and brittle, and its cover was unsecured.

‘Gentle fingers, please’, Fi whispered, indicating the end of the box lid he should grasp. Together they lifted it, slid it across the room and laid it on the floor. Gill returned to the box and looked inside. Five long bundles were laid lengthways, the upper two resting on three slightly smaller ones below. The fabric was old and intensely fragile, like mere smoke clinging to shapes that left little to the imagination.

‘You can see cuneiform bones protruding from the upper two parcels’, said Fiona. ‘The metatarsals are gone, but they might have fallen lower in the box.’

‘Bizarre’, said Gill.

‘Gets stranger’, said Fiona. ‘Get close and have a sniff.’

Gill leaned reluctantly into the box and took a slow, shallow breath. ‘I’m getting camphor oil. And something else.’ He stood up, cleared his lungs, and leaned forward again. ‘That’s weird. I’m getting road tar. Do you get that?’

‘It’s bitumen’, said Fiona, her head torch pitching and nodding. ‘If you’ve smelt it before, you never forget it. Means the bodies are embalmed.’

‘Taken any samples yet?’

‘Wood, bone and wrappings. Just not sure where to send them. Normally I’d involve St Andrews, but as we’re on opposition territory here …’ Fiona shrugged.

‘Aye. Even though Glasgow Uni swerved this dig, they’ll want to take a look now. I’ll give the archaeology professor a call.’ Somewhere in his head, his brain connected her earlier pun, and he rubbed his face to chase away the smile. ‘Thanks for letting me meet your mummy.’

Fiona laughed, delighted. ‘Right, you look about ready to get out of here.’

Gill led the way back up the stairs and into the fresh air. He stood stretching and looking around the site. 'I'm trying to relate that chamber to the rest of the building. It looks well below the foundations of the old hospital.'

'I'd say below even the foundations of the inn. Probably a cellar to that building.'

'I'm not sure', said Gill. 'That vaulted ceiling looked monastic.'

'I could believe that. Religious buildings often saw second uses as hostelries.'

'How come that old basement is so pristine? Why have those remains not been disturbed?'

Fiona knelt by the opening they'd crawled through earlier. 'At some point, the chamber has been abandoned. Maybe whoever bricked it up felt squeamish about the bodies.'

'Yeah. It became a kind of tomb. You were lucky to find it.'

'When we dug out this area, the bricks just fell away. I wouldn't normally be so gung-ho, but the schedule we're working to here …'

Gill nodded. 'This is great work. Look, I'll leave you to finish up while I go and make some calls.'

On Thursday morning, Gill gathered the editorial team to update them on the Glasgow dig.

'Okay, our routine excavation just turned up something unexpected. Preliminary inspection by my university contact in Glasgow confirms the bodies in our west-end basement are embalmed and very old. Based on their size, we suspect they're children.'

Larry shook his head. 'Shite, man. And I thought Dundee was weird.'

'What's the plan?' asked Cassy.

'Obviously, this is an anomaly. Something has turned up where we didn't expect to see it. Either the Scots were trying their hand at embalming five hundred years ago, or more likely, someone brought the remains from another country. So what I need is data. We need to hit the Libraries and figure out a rational reason why Egyptian mummies exist in sixteenth-century Glasgow. Then we need every clue about the history of the buildings on our dig site. Finally, for context, I want to understand any links between Glasgow and the Middle East, be they trade, military or cultural.'

The team went silent.

'Bloody hell, boss', said Craig, eventually.

Gill looked around. 'What?'

'You promised we'd have no more weekend working', said Cassy. 'What you're proposing isn't practical with the current manpower.'

'Aye', said Larry. 'Aw tha' work on top 'o the day job. You're killin' us, man.'

Gill tied not to look stung. This was the first time he'd experienced pushback from the team. 'Anybody got any suggestions?'

Cassy waved a hand. 'We're producing so much material in-house, we're underspent on contract writers. We could use the spare cash to pull someone in for a couple of months and give them all this desk research.'

Gill shook his head. 'Just finding someone. Then bringing them up to speed. We'd have to invest serious time and energy into any new starter before they give us extra capacity.'

Cassy smiled. 'Not unless I've already thought of someone, vetted them and informally interviewed them.'

Gill caught Craig's eye. 'She should be doing my job.'

'Won't be long', muttered Craig, looking away.

Larry held out an arm. 'Go on, Cass. Who've you got?'

'Mhairi Dodd. She has an MA in Classical Civilisation from Edinburgh Uni. Currently, she lives with her parents in Dundee, slaving in hospitality. She'd bite your hand off for this kind of work.'

'Sounds quite high brow', said Craig. 'How do you know her?'

Cassy hugged her iPad to her chest and swelled with pride. 'Now I've got my weekends back, I've started a ceilidh band. Mhairi is our accordion player.'

'You manage a ceilidh band?' said Larry. 'That's mental.'

'It's not my first gig', she sniffed. 'But *Calum's Road* is my first attempt to make the big time.'

Larry choked. 'Big time! In a ceilidh band?'

Cassy scowled at them all in turn. 'Someday soon, we'll be on the BBC at Hogmanay. Then you guys will be grateful you ever knew me.'

Gill raised his hands. 'Offer her a trial week, followed by three months' work, then bring her in. Start her on Monday if you can.'

Cassy beamed. 'Got it.'

'And we need tae think aboot the media', said Larry. 'If we have a bonnie wee story in Glasgow, I'd gee us twenty-four to thirty-six 'oors before some twat tips off the Daily Record.'

Gill nodded. 'Tony has a contact at the publisher. We'll give him a call tomorrow. Meanwhile, we need to get ahead of this. If we manage this right, we can use our online content to plant a tonne of questions in the minds of our readership. This could be the highest-selling issue of the year. Right, let's go. Regroup here, please, at 4 pm.'

Thursday afternoon was a whirlwind of meetings and calls concerning the Glasgow discovery. The Procurator Fiscal had cleared the mummified remains for removal, allowing Fiona's team to recover them to a nearby University lab. The results from a battery of tests were coming in quickly, and Gill started assembling various theories. A call from a professor of Ancient history based in Durham put him on the trail of a likely explanation. By the evening, he was already working on a draft article. His only leisure time was a long call with Salina, who promised she'd be back in St Andrews the following evening.

'I hear you saw my dad yesterday', she said.

'Yeah. He's sizing me up as a potential investor in a new restaurant he's buying.'

'Really? You think that's what he was doing?'

'We talked numbers and everything. Even though I told him I couldn't raise the cash.'

She laughed. 'You're so sweet. You always think the best about people.'

'Are you saying there was a subtext to our conversation?'

'Oh, Gill McArdle!'

They joked around for a while until Salina couldn't suppress her yawns. She'd had a series of early mornings, so reluctantly, he let her go. Then, with the office quiet, he worked alone late into the night.

The following morning, Gill was tired but looking forward to the publisher's meeting for once.

'We've been thinking', said Carl as Gill joined Tony at the head of the conference room table. 'It would be better if we renamed *Mys.Scot* as *Body Bag Monthly*. What do you think?'

Gill smiled and waited for the banter around him to subside. 'I think, Carl, you should stick to your toy soldiers and leave the news stories to proper journalists.'

Raucous shots around the room stung Carl to respond. 'You look stressed, Gill. Maybe you should spend more time with your mummy.'

'Thank you, boys and girls', Tony interrupted. 'I know it's Friday afternoon, but the sooner we get this done, the faster we can all be on the road. Let's start with the hottest topic. Gill. How are you playing this?'

Gill outlined his findings from the last two days. 'We know from our prep work that a monastic building existed on the site. In their heyday, many monasteries offered medical support to their adherents, plus the local population. And it was very common to erect new buildings on top of the old.'

'Someone built an inn on the foundations of the old monastery?' said Tony.

Gill nodded his confirmation. 'The result was to entomb the children's remains.'

'Don't think I'd drink in that pub', said Carl.

Gill ignored him. 'In all likelihood, the mummies were the medicine. We found traces of herbs and other organic material, in addition to the human remains. We think the room we excavated was the store for the monastery's apothecary.'

Tony looked shocked. 'You mean, they ground up mummies for medicine?'

'Aye. It was a general cure-all during the time of the crusades.'

'Hang on. We're talking eleventh or twelfth centuries?'

'For the monastery, yes. The mummies date two thousand years older. They were likely robbed from Egyptian tombs when the medicinal fashion started to create a demand.'

As the room fell silent, Gill took the opportunity to push Tony. 'We'll be in great shape on this story by the end of next week. I'd like to break with tradition and bring our publication date forward by one week.'

Tony frowned. 'I've got a print contract, never mind what the distributor would have to say about that.'

'I just think we should be quick off the mark with this one.'

Tony made some notes. 'I'll get back to you. How's the rest of issue sixteen looking?'

The meeting fell back into the routine, with Gill outlining *Mys.Scot's* plans for the following two issues. Then it was time for the other editors to run through their material. The meeting was close to wrapping up when Cassy put her head around the door.

'Sorry, guys. Gill, an urgent call for you.'

As she held the door open for him, something in her eyes startled Gill. He apologised to the group and left Tony to finish things up. Exiting the conference room, he had a rising sense of dread. 'Let me guess. My dad's nursing home?'

Cassy shook her head, her expression impenetrable. 'Jenny Struan at ScoCion', she said. 'Insists she speaks to you before close of play.'

Gill nodded and picked up his phone. 'Jenny. How are things on Orkney this lovely Friday afternoon?'

Jenny paused before she spoke. 'Gill, I wanted to let you know before you hear about this some other way.' She paused. 'I'm afraid there's been an accident today at ScoCion. I'm very sorry to have to tell you David Trevelyan was killed.'

Chapter 19

On Saturday morning, the short drive up to Montrose became a solemn moment for Gill. Having been reunited with an old friend and then losing him so suddenly made fate seem cruel. He was beginning to realise he had an uncomfortable relationship with death. And these last couple of years, there seemed to be so much of it around.

His plan was to spend a couple of hours at the care home, then the rest of Saturday and the first half of Sunday in his father's old home in Stonehaven. He wasn't ready to start clearing out his father's stuff. For now, he just wanted to assess the scale of the task. Physically and emotionally.

His time with Gordon started with a one-way conversation that demanded more energy than he had in his reserves. As Gill sat in Gordon's bedroom, fiddling with the family photo he'd left at his dad's bedside, he struggled to find words. Resolving to talk, he placed the frame back on the shelf and took a breath. 'Do you remember David Trevelyan, Dad? I shared a flat with him in St Andrews in third and fourth years. You probably won't. You and I weren't talking much in those days.' He leaned over and touched his father's unresponsive hand.

'He was a great guy. We stayed friends for a few years, then lost touch. Life and work, you know the kinda thing. Anyway, he's dead. Killed in an accident at work. And the crowning sorrow is that we'd just got back in touch.'

He stood up and walked to the window. The road heading out of town was steady with traffic, folk going about their everyday Saturday afternoons. 'I was going back to Orkney to see him in a few weeks, maybe take Salina. Now I'm going up this week for his funeral.'

His forehead dipped gently against the window, and he relished the cold glass against his skin. He stood like this for several long minutes listening to his father's ragged breathing. 'Why do the best people die on us, Dad? Really pisses me off.'

He thought for a second about Salina. It had taken her time to get back in a boat after the Loch Ness incident. But she'd had some counselling and got herself back in the water. This week she was working in the North Sea, studying the ecosystems accumulating on retired oil rigs. And in a couple of weeks she was taking a team to Iceland. Sub-sea vents. She was really excited.

But he was scared. Always scared for her, with a fear he'd conjured while diving with her in Loch Ness.

The cold glass now stung him, and he pulled back and rubbed his forehead. 'I'm not sure I'll be here next weekend. I'll need to see how things go.' He walked back to the bed and gently lifted his father's hand. 'Love you, Dad. I'll pop in tomorrow on my way home and update you on all the Stonehaven gossip.'

First thing on Monday morning, Gill met Mhairi Dodd in reception. Sitting on a flimsy plastic chair, she looked uncertain about her new working environment.

'Don't worry about first impressions', he said, nodding at the drab décor. 'It's our publisher's attempt to convince his investors he runs a tight ship.'

They made small talk as they walked the two flights up to the *Mys.Scot* office. A long-haired brunette in her middle twenties, she was carefully made up and graceful in the way only tall women can manage. To complete her professional impression, she spoke with clear Southern English pronunciation.

'Your parents live in Dundee', he said, by way of conversation. 'Were you born locally?'

'No. Canterbury in Kent.'

'I love your accent', he offered.

She smiled, puzzled. 'What accent?'

'Exactly!' he replied. 'I can hear every word you're saying without needing a translator.'

With all necessary formalities completed, Gill sat with Cassy and Mhairi in the glass-walled conference room.

'The problem with most archaeology', he continued, 'is that when you reach an impasse, you can't just google the answer.'

Mhairi nodded. 'Cassy mentioned that you have working theories for several projects, but you need to source collaborating material.'

'That's it in a nutshell. My problem with the Glasgow mummies is that we need to add meat to the bones of our initial speculation. Where might they have come from? Is medical utility the only explanation in the frame?'

'We've carbon-dated the human remains to 1200 BCE', added Cassy. 'That's a lot older than the box they were in.'

Mhairi nodded. 'So we're thinking about how the physical remains reached Glasgow. Trade routes, that kind of thing?'

'Yes', said Gill. 'But also the flow of ideas. How does an ancient Middle Eastern therapy find its way to Glasgow a couple of thousand years later?'

She smiled. 'I understand.'

'I'm going to ask Cassy to bring you up to speed on a few of our other ongoing researches. We've got a couple of projects on Orkney, for example.'

Mhairi glanced at Cassy. 'The book with all those numbers? Not sure that would be my cup of tea.'

Cassy shook her head. 'Craig's got that. He's our chief geek. Which reminds me, Gill.' She dug into her folders and pulled out the book of numbers. 'If you're going back to Orkney, you'd better have this. Craig has scanned it so he can expand some of the text on his PC.'

While Gill took the book, he spotted Tony coming down the corridor. 'If you'll excuse me, our publisher has just walked in, and I need to grab him for a minute.'

Gill took a few seconds to clarify what he wanted to ask, then tapped on his boss's door before walking in. 'Hey Tony, sorry to barge in. I need to beg a couple of days off.'

Tony stood and moved around from his desk to grip Gill's hand. 'Cassy mentioned about your friend. Did he have family?'

Gill shrugged. 'A young son and twin girls. Barely more than toddlers.'

Tony winced. 'That's tough. You're heading to Orkney this afternoon?'

'Aye. Got a flight at 2 pm. I've left the return open for the moment. I'm hoping to push some of our research projects forward while I'm there.'

Tony nodded. 'Okay, but take some time with your friend's family.' He released Gill's hand and slipped back to his desk. 'I've been thinking about your idea to bring forward the next publication date.'

'Don't worry about it. In the light of this, let's keep to the original schedule.'

Tony's face became more assured. 'I think that's for the best. No need to have avoidable pressure at a time like this.'

'I'll get the guys all prepped before I leave', said Gill. 'The team is in good shape.'

'Cassy mentioned you've got a temp joining this week.'

'Aye, someone to pick up the load on desk research. Just a few weeks. We'll see how it goes.'

'Okay. I'll pop past and introduce myself later in the day. You take care and stay in touch through Cassy.'

Gill stood outside David and Alice's house and leaned back against the door of his small hire car. It was only 6 pm, but the leaden grey sky made it feel like dusk. He stared at the house, wondering what he might say to Alice in the face of her loss. Lights were on in every room, set in stark contrast to the blinds drawn across the windows of every other house in the cul de sac. To heighten the sense of unrealism, he could hear voices spilling from the house, the appealing warmth of a dozen conversations. From one of the rooms, music was playing.

He'd had to muster all his courage to come here. Mindful the bereaved are easier to bear on a funeral day if you've crossed their threshold first; he had resolved to sit with Alice for a few minutes. He would say a few words about how much he had enjoyed meeting David again and then make a polite exit, leaving Alice to the sober comfort of an older friend or relative. He'd been ready for that, but not for this. This crowded house with all its noise, which was one base-beat from sounding like a party. But he was here, so he pushed off the car and walked up the drive.

He tapped the door, and finding it ajar, he walked on in. The hall was full of people; overspill from the living room, some younger folk dressed like they were going to a dance sat talking on the stairs. Dressed in black trousers and open-neck shirt, the first person he recognised was Mack, in conversation with another older man. Spotting the new arrival, he broke away and offered Gill a stiff male embrace.

'Alice will be so glad to see you. Sorry it isn't under better circumstances.' He pulled back and nodded to a friend. 'Can Graham get you a drink?'

Uncertain, Gill nodded. 'Please. Water.'

Graham acknowledged this and turned away in the direction of the kitchen.

'See if you can find a drop of malt to dilute that', called Mack to his back. He gripped Gill's upper arm. 'Come and say hello to Alice.'

Mack led the way into the living room, squeezing among the crowd towards a space beside the main settee. Dressed in a work blouse and skirt, Alice sat deep in conversation with two older ladies. Without makeup and her eyes red-rimmed, she sat with her legs curled under her. One of her friends leaned closer to Alice and said something Gill didn't catch before Alice brought her hand to her mouth and laughed. Mack pushed through some invisible cordon around the sofa and edged into the empty space to catch Alice's attention. With her face bright and her eyes still sparkling from her friend's remark, she spotted Gill for the first time. Alice threw her arms out towards him, warmly smiling as she uncurled herself to stand. They faced each other for a few seconds, and he moved to gently embrace her.

Alice was shoeless, making her seem a head shorter than Gill. She clung to him modestly at first but then fiercely, her head pressed under his chin. He stood holding her, uncomfortable with the intimacy and utterly uncertain of what to say. Finally, he settled for a whisper. 'Alice, I'm so sorry.'

At this, her body began to shiver, then shake, suddenly buckling at the knees, forcing him to keep her from falling. But she slithered from him, and he followed her into a crouch on the floor. She cried without restraint now, her face still pressed into Gill so that his shirt ran wet with her tears. They sat like this for many minutes while all around them, people drank and talked as if this was the most natural thing in the world.

'You doing okay?' said Mack a few minutes later, passing him his drink after Alice had peeled away into the arms of another friend.

Gill sniffed the glass. Reassured Graham had only mildly touched it with whisky. He took a long sip. 'Yeah, fine.'

Mack glanced to where Alice was composing herself again, settling back on the sofa; the two ladies switched for another set of friends. 'She's been like that all day. All sunshine and showers.' He nodded grimly. 'It will be a day or two before this reality sinks in.'

'You bury folk quickly up here. I wonder if that's a help or a hindrance?' observed Gill.

'Aye, we don't hang around. Never have.' Mack took a slug of amber liquid and lowered his voice. 'This will be a trickier funeral than most.'

'How do you mean?'

'I've done a few funerals for guys lost at sea. The absence of a coffin, of a physical body, makes it harder for the family.'

'Mack, I'm not following you.'

Mack looked startled. 'I'm sorry, I thought you knew?'

'Know what?'

Mack paused and steered Gill further away from the sofa. 'We can't bury David's body. It was completely vaporised in the accident.'

Gill's mouth dropped open, and he quickly closed it again. 'All of him?'

Mack glanced over at Alice, then back to Gill. 'Every last scrap.'

Chapter 20

Drained from his encounter with Alice's grief, he was locking his car outside the B&B when his phone rang. 'Gill, it's Craig. Have you got a moment?'

'You're working late. What's happening?'

'I've had a breakthrough on the Orcadian monuments. Cassy says you're on Orkney right now?'

Gill laid down his bags and slumped back against the car. 'I am. For a funeral. And I'm just back from the weirdest wake.'

Craig left a pause. 'As in, *Mys.Scot* kinda weird?'

'No. As in, people are intense, kind of weird. Sorry, what's up?'

'Listen, I think I know how the neoliths managed to code scientific constants into their monuments.'

Gill groaned inwardly and gripped a handful of his own copper-coloured hair. 'I'll do my best, Craig. But my head's pretty full.'

Craig leapt straight in. 'I looked at the estimated ages of all the monuments and arranged them in date order. Gill, the key is Brodgar.'

'Okay. Tell me why.'

'Other than a few single landmark stones, Brodgar was the last monument built and by far the biggest. Its size is important. It means the exact centre of the circle is very precise despite the crude quality of the building materials. It's the precision of this spot that marks the baseline through the Ring of Bookan, and from this line, we calculate the angles with the pre-existing stones.'

'Okay. I hear you. Giving you the hands on the clock. What's the new discovery?'

'Brodgar was the last big monument constructed. That means whoever built it could look at the pre-existing stones and choose an exact location that would allow the calculation of the important numbers.'

Gill was silent for a long moment. 'You're telling me your Orcadian clock didn't evolve over two thousand years?'

'I don't know how long it took to build', said Craig, dropping his voice. 'But with the right maths, it could have been conceived quickly. After that, it was just the toil of manual labour to put the stones in the ground.'

The following morning, Gill stood in the car park at Tormiston Mill and gathered his thoughts. Last night, his urge to take Craig's theories to Juliette Morrison seemed like a positive next step. But now, the risk of presenting this extraordinary idea to her forensic scrutiny scratched at his own misgivings. He was distracted by the distant sound of dogs barking and scanned the isthmus for the source. Several men with German shepherds were working across the moor in a rough line. Perhaps a security firm training its dogs or police looking for Euan Mearns? He made a mental note to ask Juliette, then walked into the building.

Juliette looked surprised when Gill tapped the doorframe of the cramped office she shared with the rest of her team. 'Gill, I didn't realise you were on Orkney.' She stepped towards him and gave him a fleeting embrace. 'What do we owe the honour?'

Gill stared into the long-distance for a moment. 'I'm on my way to a funeral this morning. A friend who worked at ScoCion.'

'Oh, I'm sorry. I'd heard about it but didn't realise you knew him.'

'Ach, you know. He and his wife were pals of mine at Uni. I wanted to come back and see how Alice and the kids are getting on.'

Juliette smiled sadly and reached out to rub his arm. 'That's a good thing to do.'

'And while I'm here, I've had a few thoughts towards solving that little Chi Rho puzzle we were discussing.'

'Okay. Do tell.'

'It's rather complicated', said Gill. 'Do you have anywhere we could spread ourselves out for half an hour?'

Juliette thought for a second. 'The coffee shop isn't open yet. We can grab a table in there.'

Quietly and slowly, Gill laid out the cypher from the book of numbers. He grew nervous as the colour gradually drained from Juliette's face. His typically polished presentation disintegrated into stutters with hands raised in apologies where he knew the logic stretched to breaking point. In the event, it took almost an hour to bring her up to speed.

When he finished, he met her gaze and asked her straight. 'Well, what do you think?'

'Let me check if I understand', she said quietly. 'Are you telling me aliens laid out the principal Orcadian monuments?'

Gill held up a hand. 'No, that would be getting ahead of ourselves.'

Juliette broke in. 'And let's agree not to get ahead of ourselves.' She reached down and spun the ordnance survey map until it was in front of her. 'Can I burden you with one fact you haven't mentioned?'

'Please. Go ahead.'

Juliette drew her finger down the Orcadian clock Craig had pencilled on the map until she reached the southern part of the island. 'You say the data derived from the principle stone monuments correspond to the eight known planets?'

'Yes.'

'What about this ninth data point?'

'Sorry, which one?'

Juliette drew her finger across the map. 'You have a line here, running from Brodgar through Stenness.'

'You're right. But that data point doesn't correlate with a known planetary body, so we've discounted it.'

'But according to your book, it's in the data. So somehow, using this clock of yours, you would expect it to represent a significant relationship?'

'Agreed. Other arms of the clock account for all the planets, so maybe this one hasn't been discovered yet.'

Juliette frowned at him and spun the map again until it reorientated in front of him. 'Come on, Gill. Look at your so-called outlier. Extrapolate the line and tell me you can see what I mean.'

He shook his head. 'It's empty space.'

Juliette sat back and sighed theatrically. 'Here's a clue. Think about any buildings added since this map was published,' For emphasis, she drew her finger from Brodgar to Stenness and out across the bare hillside.

Gill felt his jaw drop a fraction. 'The ScoCion site.'

Juliette's expression was challenging but not cold. 'Rumour has it ScoCion's continued funding is in doubt. That place might be hanging by its fingernails.'

'It's in the data', said Gill. 'From the book of numbers.'

Juliette sighed. 'Have you considered that you might be the victim of an elaborate publicity stunt?'

Gill said nothing for a few moments. 'Not really.'

She mustered an encouraging smile but said nothing.

He glanced at his watch. 'Thanks for taking a look.' He ran his eyes over the map again, straining to see anything else he'd missed.

'This funeral', he said at last. 'I'd better go and change.'

As Gill got out of his car beside *The Fish Shed*, the band was already in full swing. The crash of drums and the strong, clear pitch of a woman's singing voice signalled a festival, not a funeral. Gill took a deep breath and moved towards the building. A group of David's work colleagues were standing outside the main door. Jenny Struan, dressed in black, stood smoking a little way from the group. Gill shook hands with one or two, doing his best to recall their names. He remembered Doug from the control room and lingered by him for a few seconds.

'Professor Harley already inside?' Gill asked.

Doug shook his head. 'Don't think he's going to make it. Feels a bit responsible. Not that he is, like. Doesn't want to make a fuss.'

'I'm sure the email said 11 am, but it looks like we missed the start', said a woman Gill recognised from ScoCion reception.

'Don't worry, Prisha. It's the way they do things here', he said, grasping the door. 'Brace yourselves. This probably won't be like any funeral you've ever been to.'

He held the door for them as they filed into the foyer. Jenny was last, reluctantly tossing away her cigarette. Gill stared at her, hoping to catch a few words, but she slid past him and avoided eye contact.

Stepping inside, Gill led the way towards the music and guided the group towards empty seats at the back of the auditorium. If anything, it was busier than his recent Sunday visit, minus the youth. The ScoCion group flashed uncomfortable looks at each other as if some explanation would collectively dawn on them. Gill was too tired to share in their stress, so instead, he closed his eyes and let the experience wash over him.

After twenty-five minutes of devotional music, Mack stepped up and faced the room. Gradually things quietened down, and people took their seats.

'Folks, welcome', said Mack. He paused and took a long slow look around the room. 'Look, we're friends here. We're not going to say a lot of things that don't need said. Can we just agree David's in a better place?'

Murmurs of ascent floated around the room, accompanied by a ripple of applause.

Mack's pause looked genuine, and even Gill, from the back of the room, could see the older man was struggling. 'But that doesn't make his absence any easier to bear.' Mack cleared his throat and sipped on a water bottle. 'On behalf of Alice and the children, thank you for making room on a weekday to come and remember a friend.' Mack turned to face the front row of seats. He said nothing, but just waited. After nearly a minute, Gill spotted Alice for the first time, getting slowly to her feet and walking with Noah to stand beside Mack. A few moments later, the twins followed, having escaped whatever restraint their mother had conjured for them. She bent to scoop up Grace while Esther made for Mack, who stooped to carefully pick up the child. Gill felt a lump rise in his throat while the whole congregation broke into more applause.

Mack beamed around the room, and for a moment, even Alice managed to smile. Eventually, as things quietened down, Mack spoke again. 'Folks. What we're going to do here, is give anyone who wants to say a few words, the chance to step to the front. You can speak for one minute max and tell us a story to help remember David.' He glanced at Esther, who was now wrestling him for the mic. 'Looks like we've got our first volunteer. Esther, tell us something about your daddy.'

Esther stared up at Mack's collar as if perplexed by the presence of a tie, and in the long seconds that followed, Gill wondered if the pastor had pushed his luck too far. But the little girl looked up at him brightly and said, 'He's very good of building sandcastles.'

Spontaneous laughter erupted to lighten the tension of the moment. Strengthened by that, the rest of the family stepped forward to say just a few words. 'Best dad ever', said Noah. 'Funny', whispered Grace. And Alice, after a deep breath, uttered, 'Quite simply, the love of my life.'

More applause, and then one by one, many of the congregation stepped forward to express their memories. Out of the corner of his eye, Gill noticed Doug staring at him. He was suddenly aware he could feel tears streaming down his face and realised he didn't care.

After half an hour, Mack drew the reminiscences to a close and stepped up to say a prayer of thanks for David's life. Then he indicated the end of the service and pointed to where refreshments would be available in the café area. Then the music started again, and people began to file out of the room.

'That was intense', said Doug once they were back outside.

'Amazing though', said one of his colleagues.

'I'm wrung out', said another. 'Anyone fancy a beer?'

Quickly the group arrived at a consensus on a venue. 'Joining us?' asked Doug.

'Thanks, but no', said Gill. It was sunny and barely lunchtime. Despite the appealing anaesthesia of an afternoon spent drinking pints, he knew he needed to think clearly. He noticed Jenny had slipped past him and was already at her car. 'Guys, I'll catch you again.'

After rushed farewells, he jogged down to where Jenny's car was reversing, but it seemed she had resolved not to see him and drove off without as much as a wave. Gill watched her go and found himself reconsidering the offer of a beer. He glanced at his watch and then at his phone. He sighed, spotting several emails from his office, plus a text from Juliette Morrison asking him to call her urgently. He watched Doug's group file off towards town, the whole party suddenly in better spirits. He suppressed the urge to follow them and dialled Juliette's number.

'Hey, Gill. How was the funeral?'

'Weird. Well, I think it was a funeral. Hard to say when you don't have a body.'

'Gosh, sorry, I didn't realise. Terrible business.'

Gill made a non-committal grunt into the phone and waited for Juliette to get to business.

'Look, I was thinking after you left this morning, and I hope I wasn't too hard on you.'

'No problem. You very politely found a reasonable flaw in a scheme that already looked too good to be true.'

'That issue aside, the rest of it looks intriguing.'

'Yeah. It does.'

'So I might have an opportunity for you.'

'Sure. Go for it.'

'Can you come up to the Brodgar circle? I mean, right away?'

Gill accepted and hung up. Instead of stepping back into work, he knew he'd far rather go drinking and reminiscing with David's colleagues. 'But, hey! Life goes on', he muttered to himself and headed for his car.

Chapter 21

You scrub up well', Juliette offered huskily as he gingerly stepped over the heather in his best shoes.

'For once, if you offer me a brush and trowel, I will be forced to decline. What's going on?' said Gill. They were standing beside a large blue tarpaulin covering the centre point of the Brodgar standing stones.

'I forgot to mention to you this morning. I'm getting nowhere with Historic Scotland regarding a formal dig at the circle's centre.'

'Aye. Doesn't surprise me.'

'Then you came in this morning with all your Orcadian clock bullshit.'

'Yeah, thanks.'

'But then I got to thinking about your scans in the centre of Brodgar circle; the ones with the faint hexagon shape.'

'Aye.'

'And then I thought, if we did find a hexagon, then maybe the clock idea wouldn't be bullshit after all.'

'Look, Juliette ...'

'And this is where I admit I've been a rather naughty girl.'

Gill raised an eyebrow. 'What have you done?'

'For the last few days, I've been collecting soil samples, inside the circle, at ten-centimetre increments within an area of four metres square.'

'Okay. Why?'

'For a carbon dating study. There's a long-term question around whether this whole area was urbanised at one time. You know, looking for post holes, trackways, all manner of human detritus. It's moorland now, but four thousand years ago, this whole area was buzzing.'

Gill glanced down at the tarp, realising that she'd sampled the ground where they were standing. 'Right, I get it. You want to find out if the period of urban development preceded or followed the placing of the circle. We would normally expect the development to come after the stones, in which case the soil in the circle should be pretty much undisturbed.'

'Exactly. We still hold samples from previous studies, but they were from a hundred years ago. A while back, the trust agreed to extract a fresh batch. I've sat on it until, frankly, I could be bothered.'

'And you're bothered now?'

Juliette stood with her hands on her hips, looking smug. 'With it being the end of the season, and I've got an urge to be proactive, guess where I decided to take the samples from?'

Gill looked at her and smiled. 'You're a complete chancer. They'll bloody fire you if they realise what you've done.'

Juliette knelt on the dirt to start rolling back the covering, and reluctantly, Gill followed her lead. 'They won't if I make an exciting discovery.'

Gill's inhibition about getting mud on his trousers suddenly vanished. 'What have you got?'

Juliette pulled back the last covering to reveal a small area of exposed bedrock. The surface had no crack or blemish other than the presence of typical sedimentary lines. Gill looked up at her. 'I'm sure it's brilliant, but humour me and tell me why I should be impressed.'

Juliette hung her head in frustration for a moment, then fixed him with a mothering glare. 'The thirty-four surviving Brodgar megaliths are a local yellow sandstone called Stromness Flagstone. We reckon they were cut from a hillside just over there, in the direction of the village.'

Gill nodded.

'The bedrock you're looking at, however, is Rousay flagstone. It's a grey colour where I'd expect to see yellow. And when I look closely, I see a crack and different coloured stone on either side.'

'Rousay flagstone. Is that significant?' asked Gill.

'It comes from the other direction.' She rubbed the surface of the exposed rock. 'It shows signs of being weathered by the sea and is exceptionally hard.'

'Then it must be what we anticipated', said Gill triumphantly. 'A capstone.'

Juliette nodded. 'It certainly points in that direction. And I've noticed something else.'

'What.'

'Based on your scans, this thing is about three metres square, right?'

'Yes. That's enough to cover the hexagonal stone beneath with room to spare.'

'Well, look around you. You couldn't have brought a stone as big as that in here as an after-thought.'

The implications of what Juliette was saying struck him hard. 'Whatever is down here was built before the henge?'

Juliette sat back on her haunches and blew hair out of her face. 'Whatever is down here might be the very reason the Brodgar circle exists.'

'I have to admit, it looks promising', said the rugged face on the other end of the Zoom call. 'But you can't honestly be proposing a late autumn dig. I'd imagine a six month lead time at the very least.' Charles Downshire was a straight-faced Ulsterman and Juliette's line manager based in Edinburgh. They were calling him from Juliette's office at Tormiston.

'Agreed', Juliette replied. 'But I still have a panel of willing volunteers, plus the financial support of *Mysterious Scotland* if we can get it done this year.'

'Sounds like Mr McArdle is twisting your arm', said Charles.

'If I can butt in', said Gill. 'My year-end runs to the calendar year, and I've got a little money left. If we leave this project to the new year, I'll have a whole host of things to consider. This potential project becomes just one of many.'

'Be that as it may, Gill, the timescale you're proposing doesn't leave room for consultation.'

Juliette cut back in. 'Another reason an immediate dig is so attractive is the favourable weather window. We have a low-pressure system coming through tonight, and then we're looking at a week of settled weather. You know what it's like up here, Charles. These kinds of conditions are a gift.'

Charles dipped his eyes for a moment, then looked up again. 'What about site preservation and restoration? We can't go into the winter with Brodgar churned to a quagmire.'

Gill cleared his throat. 'We have a local hire firm willing to lay protective trackways across the site, and all staff and volunteers will adhere rigidly to their use. We've also spoken to a construction firm working on a jetty extension at Kirkwall. They have a heavy lifter with a long-reach crane they can rent to us for a few days. The crane would sit well outside the circle. We would do a primary lift to transfer the capstone onto pallets laid within the circle. Then, if the hexagonal stone's condition is good enough to lift, we'll recover that to Tormiston Mill, investigate what's underneath, and conclude the dig by placing the top layer capstone back in situ.'

'We would lift the turf in single cuts from surface to capstone', said Juliette. 'That way, we can keep it moist and in the same configuration as it came out, then pop it straight back afterwards. Come the spring, all visible signs of the dig will be gone.'

Charles nodded. 'Okay, that's prudent.'

Gill and Juliette waited while the older man thought.

'Look, I'll need to run this past a couple of the experts. I'd like you to send me your "Scope of Work" documentation. Today if possible. I want to know every detail down to the last spade cut. If that's in order, and no one down here raises an issue, I'll wing it out to the Trustees marked for a twenty-four-hour response.'

'Thanks, Charles, you're a star.'

'No promises, Juliette. But I suspect Gill's reputation might just swing it in your favour.'

The call ended, and Juliette beamed at Gill. 'We might actually get to do this!'

Gill was already cracking open his laptop. 'Hold back on the champagne. We've got a lot of planning to do.'

Gill's Wednesday morning began with a run, followed by a pre-arranged call with Cassy and Mhairi.

'The idea that the mummies were utilised for medical purposes seems the only credible theory', Cassy began.

'The carbon dating on the box', said Mhairi. 'It's consistent with the date when the Egyptians stopped trade in human remains from their territory.'

'This had been going on for a while then?' Gill asked.

'It came from a Persian idea. Then it was corrupted in translation', said Mhairi.

'Tell me about that.'

'Persian medicine used bitumen as a general cure-all. It washed up on the shores of the Caspian Sea as hard pellets. The Persian word for bitumen is "mumia". Unfortunately, when the Europeans got hold of the idea, "mumia" translates in Latin as mummy. As in, ancient Egyptian mummy.'

‘Hang on’, said Gill. ‘Not only were the Europeans sipping potions made from human remains, but they were doing it based on a translation error?’

‘Aye, that and the fact that embalmed bodies smell similar to pure bitumen.’

‘How could they make such a fundamental mistake?’

‘By the middle ages, Persia was long gone, so we can’t check the original sources. We only know what we do today because of archaeology.’

‘Nice wee spin for our story. But it doesn’t say much for the flow of ideas across the millennia.’

‘I’m not sure I’d agree. Persia was the world leader in various ancient technologies, including medicine. The fact that somewhere along the line, someone mistranslated the main ingredient doesn’t disprove clever ideas flowed out of Persia and its succeeding kingdoms.’

‘I wonder if any ideas flowed to Scotland?’

Mhairi paused for a few seconds before answering. ‘Tough call as Scotland didn’t exist as a distinct nation until the eighth century.’

‘Fair point.’

‘I’ll have a look. My training is more Greek than Persian, but I can talk to Adina Mofaz again. She mentioned possible cultural exchanges between the ancient Middle Eastern civilisations and an advanced European culture loosely translated as “The Northern Kingdom”.’

‘Thanks, Mhairi, this is excellent. Listen, we have a section on our website called “Sidewinders”. It’s where we place anecdotal stories linked to our main editorial thrust.

I'd like you to write some of this up. Cassy will show you the format.'

'Great. Will do.'

'And can I borrow your skills to get hold of another historical document?'

'Sure.'

'I'll text you details. For the Orkney dig, I'm referencing a book written in 1851 by a chap called Wilson. I believe he wrote a second volume about five years later. I'd love to get hold of it.'

'Do you know the title?'

'No. The name of the first one was a bit of a mouthful, so the second might be too. I'll send you what I've got.'

The call ended a few minutes later, and Gill thanked the heavens that Cassy had come through for him again. Mhairi Dodd was excellent. But his burst of satisfaction was short-lived. He remembered he had a house call to make, and sadness bubbled up in him again.

Gill sat in the front room while Alice fetched coffee for them both. In another part of the house, he could hear Alice's mum playing with the twins. Meanwhile, Noah sat opposite Gill, his small hands gathered between his legs, oblivious to the TV cartoons, playing with the volume on mute. He and Gill studied each other. At first, Gill didn't know what to say. He had no words for this moment, and after a few more seconds, Noah just looked away.

‘Noah, go and see if granny needs any help’, said Alice, laying a tray with two cups down on the table. She looked pale as she sat down. Her straw-blond hair pulled back in a straight ponytail that wasn’t her usual style. Without acknowledging her request, Noah obeyed.

‘I thought you were all very brave yesterday.’

Alice dropped her forehead into the palm of her left hand and couldn’t suppress a smile. ‘Poor Esther. We can always rely on her to break the ice.’

‘She did great. You all did.’

Alice gave a barely perceptible nod and stared at the floor. ‘Thing is, Noah realises that his dad is gone. My GP says it might be months before the girls understand David isn’t around anymore.’ She shook her head. ‘For me, the only good thing about yesterday was finally realising this is actually happening.’

‘How do you mean?’ said Gill gently.

Alice pulled a mystified face and held her hands aloft. ‘No one at ScoCion seems very clear about what happened. I mean, it was hours before they even started to use words like “dead”, or “killed”, or “fatality”. It sounded like they were expecting David to come waltzing in at any moment with a bag of spanners, wondering what the fuss was about.’

Gill looked away. ‘I’m sorry. That wasn’t very considerate of them.’

‘I mean, I talked to that guy Harley and asked him to explain what happened to David. All I got was mumbo jumbo and eighty zillion hertz and absence of grounding to earth, and a deep flaw in safety mechanisms. I didn’t understand a word of it.’

‘I take it he apologised at least?’

'Oh yes. Said ScoCion admitted full liability and that I could expect a big settlement.'

'That's some comfort.'

Alice peered down into her coffee. 'A million quid or David back home again? No contest.' She balanced her cup in one hand and wiped away a single tear with the other. 'Sorry, I'll stop bloody crying one of these days.'

Gill smiled but said nothing.

'David was so excited about seeing you again. He was really looking forward to being back in touch and meeting your girlfriend.'

'Aye, we'd been texting since I was over. We had this rolling chess game …' Gill trailed off, remembering the game they'd never finish.

'What am I going to tell the kids when they get older? Noah wants to know right now.' Alice threw Gill a startled look. 'I'm worried about him. I heard voices in his room last night and thought one of the girls was out of bed. But when I looked, Noah was alone. Then I asked if he was praying out loud. He said, "no", he was talking to "the man".'

Gill nodded sympathetically. 'What man?'

'He refused to say. And he didn't seem scared. He just lay down and went back to sleep. That behaviour isn't like him.'

'Would it help if I spoke to ScoCion?' said Gill. 'I could ask to see the preliminary safety reports on behalf of the family. I met a journalist last time I was over who might be able to translate it into meaningful English.'

Alice thought for a second, distracted by the sound of small feet coming down the stairs. 'Yes, please, Gill. I'd like that very much.'

Chapter 22

Walking into ScoCion early that afternoon, Gill was aware of a sombre hush throughout the building. He recognised the receptionist from David's funeral and approached her quietly. 'Hey, Prisha. Is Professor Harley available? I'd like to have a few words.'

Prisha glanced down at her desk while she considered her response. 'I'm sorry, Gill. The professor isn't giving any interviews at the moment.'

'This isn't a professional call', said Gill. 'The family has asked me to liaise while the accident reports are prepared. Alice Trevelyan didn't want to come up here herself, and she'd like to avoid the formality of using a solicitor.'

'Okay. I can certainly let Professor Harley know about your request. Perhaps schedule something for later in the week? How long are you on the island?'

'I'm hoping to get away on Friday. I don't need a big slug of his time. Maybe a few minutes to establish a basic understanding. After that, he can just email information as it comes available.'

Prisha nodded and tapped her keyboard. 'I'll just check his diary for Thursday.' She shuffled between screens for a few moments, then apologised. 'Excuse me a second. I don't think this is fully up to date.' She left her desk and walked to one of the larger offices against the outside wall of the building. She put her head around the door, and Gill could hear a muffled conversation. Eventually, she nodded and left the door ajar as she headed back to her desk, with Harley following behind.

Harley offered Gill an outstretched hand. 'Gill, thanks for coming in. Prisha tells me you're going to be our link man to the family.'

'It's my way of helping out. Given the violence of the accident, Alice isn't up to working through the detail at the moment.'

Harley leaned back and briefly closed his eyes. 'I'm devastated by what happened. David was a friend as much as a colleague.' Harley beckoned to Gill and steered them towards his office. 'Talk to me about what you would like to achieve here. I'll drop what I'm doing and try to help you any way I can.'

Gill nodded his thanks. 'The first and most important thing is to understand the accident, Professor. What led up to it? What happened in the moments before David was killed? What's going to change in the future?'

Harley's expression grew even more sober, and he rubbed his chin with his left hand as he thought. 'I want to start this process by being open and thorough. Let me take you down to the control room, and I'll walk you through exactly what happened.'

A few minutes passed while Harley spoke to Prisha before reappearing with white coats and hard hats. He checked his I.D. access card and gathered a pouch of keys. 'These are amongst the items David would have had on him the day of the accident. All the locks are key card operated, but we have mechanical overrides in case of a problem.' He patted his pockets. 'Okay. Are you alright for a bit of a walk?'

They set off together down a long tunnel that linked a secure door at the back of the offices down towards the apparatus built deep into the hillside. The walls were steel-lined and faintly downhill, and Harley talked about the construction challenges to pass the time.

'By the time the boring machines had finished their work, you can imagine what the locals were saying. One of the taxi drivers spread a rumour we'd put a laser on top, and next thing I knew, they'd all started calling me *Goldfinger*.'

After six minutes of walking, they diverted into the control room with its viewing platform, where Gill had sat on the day of the failed test.

'We'd fixed the targeting issue that had scuppered test thirty-six, and essentially test thirty-seven was a re-run of that experiment. You can imagine how frustrated we all were when we detected another problem with less than twenty-eight minutes left on the countdown.'

'Why was the timescale so important?' asked Gill. 'If you hit a problem, couldn't you just kick the whole thing back a couple of hours?'

Harley's face took on the air of a college lecturer. 'Each test fire takes an immense amount of charge, precisely delivered. We start loading up the capacitors eighty minutes before each firing. A reset can take days.'

'So, what was the problem?'

'The ion source for the targeting beam is a radioactive isotope. It's nothing very deadly, but it's only exposed to the air in the minutes before firing. We got a red light as soon as the protective cap wouldn't retract to reveal the ion source.'

'Sounds simple.'

Harley shrugged. 'It was bloody typical. You have a billion-pound installation, and then you're let down by one hundred quid's worth of electric motor. Anyway, the safety officer moved to cancel the test, but David wasn't having any of it. He decided to enter the ion chamber mid-count and address the problem himself.'

'And he did this with half an hour on the clock?'

'Less than that. Because of the radioactive source, plus the strong magnetism of the targeting mechanism, he had to put on a radiological suit. So the clock was standing about T minus nineteen minutes when he entered the chamber.'

'What happened then?'

'By T minus twelve minutes, he had reached the isotope shutter and fixed the mechanism. Then by six minutes, he signalled he was out of the chamber and that the count could proceed.'

'Did anyone verify this?'

Harley shook his head. 'We were all hands on deck up here, and David had gone down alone. Preventing a solo expedition like that is one of the primary safety recommendations I'll be making to the board.'

'Did nobody notice he wasn't back in the control room before the apparatus fired?'

Harley leaned back, his arms outstretched in front of him. 'Going via the safety room where the rad suits are stored, it's another six hundred metres from the ion chamber back up the access hallway to this room. When he didn't return immediately, we assumed he was taking his time changing his clothes.'

Gill said nothing for a moment. Then he took a breath and continued. 'Any idea why David was back in the chamber when the apparatus fired?'

Harley shrugged. 'That's a mystery, I'm afraid. It's not like David was a tinkerer. He wouldn't have thought, "Oh, while I'm down here, I might as well tighten that gasket". No, he was much too considered for that and completely aware of the danger this apparatus represents when it's active.' Harley walked over to a control panel and drew up a live feed from the inside of the particle cannon. 'I've no idea what drew David back into the chamber to risk his life.'

'And he didn't communicate with you between leaving the chamber and his death six minutes later?'

Harley shook his head.

'This feed. Did you record David when he was in the chamber?'

'We have him while he's working at the firing mechanism. There are two cameras at that end. Then we have cameras on each of the two exits, but unfortunately, they weren't working that day.'

'It's a pity you didn't test them beforehand', Gill observed.

Harley held out his hands. 'And that'll be another recommendation.'

'This might be a daft question, but how do you know David is even dead? You don't have a body.'

For the first time since he'd arrived, Gill saw Harley properly look him in the eye. 'We only have his rad suit. We found it in the ion chamber. We did a manual sweep of the place as soon as we realised David was missing.'

'But no, David?'

Harley grimaced and turned to face the lifeless instrument panel. 'The suit and everything metal on David's person; his watch, his ring, survived the firing. His phone, too, though that was fried. But David, and his cotton undergarments, were all gone. As I'd expect when that amount of energy hits anything organic.'

'Can we go down there?' Gill heard himself asking.

Harley was silent for a few seconds. 'I don't see why not. Everything is switched off, so it's perfectly safe.'

Gill followed Harley down another two hundred metres long passageway in silence. Harley pointed to a corridor leading to the safety room where ScoCion stored protective garments. Then they moved to the access hatch into the ion chamber itself. Harley swiped his key card, and the solid metal door clicked a few times, then swung open about ten degrees. Harley hauled on it and, after glancing at Gill, stepped inside. He pointed to a key slot in the door casing. 'This is the manual override. Even if the electronics weren't working, you could affect an emergency egress without much effort. He pointed down the ion chamber. 'This way.'

'I've wondered why David's suit didn't protect him?' Gill asked as they walked.

Harley grimaced. 'Not against a full ion beam discharge. This tube has been characterised as the biggest microwave on the planet. The suit protected him from radiation given off by the targeting isotopes.' He mustered an encouraging smile. 'For your peace of mind, it's all shielded while the machine is dormant and the batteries are spooled down. There's no danger.'

They walked for several minutes until they approached a second hatch. The rough outline of a man was discernible in yellow paint sprayed on the ground.

'Like a bloody crime scene', said Harley.

Gill knelt. For a long moment, he said nothing, his hand lingering on the edge of the coarse yellow lines.

Harley cleared his throat. 'Again, I'm so sorry.'

'Would he have felt anything?' Gill asked.

Harley sighed and gave his trouser legs a slight upward tug so he could comfortably join Gill on the floor. 'To have been so utterly destroyed, it would have been instantaneous. He wouldn't have known what hit him.'

Gill looked Harley full in the face. 'Why the hell was he down here? He must have known the risks.'

Harley grunted as he struggled back up to full height. 'We don't know, Gill. We might never know.'

'Then speculate, Professor. Please. Come up with a theory.'

Harley lifted a hand. 'The health and safety people asked the same question. Rather than risk upsetting you, I'd rather leave it to their report.'

Gill got to his feet. 'Okay. Can I ask about this second hatch? Why would he have come down this far?'

Harley sighed. 'That's a puzzle. This one is purely an emergency escape hatch. I'll show you.' He reached for a wheel recessed into the door and spun the lock quickly on its well-oiled mechanism. The door clicked open, and Harley swung it inwards and stepped into a short corridor beyond.

'There's a similar locked door in the next wall. I'd prefer not to open it as we try to keep the ion chamber dust-free.'

'What lies beyond?'

'A simple brick corridor. Then a very long metal ladder up to the surface across a dozen stages. At the top, I think the layout is another small room with a door leading onto the moor.'

'You've not been?'

'Not since the construction phase. The exit is out onto the moor on the south-facing slope of Rusky Hill.'

Gill nosed around for a minute, and with little else to see, he followed Harley back into the ion chamber.

'To come down here, could he have been confused?'

'We don't think he was disoriented. He knew this facility like the back of his hand. And he was cool and rational on the day of the test. No signs of stress, nausea, giddiness.'

'Do you see any possibility someone abducted him?' said Gill, trying another tack.

'We did consider that possibility because of the massive commercial potential of this project. Some form of industrial sabotage isn't out of the question. But it's not likely. If you wanted to kidnap David, I could think of a thousand easier places.'

Gill stared at the floor while he thought about what Harley was saying. Then he looked up again and asked, 'Any other theories?'

Harley let his hands slump into his pockets as if searching for words. Then he stood up and peered through the narrow porthole on the escape hatch. 'Gill. Let's not do this.'

Gill stepped closer to Harley, cramping the man's personal space. 'If you have any ideas, I'd like to hear them.'

Harley turned around to face him. 'I can see only one possible explanation.'

Gill waited for Harley to continue.

'Oh, come on, Gill. When you look at all the circumstances, and you discount foul play or an accident ...' Harley held a hand out to Gill, expecting him to take up the logic. When he didn't, Harley continued. 'David knew this apparatus. If anyone ever wanted an instant and painless death, what better than the world's most powerful microwave?'

Gill was briefly stunned. 'Suicide! Really? Why would he do that?'

Harley's hands flew out defensively. 'I dunno. A marriage on the rocks, shame, powerlessness, debt? I gather he had religious convictions, so maybe it was a crisis of faith. There are a hundred possible reasons.'

Gill stared at Harley. 'Knowing the guy, I think that's unlikely.'

'You did ask me to speculate, against my better judgement.'

'Maybe', said Gill. 'If I can be blunt, I don't have any data pointing to that conclusion.'

'We'll see what the accident enquiry concludes.'

Gill shook his head and turned away. 'Look, I need to go now. Thanks for the tour.'

Harley followed Gill and caught up with him as he stepped gingerly around the yellow marks and walked back down the ion chamber. 'Look, I'm not absolving ScoCion of blame. It shouldn't have been possible for David to enter a high-risk area unaccompanied. I get that. You asked me to speculate. So don't shoot the messenger, alright.'

Gill stopped suddenly, making Harley drop back a couple of steps to get beside him again. 'You're right. Nothing excuses the fact that he was in here alone.' The two men met eye-to-eye for a few moments. 'And I agree, suicide is one legitimate line of enquiry, but you'll understand if I find it upsetting.'

Harley nodded, relieved. 'Do you know of any reason he might have put himself in harm's way?'

'No. But I'll ask around.'

'Good', said Harley. 'Thank you.'

They walked the rest of the way back up into the administrative block in silence. Harley hesitated at the door of his office. 'As you're the family representative, maybe you'd help me with one thing.'

Gill nodded.

Harley stepped into his office, returning a few moments later with a small, neat cardboard box. 'These are David's personal effects. From inside the suit, plus some personal things from his desk. Would you mind giving them to Alice? Again, with my profound condolences.'

Gill nodded and took the box.

Without another word, he left the building.

He sat in his car for ten minutes, pushing away the dread that David could have died at his own hands. Needing to pull him closer again, he opened the box and inspected each item. A picture of Alice and the kids. A phone charger. And the phone itself, dented and discernibly blackened. Near the bottom was David's watch. A Breitling Aviator and a gift to him from his father, it lay fused at the date and time of its owner's demise. Finally, a thick gold wedding band. Gill picked this out and held it between the thumb and forefinger of his left hand. The ring was a plain band, but Gill could discern three words engraved on the inner surface. He held it at a distance and squinted at the writing.

"The Heavens Declare", he read.

He placed it carefully back in the box, and for five therapeutic minutes, he let himself cry freely.

Chapter 23

A little later, Gill waited outside *The Fish Shed* while two men on ladders took down the church's name board. As he watched, he felt a twinge of sadness and wondered whether Kirkwall would be darker place without this lively gathering. After a shout of thanks from the guys with screwdrivers, he passed into the building and found Mack in the church office, surrounded by boxes and a bevvy of glum volunteers.

'Goodness. Looks like the end of the empire in here', said Gill, trying to sound cheerful.

Mack murmured a few words of encouragement to one of his staff and steered Gill with a touch on his shoulder. 'Take me away from this for a few minutes. We can grab a coffee in the kitchen.'

'Second thoughts?' Gill asked.

Mack shrugged. 'Orders are orders unless the man upstairs changes his mind.' He checked the kettle held water and flicked it on. 'Some of the members are finding it tougher than others. We're trying to disseminate our resources and clear out unnecessary paperwork. I think the finality of it all is hitting people.'

Gill looked at the older man. 'Still think it's madness myself. You've got such a sense of community here.'

Mack smiled sadly. 'I agree. But somehow, the church seems to survive, even when it's scattered.'

'Sorry, Mack, but from where I'm sitting, this looks like a self-inflicted wound.'

'Maybe. Or perhaps an invitation to a fresh start. I'm a tiny bit curious what God will do next in our community.'

'And in the meantime, all the people who helped you build this simply let it go? Just because you say so?'

Mack looked away. 'Never follow another man's faith, Gill.'

'Beg your pardon?'

'I'll go further. Don't even become a believer. Not unless you have overwhelming supernatural proof that what you're getting is the real deal.'

'But aren't pastors meant to ...' Gill was uncertain how to finish.

'Proselytise? Sell you their religion? No, my job is to teach people, not make converts.'

'Most pious folk I've ever met were quite happy to flog me their religion.'

'Agreed. Sign on the dotted line for health, happiness and as much prosperity as you can handle. But I've seen folk made miserable by a faith built on logic or tradition. They assemble a mental construct that doesn't survive the storms of life.'

'Over-whelming supernatural proof?' Gill observed.

'An actual encounter with this entity we call "God". An experience that is so irrevocable we can choose thereafter to ignore it but can never deny its implications.'

'Even if in your case, the implication is that you should dismantle your life's work?'

'Think about it', said Mack, waving his arms around him. 'If God really exists, do you think replacing all this will be a struggle for him?'

'I guess.'

'For example, have I tried to convince you of anything?'

Gill shook his head slowly. At this moment, he didn't know if Mack was mad, deluded or inspired.

Mack reacted to Gill's expression and dropped his outstretched arms. He poured the coffees and passed one to Gill. 'Anyway, you came to ask me something, and I should be grieving on mute. How can I help you?'

Gill gathered his thoughts. 'Alice has asked me to act as a liaison between her and ScoCion.'

Mack nodded. 'Yes, I called by earlier, and she mentioned you.'

'I visited this afternoon, and Professor Harley was good enough to see me immediately and walk me around where David died.'

'Okay. That's positive.'

'Thing is, he's got a theory that David might have put himself in harm's way.' Gill raised his hands to calm Mack's startled reaction. 'He has no proof, but he might lead the accident enquiry to consider it. Look, you were his friend, his mentor. I'm just asking if you know of any reason why David might have wanted to take his own life?'

Mack slowly drew a chair off a stack and wearily sat down. He stared into the middle distance for the best part of a minute, then shook his head. 'I can think of a thousand reasons why he wouldn't want to kill himself.'

'You're sure? No marital issues, or mental health? Anything?'

'No. Absolutely, no.' Mack looked up. 'Don't go saying this to Alice. You'll break her heart.'

Gill shook his head. 'Just between you and me. And for what it's worth, I agree with you. I just needed to ask someone who knew him better.'

Gill's phone rang, and he glanced at the number display. 'Sorry, Mack, I need to get this.' He stepped out into the corridor and picked up the call. 'Hi, Juliette. How's it going?'

'Good news or bad news?' she said without a greeting.

'Always prefer good news.'

'The dig is approved.'

'Excellent!'

'But not until next May.'

'Dammit', said Gill.

'Yeah. Shite', said Juliette. 'Speak to you in a day or two.'

He hung up the call and thought. It would have been handy to press on with the dig immediately, but these things always took time. From an editorial standpoint, the story would keep. But Brodgar had scratched his curiosity, and now he'd itch until he got back here.

He took a deep breath and put his phone away. Then he walked back to where the older man was waiting. 'Listen, Mack. You talk about supernatural encounters. Can I run something past you?'

On the way back from Kirkwall, Gill found a layby that commanded an excellent view over the Isthmus. He stared out over the stones and thought about his conversation with Mack. The older man had listened as Gill reported his encounters with Raphael. Without judging, he'd considered Salina's idea that the stranger might be some form of angelic being, adding that he thought this kind of encounter was considered rare. He'd pointed Gill to some Bible references and offered to meet with him again. When Gill expressed his uncertainty in the reliability of the ancient book, Mack had grown embarrassed and apologised for over-stepping. But Gill had thanked him and promised to "do a little digging."

Amid this personal reverie, his phone pinged. It was Cassy asking him to call the office. It had been a couple of days since he'd been in touch, and the team wanted to connect.

'Making any progress on the next dig?' Cassy asked.

'The trust is letting it go ahead, but not until next summer.'

'What are you up to in the meantime? Not like you to be so quiet.'

'I've been spending some time with David's widow. Help her sort out a few things.'

'How's she doing?'

'Comes and goes. It's bad enough to lose a loved one, but if David had been hit by a bus, at least the family would have had a grave to gather around. David's accident feels more like a missing person's case.' Gill took a few minutes to fill her in.

'Anyway, none of that is the magazine's business. What's happening at your end?'

He heard Cassy switch her phone from one hand to another. 'All pretty routine. The guys have mailed you various layouts to take a look at. We're monitoring a couple of small stories, but nothing worth talking about – I'll message you. Oh, and Craig wants to bend your ear about something.'

'Okay. I'm going on my laptop as soon as I'm back at the B&B. No doubt I'll speak to you tomorrow morning.'

'Cool. Transferring you to Craig.'

'Boss. I've been working on those planetary positions I derived from the stones.'

'Having second thoughts about your theory?'

'No. Just refining it a little. A wee reminder to you that our guy calculated the orbits from the stones to five significant numbers.'

'Aye, and you found numbers within each planet's minimum and maximum orbit.'

'Well, that's the thing. It bothered me he'd gone to so much trouble to find the exact position of the planets. And then I realised that each planet's number would only be valid twice during any one revolution around the sun.'

'I'm with you', said Gill. 'During the planetary swing towards the narrowest part of the orbit and again on the way back to the widest.'

'And that's twice a year for planet Earth but only once every sixty years for Neptune, the outermost planetary body referenced on the clock.'

‘Okay. What’s the significance?’

Craig left a dramatic pause. ‘In effect, it’s a calendar. The planets might only fall into the alignment implied by the Orcadian clock once or twice in an aeon.’

‘And you’re going to tell me you’ve worked out a date.’ Gill felt his excitement rising.

‘Before I tell you, you need to remember you could get a date from the time of the dinosaurs to a date far, far into the future.’

‘Okay, Craig, I’m with you. And the date is?’

'Honestly, man. You're not going to believe it.'

'Craig!'

‘15th August. This year. THIS year, Gill.’

The line went silent until Craig spoke again. ‘Boss, you still there?’

‘Yeah’, said Gill. ‘Let me rewind to make sure I get you. You are saying the layout of the monuments in the Brodgar area, built thousands of years ago, point to a date less than two months ago?’

‘That’s it. Does the date mean anything to you?’

Gill let out a long sigh. ‘Not a thing.’

‘Me neither. I did an extensive web search for that date, expecting to see a UFO spike or something. I found nothing.’

‘And you’re sure you’ve done your sums right?’

‘Double, treble checked. Cassy’s about ready to fire me.’

‘Okay, I’ll ask around up here. See if it sparks anything.’

Gill thanked Craig and rang off. Almost immediately, his phone rang again. It was Alice. She must have had him on auto-redial.

He heard Alice suppress a sob, her voice shaky as she spoke. 'Gill. David's car …' she broke off.

'Oh, I'm sorry. I was at ScoCion this afternoon. If I'd thought, I could have picked it up.'

'No, you couldn't. It's parked at the airport, in a rental bay. Gill, why would David's car be at the airport?'

Gill was already leaning over the passenger seat. 'Alice, just bear with me a second.' He switched his phone to his left hand and reached for David's box of possessions in the footwell. He tipped it up and rummaged. Sitting back again, he forced calm into his voice. 'ScoCion gave me a box of David's personal stuff. Alice, there aren't any keys here.'

Chapter 24

'Thank you again for your patience. Appreciate it. Bye now.' Gill finally hung up on the banking services call centre that had taken the rest of his evening.

Red-eyed, Alice still sat beside him after answering the security questions at the start of the call. 'Nothing?' she asked.

Gill shook his head. 'No activity on any of David's bank cards since the day he disappeared.'

Alice's head dropped slowly onto the table. 'Oh, God. I can't do this.'

She started to cry again, and Gill slipped an arm around her shoulders. 'We'll find out what's going on.'

She pulled her left arm against her forehead. 'How did his car get to the airport? We don't have a body, and now this. What the hell's going on?'

Gill sighed. 'If it's okay with you, I'll talk to the police. They're the only people with the resources to discover if David is still alive and has left the island.'

Alice's face spun round to his. 'You think he's alive?'

'No, I didn't say that. It's just that we're limited in what we can discover on our own.' Gill paused. 'Look, we need to keep our minds open to the likelihood someone moved David's car maliciously.'

'But why?'

'Perhaps by suggesting he left the island, Perhaps someone benefits by creating doubt about the accident. I dunno. Maybe ScoCion would try to wriggle out of the blame for what happened.'

Alice's face sank forward again. 'That would be too cruel.'

'Look, I need to ask you another question. And it's going to seem a bit random.' Alice nodded, so he pressed on. 'Does the 15th of August mean anything to you?'

'What about it?'

'That date cropped up in a conversation this afternoon. I plan to ask everyone I know on Orkney if it means anything to them.'

Alice concentrated for a second, a thin smile appearing through her tears. 'It's our wedding anniversary. David and I.' Her smile faded. 'Not that you would have known it this year.'

'How so?'

'David worked late that night. That wasn't unusual, but I'd cooked a nice dinner, so I was pissed at him. Seems so petty now.'

'Any idea what he was working on that day?'

Alice shrugged. 'Could have been any of a million things.' She thought for a few seconds. 'It was a test, I believe. It sticks out in my mind because it was an unqualified success, apparently. I remember because not many of them are.'

'Any idea what the test was about?

'I was about ready to throw his dinner at him', said Alice sadly. 'I don't remember asking him about his day.'

'Sorry. I remember he could lose all track of time when he was busy with something.'

'Yes, he could', said Alice.

Gill heard the sound of the front door opening and closing. Shortly after, Alice's mother shouted a greeting as she passed the doorway carrying two bags of shopping. 'Reinforcements', whispered Alice, forcing a smile. 'Best make a dash for it while you can.'

The following morning, Gill drove up to the ScoCion facility. He waited for almost an hour before Harley came out to see him. He rushed through a quick handshake and refused Gill's invitation to sit for a few minutes.

'I'm sorry, Gill. We're working very hard to get back up and running here. My apologies. I don't have time for a long conversation.'

'I take it you heard about David's car?'

Harley nodded quickly. 'I heard.'

'What do you make of it? You seemed confident that David couldn't have exited the ion chamber without being detected.'

'I did, but then David was the chief engineer. Perhaps he bypassed the systems.'

'You're not suggesting that's what actually happened?'

'It's a matter for the accident investigators. And if it transpires David Trevelyan left this facility with commercially sensitive material; it will become a matter for the police. Now I really must get back to work.'

'Okay. Just one more question. What happened here on the 15th of August?'

'I beg your pardon?'

'The 15th of August, Professor. Six weeks before David's accident. Your website doesn't record any test, but Alice Trevelyan clearly remembers David getting home late. A test had gone well, and she recalls David was delighted with his day.'

Harley waved a hand dismissively. 'At some level, we run machine tests every day. All of which are important in and of themselves, even though they are just tiny parts of the bigger effort here. David took his work seriously. If he'd been battled successfully with a lightbulb in the canteen, he'd have gone home happy.'

Jenny Struan strode into the reception area but stopped abruptly when she found Gill and Harley glaring at each other.

'I'm really desperately busy, Gill. I'll leave you in Jenny's capable hands.'

Jenny looked like she'd rather do anything else than talk to Gill. They stared at each other for a long moment. 'Have I offended you?' Gill asked.

She glanced at Harley's retreat and steered Gill towards the coffee area. As soon as he was out of earshot, she dipped her head. 'Why were you talking to Professor Harley?'

Gill indicated a sofa, and they both sat. 'Alice Trevelyan has asked me to liaise with ScoCion in regard to David's death. The professor was quite helpful yesterday, but today I'm not so sure.'

Jenny stared at her feet but didn't say anything.

Gill's eyes narrowed. 'You know something, don't you?'

She looked up, and he could see the stress she was under for the first time. 'David's death affected all of us. I'm sure Professor Harley is doing his best.'

'Come on, Jenny. Talk to me.'

'I've arranged counselling for a number of the staff here. If you think you might benefit, I'm sure the company would extend an invitation.'

Gill raised a hand. 'Enough, Jenny. I'm going to go now. If you ever feel like an honest chat, you know how to reach me.'

Gill sat in the car park, wondering what had just happened. Harley had been so approachable the day before, but now his body language had closed like a clamshell. Gill sat, trying to figure out the exact moment Harley's posture changed. Was it when he mentioned the 15th of August? Or was it before? Perhaps the discovery of David's car put a different spin on things? One thing for sure - the easy flow of circumstantial data from Harley was finished. And Gill still couldn't tell Alice what had happened to her husband.

'Time to call in an expert', he muttered to himself as he dialled Arnold Broadbent's number.

'Good morning, matey boy. You looking for some solid science to pop into your little publication?'

'In a way.' Arnold had heard about David's accident, and it only took Gill a couple of minutes to fill him in on what had been happening.

Arnold cleared his throat. 'The key question I'm hearing is, did David do a runner, or did he die in the chamber?'

Gill thought for a moment, then confirmed Arnold had gripped the main issue.

It was a long moment before Arnold spoke again. 'I've been keeping an eye on the accident enquiry. It's not finished yet, but the initial finding is David's body vaporised when the energy beam discharged in the chamber.'

He waited until Gill murmured his agreement.

'But the thing is, I've seen the specs, and I know the ion cannon is full of sensors. If the atmosphere in the chamber changed, they would have spotted it.'

'Sorry', said Gill. 'I'm not following.'

He heard Arnold sigh. 'If David had been vaporised, then they would have detected it. Carbon oxides, water vapour, amino acids. Even if he'd been blasted to smithereens, their sensors would have lit up like a Christmas tree.'

'Let me check if I understand. We can't be sure where David's body is but we do know it's in one piece.'

'That about sums it up.'

Gill suddenly remembered seeing teams with dogs searching for something on the moors. 'Thank you, my friend. I owe you.'

Gill processed the reality of what Arnold was saying. Knowing that David's body could be intact seemed almost a relief. Now he just needed to work out where it was. He set off again, intending to return to his B&B to prep for a team meeting. He was almost at the bottom of the ScoCion approach road when a text came in from Juliette asking him to call. As he was just a few minutes away from Tormiston, he decided to drop in and see if she was there.

He found her pacing in her office, phone in hand, negotiating with a contractor. She scowled and waved him into a seat while she ended her call.

'I'm going to take a risk', she said.

'Hello to you too.'

'I've decided to push ahead with the dig straight away.'

'But I thought ...'

Juliette cut him off. 'It's the right moment. I've got an active volunteer base. I've sourced a crane locally; they're scarce on Orkney. And, of course, you're on hand as well.'

Gill frowned but said nothing.

'I've even got a weather window. So, I'm making an executive decision, and we're going for it. Tomorrow.' She studied his face for a few moments. 'Are you still in?'

Gill's response wasn't immediate. 'Yeah. Of course. As long as you don't get into trouble for this.'

She shrugged. 'I think it's too important to wait. If this dig is still in someone's in-tray next spring, it might never happen.'

'If you waited until the spring, it would still be in your in-tray. Wouldn't it?'

Juliette stopped pacing and leaned towards him. 'I'm impatient. Call it a character flaw. But I'm doing it, with or without you.'

Gill nodded slowly. 'I'm in. What can I do to help?'

'Bring yourself in working clothes. Be my minder and stop me if I'm about to make a bollocks of anything.'

Gill thought, then smiled and nodded once. 'Okay. Kick-off time?'

'If I can get that contractor sorted out, we'll be laying trackways by 8 am.'

Gill stood. 'Okay. I'll see you then.' He raised a hand in farewell and turned to leave.

'Gill …' called Juliette as he reached the door.

He turned and waited a few seconds for her to speak.

'Actually, never mind. I'll see you tomorrow.'

The team meeting later that day was a helter-skelter dash through page amends, positioning requests for adverts and evaluations of editorial material for future issues. Mhairi sat quietly throughout all of this until Cassy, Larry and Craig exited the call.

'Gill. Based on the credentials you gave me, I believe I've found Wilson's second book.'

'Girl, you work fast. The rest of the team will thank you for showing them up.'

'Ach. Easy really. A call to the British Library and a chat with someone who's good at their job. The best news is, the book is part of their digitised collection, so I've been able to email you a copy.'

'That's great. And is the book title a full paragraph like volume one?'

'No. Quite pithy. It's called, *Temple of the Stars.*'

'Great. I'll try to get into it later. Are you able to talk me through his material?'

'Yeah. Cassy said you would ask. How much detail do you want?'

Gill thought for a second. 'Wilson's first book recorded the physical Orcadian monuments but didn't speculate on their purpose. I'm hoping he covers that in his later volume.'

'He does', said Mhairi. 'In the introduction, he records a Persian myth about a temple in a far north where the sun never sets.'

'Interesting. Is it about sun worship?'

'No. Wilson believes the temple is a map of the stars.'

Gill gripped the phone a little tighter. 'Have you spoken to Craig about any of this?'

'No.'

'Well, please don't. You're both studying different source documents that might point to the same thing. Tell me more about the book.'

'Wilson admits the "stars" are probably best interpreted as the solar system. He gets incredibly excited because the Persian source includes the eighth planet, even though Neptune was only discovered by modern astronomers a year before he wrote his book. It was this confirmation that compelled him to publish his second volume.'

'The Persians knew of eight planets before they were confirmed in the modern age?'

'If his source document is credible, then yes. And more than that, they seem to have had a pretty fair insight into their orbits.'

'Listen, Mhairi, this is important. I'll struggle to read this over the next few days. I need you to interrogate our friend Wilson. If he lists them, dig into his source materials. We need to know if any of these ideas stand up.'

Chapter 25

On the first morning of the dig, Gill found Juliette at the edge of Brodgar, hands deep in pockets. She was watching workmen lay sections of plastic trackway towards the stones. It had been light for almost two hours, but the dense grey sky made it seem earlier.

'Wasn't in the forecast', he said, nodding at the sky.

Juliette shook her head. 'Not a problem. Windy and overcast, but no rain.'

'You're still sure you want to do this?' Gill asked.

Juliette turned to look at him for a long moment before diverting her attention back to yet another lorry reversing down the track towards the stones. 'Gill, can you tell me an honest answer to a blunt question?'

'Sure', he said to her back.

'Are you aware I'm being treated for lung cancer?'

Gill instinctively turned away from her. Words didn't come, and he found himself clasping his arms across his chest.

'I didn't think so', she said, turning to face him. 'Sorry. You never know who might be blabbing.'

She peered at him for a few seconds, then advanced into his personal space. 'Had some surgery a few years back. Hoped we'd got it. But three months ago, they picked up another mass during a routine scan.'

'I'm very sorry to hear that.'

Juliette nodded. 'I believe you. My apologies, but I needed to know.' She wagged a forefinger at him. 'You're the kind of person who gets things done. I like to get things done too, but in my present state, I'm wary I could be manipulated.'

Gill looked at his feet and slipped his fingertips into his trouser pockets. 'I lost my mother to cancer a few years back. I know it's a tough walk.'

'Aye', she said. 'It is.'

She took a couple of steps towards the stones. 'Next May, when I've got official permission to start this dig', Juliette continued, 'I likely won't be here. I'll be back in Inverness getting treatment. Or worse.'

Gill nodded at the cluster of volunteers mustering in the stone circle. 'I hope I didn't push you.'

She tilted her head back and closed her eyes. 'I've been doing this job for twenty-five years. Never had an opportunity like this before.'

Gill understood her, although he now felt conflicted. 'How long before your manager catches up with you?'

'Two days', she replied. 'Three, if I mislay the paperwork. I've not asked the local folk to lie for me, but most will look the other way until Edinburgh brings down a shit storm.'

'Uh, oh', said Gill, spying that the lorry's offside tyres had left the trackway and were sinking deep into the heather.

'Tossers', muttered Juliette.

He watched her stride off, stopping the vehicle a few moments later and bidding the crew to move their cargo by hand. In the distance, another lorry was creeping along the narrow road down from Stromness, its blaze of flashing orange lights aggravating his guilt. He strode over to where she was threatening to help the workers carry the equipment.

'Juliette, I'll do this. You're the site coordinator. This is your dig. I've left string and pegs by flagstone seven. Go and mark up where we need to cut the turf.'

Juliette stood with a sheet pulled half off the lorry and would have continued had Gill not muscled in and taken her place. Rather than fight him, she shrugged and went to find the tools.

By 10 am, they were ready to go. Volunteers, mainly from the initial dig two weeks before, stood leaning on spades, their numbers swelled by other locals who'd heard rumours about what was going on.

'Okay, folks', Gill began. 'This dig is under the auspices of Juliette Morrison. I'm here as dig sponsor and to give technical support where requested. By all means, talk to me, but the tough decisions belong to Juliette. Any questions?'

Juliette stepped forward. 'Just to emphasise our need for speed. We've had to close the monument to visitors, but it's a big site, and although we've taped off the high-risk areas, we need to stay aware of folk wandering where they shouldn't. Follow Gill's lead while you're digging, and I'll keep to a supervisory role and cover anything else that doesn't involve using a shovel.'

Gill clapped his hands. 'Okay, people. Juliette has already probed the surface layer in a few places. We'll lift the turf in neat strips within the marked boundary and lay it on the tarp. We need to number each piece so we can put them back in the same order. Buddy up, and let's go.'

The dig progressed through the morning. For speed, Gill decided the covering soil should just be laid aside for relaying later rather than being combed inch by inch for any interesting fragments. By lunchtime, a large area of bedrock was available for inspection. The pace slowed when the team switched to smaller tools to clear the stone's surface.

'That's not a weathered edge', Juliette observed, kneeling by a point where the capstone butted up to the rest of the bedrock.'

'I'm seeing the same over here', said Gill. 'It looks like they quarried out the bedrock, allowing the prefabricated stone slab to slot into place at the end of the process.'

Juliette dropped her hands to her thighs. 'But how would they lift it? Based on the thickness we estimated from the scan, it must be three or four tonnes.'

'I've got a spot here where they drilled through the stone. Let me see if I can find other holes, and then I'll give you my theory.'

By the end of the afternoon, an area of ten square metres had been cleared, revealing the irregular shape of the capstone, plus the apron of rock in which it nestled. The volunteers dispersed for the day, and Juliette stood with her hands on her hips, bristling with uncertainty.

'This is ridiculous. The Neoliths didn't use manual drills. And I doubt they could build a tripod pulley of the scale required to lift a stone this size.'

Gill raised his hands slightly and gently patted the air in front of him. 'Let's look at the evidence. These three holes are consistent with what fire-hardened rods can do in the right hands. We find it unbelievable because each hole would have taken a grown man two weeks and half a hazel grove to accomplish. But you admit it's technically possible?'

Juliette nodded once.

'And the position of the holes? Perfect weight distribution, I'd say, with the stone hanging from three individual ropes meeting at the apex of the pulley.'

'Yes, in theory, Gill. But in practice? Are we assuming Neolithic ropes capable of carrying over a tonne each? And your pulley! They'd need at least ten metres in height. Almost a work of art in itself!'

'Okay, let's look at this trail of nuts. We started because you found something out of context. Something ahead of its time. In the light of the Chi Rho symbol, do you think we should be surprised to see technologies ahead of where are expecting them to be?'

Gill stopped, and Juliette said nothing.

He sighed and pointed at the exposed rock. 'Can you think of any other method they might have used to chisel out a big chunk of bedrock, then fill the hole with almost laser precision using an imported stone?'

'I'm worried, that's all. Maybe we've seen some lines in our scans that just happen to fit with the exciting things we'd like to see, while in reality, they're just an accident of nature.'

Gill stooped to pick up his daysack. 'Well, in the morning, we can either use these three holes to lift the stone. Or we can lay the turf back quickly to restore the site. It'll be your call.'

Juliette looked at the naked bedrock and nodded.

'I've come across something else', said Gill.

'Don't try and tell me an alien civilisation lies buried under Skara Brae. I just couldn't take it.'

He shook his head. 'It's our old friend, F.R.Wilson. My office got hold of his second book.'

'By your face, I'm guessing it made an interesting read.'

'Aye. Wilson worked most of his life in Scotland, but after retiring from the navy, he took a job at the British Museum, interpreting Persian artefacts. He got quite a feel for their culture.'

Juliette tapped her leg impatiently.

'Long story short, Wilson explains the Persian's knowledge of the solar system was far ahead of their contemporary tools or methods. They inherited this information from an even earlier civilisation called Sumeria.'

'Heard of them, Gill. They lived a long way from here.'

'Yes, but their civilisation was contemporaneous to the Orcadian Neoliths.'

Juliette shrugged.

'Wilson says the Sumerians held in high regard a religious site in the northern kingdom called, *The Temple of the Stars*. He believes it's the source of their astronomical knowledge.'

'And your point is?'

‘It just made me think about our *Orcadian clock* theory. He uses different words, but Wilson arrives at basically the same conclusion.’

She raised a hand to her forehead and suddenly looked very tired indeed. ‘Sorry. You’re saying Persia led the world in astronomy, based on a rumour from far-away ancient Orkney?’

Gill stretched out an arm to her. ‘I think we need to consider the possibility. It might help interpret anything we find in our dig.’

Juliette gathered her jacket in her arms. ‘That’s if we dig any further tomorrow. I need to think it through. Look, I’ll see you in the morning’, she said, before trudging away.

Gill resolved he would not stress over Juliette’s decision. On balance, he believed she would come around. But if she didn’t, it wasn’t his place to press her. He glanced at the sky. He still had an hour of decent daylight, and there was something else he wanted to check out.

Chapter 26

It took half an hour to walk up Rusky Hill from the northwest and locate the emergency exit from the ion chamber. It sat at the end of a rough track, and as Harley had described, a series of concrete steps emerged out of the ground, surrounded by a low stone wall. At least, that was the little he could see. It was impossible to get close as the exit lay in the middle of an area the size of a tennis court surrounded by a high-quality fence topped with razor wire. And a heavy padlock sealed the only access gate. He made a circuit of the wire, looking for any clue David had used this as an exit route. He studied the undergrowth to see if anyone had waded through it in recent days. He examined the gate, looking for fresh scratches in the metal. But he saw no evidence to suggest anyone had passed this way in a long time. Frustrated, he decided to carry on across the moor until he reached the top of the hill.

Gill stood and looked around him. Standing in the same spot, twisting slowly through 360 degrees, he scanned the near and far distance for any other exits from the ScoCion complex. He tried to imagine the mile-long tunnel cut into the rock below him, with its myriad laboratories and facilities. He judged that the reception and office area lay some four hundred metres towards the lochs and maybe one hundred metres below him. Allowing his eyes to drift to the left, he followed the coastline until he saw Stromness. It was just a small town, dominated by an enormous concrete pier. He recalled when they excavated Rusky Hill to create ScoCion, they used the spoil to fill the foundations of the new dockside. He continued his anticlockwise scan, pausing to watch a small aircraft descending towards Kirkwall. As he watched, his eyes were distracted by the glint of sunlight bouncing off a reflective surface about a mile distant. He considered waving but paused, having the sudden sense he was being observed.

He caught the sound of a far-off vehicle, a large engine, its pitch elevated as it laboured uphill. He stared down at the Finstown Road. A small amount of traffic was winding its way in both directions, almost too distant to hear. He was still looking for the approaching vehicle when he caught the throaty roar of a heavy motorcycle on the road below. He could see it in the distance. It was a long way from his position and moving away from him. But its shape, its sound, the distinctive bulk of its rider sent a shiver down Gill's spine. Sensing danger, he began to jog down the track towards the main road.

He made good going for a few minutes, but the approaching vehicle's sound was close now, and he shuddered to a halt. A big black Mitsubishi off-roader powered up the track from the main road. Something about its pace, and the way the car pitched up and down as it accelerated up the soft track, made him feel uneasy. He waited until he could see the faces of the occupants, the gritted expression of the driver, the way the front-seat passenger bent forward with his hands on the dash. By then, he'd left it too late to look for cover. To have run away would have suggested guilt for some uncertain crime, so he stood his ground and resolved to avoid a confrontation.

'Afternoon', he called as the three occupants spilt out of the car.

'Hi', replied the driver. 'Can I ask what you're doing?'

Gill glanced around him. 'Just out for a stroll. What's the problem?'

'You were picked up on camera, sir. Testing the security fence around part of the ScoCion facility.'

'I did pass a fenced-off area. I don't know about "testing" it. I don't recall even touching it.'

'We'll leave that decision to the local police. I'm going to ask you to come with us, sir.'

'Hang on a second. I didn't trample down any private property to get here. I'm just walking.'

The driver strode up to within a pace of Gill and looked at him closely. 'If you were walking, why did you try to breach our security?'

Gill pointed at him. 'We've met before. You signed me in a few weeks ago while I was here for a test.'

'What's your name?'

'Gill McArdle. Call Jenny Struan. She'll vouch for me.'

'Stay here.' The man strode away and spent two minutes on the phone. When he returned, his demeanour had softened. 'I'm sorry, Mr McArdle. We've been running a tighter ship since the accidents. I'd still like you to come off the hill.'

'Why are you guys so jumpy?'

'Just doing my job, sir. How about we give you a lift back to your car?'

As he pulled up outside his B&B, Gill could see Jim Robertson standing at the open door, in conversation with the manageress. He groaned when she pointed at his approaching car. Having shaken off ScoCion security, he was now in the cross-hairs of the self-appointed Brodgar ethics committee. He waited by his car as Jim came striding towards him.

'Mr McArdle. We need to talk.'

Gill sighed as he locked his car. 'It's Friday night, Jim. If it's okay with you, I'd like a pint in my hand.'

Gill swept his arms around the darkly lit bar. 'Is this going to be alright?'

Jim raised a hand. 'This is fine. Orkney's a grand place to live, but we're not over-endowed with places to meet.'

'Can I get you something?'

Jim thought for a second. 'I'm driving, of course, but maybe I could have a malt first, then follow it with a coffee.'

Gill slipped to the bar and returned with a pint of *Dark Island* and a tumbler dampened with a thin measure of *Highland Park*. He placed the malt in front of Jim and led from the front.

'You've heard about the dig?' he asked.

Jim grasped his glass and stared at the amber liquid. 'Yes. I walked past it earlier. And I've got several concerns.'

'Lay them out for me. I mean, it's Juliette's dig, but let me see if I can help.'

Jim glanced up once and then away. 'For a start, where's the paperwork? Normally we get months of notice before even a spade goes in the ground. I've not heard a peep about this.'

Gill nodded. 'Sorry about that. I sat in on a call between Juliette and Charles Downshire earlier in the week. We discussed the possibility it might go ahead this year. I know Juliette was pushing for it.'

'Aye, well, that's the next thing. You know she's not well?'

Gill nodded. 'She's mentioned that. You can imagine why she feels a sense of urgency.'

Jim was stony-faced. 'I'm sorry for her. I really am. But we can't let it undermine her judgement.'

'She's involved me as site overseer. To make sure she doesn't make any mistakes.'

'And that assumes you're a passive observer, Mr McArdle.'

'What do you mean?'

Jim shrugged. 'Your job is to sell magazines. I understand that, and I don't have a problem with it. It's just that those of us with generational roots on the island want to protect our heritage.'

'I understand, but it doesn't change the fact that this landscape is always evolving. Stones erode or get ploughed under. Some fall down, and well-intentioned people pop them back up again. Archaeology studies these places before nature obliterates them forever. If you don't believe me, just look at Skara Brae.'

'Erosion is one thing. But tampering with Brodgar feels more like invasive surgery.'

'We're not moving any of the standing stones. The plan is to excavate at the centre.'

Jim shook his head slowly. 'That area is far too sensitive.'

'But aren't you curious? Suppose something important is buried at the centre of the circle. Wouldn't you like to see what it is?'

'I'm not like you. Forgive my directness, but my curiosity isn't a lust that bays for satisfaction.'

Gill decided to go on the offensive. 'You mentioned your generational roots. Reminds me of a local group I heard about. Something called "The Vigil". Can you tell me about it?'

Jim leaned back in his chair. 'What's that got to do with the Brodgar dig?'

'It's faith-based, isn't it?'

'Yes', Jim said slowly.

'Can you tell me something about it?'

'With respect, if you've come to tamper with our stones and mock our beliefs, this will be a very short conversation.'

Gill lifted his hands. 'I respect your passion, Jim. And I saw your discomfort when we lifted the first Chi Rho stone. I'm only trying to understand your point of view.'

Jim fell silent for a long moment before he spoke again. 'A few local people feel called to a special purpose. Part of that purpose is to protect the stones. In situ. Avoid any disturbance.'

'Even if that disturbance records and evaluates an artefact that will eventually be lost to nature?'

'As I said, I don't carry a burden to solve every mystery.'

'What's the significance of the 15th August 2023?' asked Gill, changing tack.

He watched as the colour drained from Jim's face. 'How do you know about that date?'

Gill kept his face expressionless. 'You could say it's written in the stones.'

Jim stared at him but said nothing.

'Unfortunately, either our maths are wrong, or the date has passed without incident. What do you think?'

'Stop a second, McArdle? How could you possibly know that date?'

Gill leaned into his bag and laid Euan's book of numbers on the table.

'What's that?' asked Jim.

'Someone has gone to a great deal of trouble to deduce the meaning of the stones, mathematically.'

'Which stones?'

'Brodgar, Stenness, Ring of Bookan, The Comet Stone, all of them.' He opened the book at random and turned the page to face Jim. 'Not a great note-taker, unfortunately, but the author does seem to conclude the monuments are linked.'

Jim suddenly looked flustered. 'These monuments weren't built quickly. If a grand plan existed, it required incredible continuity of purpose.'

'Well, that's one of the things I wanted to ask you. Let's say Neoliths built the monuments to a single blueprint. A project like that would require …'

'Incredible resources', Jim interrupted. 'Brodgar alone is estimated to have taken 80,000 man-hours to construct.'

'An entire clan and culture dedicated to its completion. For generations.'

Jim nodded, ashen-faced. 'And clearly, we have the monuments as proof that such a culture once existed.'

'Treat me as a potential convert', said Gill. 'What's the big deal about 15th August? Why should we leave the stones undisturbed?'

Jim sipped his drink. 'I'll answer your questions with questions of my own. Think about the complexity of the arrangement; an edifice begun more than four thousand years ago, taking a thousand years to build. Who could have conceived of it except God himself? And why direct all that effort towards a single date unless that date was of huge importance?'

'So the date is what? The second coming?'

Gill watched Jim grip his lips, then take a quick sip of his whisky. 'An old tradition around here talks of a powerful king who said he would be born again. I believe this king's rebirth could signal our Lord's return.'

'My apologies, but the date has come and gone without incident.'

'Once upon a time, there was a babe in a manger', Jim growled. 'It was thirty years before the world noticed his rise to glory.'

Gill shook his head. 'I googled this. Isn't the second coming meant to happen as a sudden, wham, bam kind of thing?'

Jim looked away. 'That's a neat, secularist way to put it.'

'My apologies. I didn't mean to offend.'

'It doesn't change the fact that men like you have no fear of God. You have no cause to protect and no calling to pursue.'

'While part of your calling is to protect the stones', Gill stated. 'Because the builders coded messages into the relative position of the stones.'

Jim finished his whisky and scowled at the approaching waitress, anticipating correctly she would rattle his coffee cup down in front of him as if it were a crate of vodka. He used a napkin to soak up the drops of spilt coffee. 'Perhaps the meaning of the date is obscured for now. That's the thing about faith. It requires patience.'

Gill smiled. 'I think I'm starting to discover that.'

Jim nodded at the book on the table. 'This book with all the numbers, where did you come by it?'

'It was left for me at Tormiston just before the start of my last trip.'

'I see.'

'I made enquiries last time I was on the island. I gather the author is missing.'

'Maybe he left the island.'

'Which would be a pity as I'd love to speak to him', said Gill swilling a little life into his pint. 'His name's Euan

Mearns. Another regular up at Brodgar. You must have met him.'

Jim nodded. 'Aye, I know Twitch.'

'Twitch?' echoed Gill.

Jim raised a hand and gave it a little shake. 'No offence. Euan could behave quite oddly. Someone gave him that nickname, and unfortunately, it stuck.' He reached across the table and turned the book to face him. Casually he thumbed through a few pages. 'A very private person. Sometimes seen taking measurements around the stones.'

'Have members of "The Vigil" taken offence at him?'

Jim shook his head. 'He was harmless. Juliette Morrison told him in no uncertain terms how he should behave around the monuments and the tourists. To my knowledge, he never deviated from that. I worked with the lad for awhile. Tried to steer his curiosity towards knowledge and conservation of the monuments.' He turned another few pages before laying the book down. 'It looks very methodical. Astonishing, he achieved all this on his own.'

'Indeed. And remarkable field skills for someone without training.'

'Well, that'll be another mystery for you to solve', said Jim. He pointed at the book. 'Look, I'm concerned about Euan's welfare. Can I borrow this? See if I can find any hints about where he went.'

Gill paused, conflicted. 'I need to hold on to it for now. I'm harbouring a desire to return it to its rightful owner.'

'You'll hardly get a chance when you're back in Dundee', said Jim with a hint of resentment.

Gill pulled the book back towards him. 'I've got an instinct that I will.'

Jim nodded, then sucked in a mouthful of coffee. He stood up and pushed his chair. 'Well, thank you for the drinks. I'll see you at the dig tomorrow. I'm sure you'll do the right thing.'

Chapter 27

Gill stayed on for a second pint while he reviewed the conversation with Jim in his mind. While he understood Jim's reasoning for not damaging the monuments, he was convinced the excavation of a second Chi Rho stone was a solid piece of research. The artefact was buried below ground, if it existed at all, so it wasn't be part of the Orcadian clock. He'd done his best to listen to Jim, but the man's response rose from dogma rather than reason. On that basis, Gill decided that if Juliette continued with the dig, he was in.

As he walked back to the B&B, he analysed what he found difficult about Jim. The man demonstrated the moral certainty of the devout, which never sat well with Gill. But he had to admit that he'd never done much reading when it came to matters of faith. On that basis, he was as guilty as Jim, substituting religious dogma with his agnostic default. He had shoved faith, morality, and religion into a mental kitchen drawer to sort out somewhere down the road.

Arriving in his lodgings, he resolved to change that. Sitting on his bed in a pool of weak orange light, he googled the phrase he'd seen on David's ring; "The Heavens Declare." He found it was a reference to Psalm 19, so he dug into the bedside drawer and pulled out the hotel Bible. 'The heavens declare the glory of God', he read. 'The skies proclaim the work of His hands.' He intended to ask Alice why David had chosen those words. For now, he did a little web research, following a trail of suggested references until he lost himself in a tangled chamber of science, mysticism and faith. Eventually, he achieved a sense of what the

Psalm's author had been trying to express. In his pursuit of science and unravelling nature's secrets, David Trevelyan acknowledged a higher power; far above himself.

Gill laid aside his phone and went back to the Bible, looking up the references Mack had given him after their conversation at *The Fish Shed.* They outlined moments when supernatural messengers intervened in human affairs. A man called *Abram* is told he will father a nation. Joseph, the father of Jesus, is warned of danger in a dream. The Apostle Paul is shaken back to courage by an apparition who promises survival in an imminent shipwreck. He closed the book and doubted he was in the same league.

Noticing the time, he laid it aside and dialled Salina at home. The phone rang five times, and Gill considered what he would say if he had to leave a message. When Salina answered, she sounded sleepy.

'Hey, mystery man.'

'Hi Sal, just checking in. Hope I'm not disturbing you.'

'No, you're fine. I was hoping you'd call. Now I can turn off the light and get some proper sleep.'

'Funny to think of you being nearby in the North Sea these last few days. How was the Brent Field?'

'Interesting. Tangible signs that the concrete legs of the old rigs are becoming natural reefs, at least the ones they toppled. Foul weather, though. Barely slept a wink.'

'Did the boat behave herself?'

He could hear the smile in her voice. 'Yes, my non-cognisant deep-sea vehicle performed within acceptable parameters. Oh, and Ellie says, "Hi".'

It was Gill's turn to laugh. 'Miss You.'

'I should hope so.'

'Look, I'll be staying here a couple more days.'

'That's okay.'

'I've been helping Alice with a few things, and I think it's making a difference.'

'I'm sure. You're a decent human being, McArdle.'

'And my second dig got approved.'

'You're kidding. In October?'

'Technically, the permit starts next May, but we're going to risk it and do it now.'

'Can you do that?'

'My local contact has taken the call. She'll feel the pain if we mess things up, or worse, if we don't find anything.'

'And what are you expecting to find?'

Gill paused. 'Not sure. My instinct says it'll be something significant.'

The conversation slipped into a natural lull until Salina said, 'What's up?'

'Why should anything be up?'

'You're my man. I'm your woman. It's really that easy', she replied drowsily.

He took a deep breath. 'I saw Raphael again today.'

He heard a flurry of bedcovers and a creak of plastic on plastic as she grasped the phone more tightly. 'Okay, fully awake now. What's going on?'

Gill sighed. 'He was a long way away, but I knew it was him.'

'Tell me. Tell me right from the beginning.'

Gill gathered his thoughts and explained why he had been on the hillside and how the ScoCion security people had challenged him.

'Pity you didn't get to talk to Raphael', said Salina. 'You could have asked him if he really is an angel.'

'Yeah. Just a chat, guy to guy. "Say, what's life like as a supernatural being?"'

Salina blew out a breath but didn't speak.

'Blunt question', said Gill. 'How do you know God exists?'

He listened to her inhale. 'You asking me personally?'

'Yes, personally. I don't know of any scientifically accepted test.'

'You know why I believe.'

Gill sighed and parroted her mantra. 'Science tells us how stuff works but explains none of the why.'

'Yep. From Big Bang to evolution, through to what I chose for my lunch today. God sees it all, and intervenes where he chooses to.'

'I get that', said Gill. 'But God, the God of the Bible, is it really that simple?'

'Most folk don't believe it', said Salina. 'So it's not simple.'

Gill grunted. 'Most folk aren't interested. I know how they feel. Too much kirk for too many years.'

‘And now we’re both being stalked by a supernatural being who appears at critical moments in our lives. What’s boring about that?’

‘It’s not funny, Sal. The guy carries two swords. What’s that all about? The biggest miracle here is that nobody arrests him!’

Salina shushed Gill gently. ‘I think he operates in a slightly different context to us. Being arrested probably isn’t a risk for him. My concern is whatever you’re involved in seems to merit his attention. Remember, he generally only appears when he needs to stop you from dying or something.’

Gill sighed. ‘I know. I’ve been on edge all evening.’

‘Listen, Gill’, said Salina. ‘Stay sharp. If Raphael is around, you need to keep your wits about you.’

Chapter 28

After his call with Salina, he hadn't slept well. She'd made a good point about Raphael; his appearance had elevated Gill's sense of imminent danger. So, after tossing and turning for an hour on that Saturday morning, he surrendered to an early start. Grabbing the sandwiches his host had left for him in the kitchen, he slipped out of the B&B soon after 7 am. He'd decided to forgo his morning run, knowing the day ahead would hold enough physical challenge. Instead, he wanted to arrive at the dig site early, walking out from the excavation in different directions to check he hadn't missed any context.

Pockets of mist hung in the cool morning air. Like the teeth of some great beast, the tips of the Brodgar stones rose above the swirling grey air. Gill had taken several strides into the stone circle before he made out the figure of a man standing in the centre of the exposed rock. Not wanting to startle him, he called out 'Hello', and as the man turned to face him, Gill realised it was Jim Robertson.

'Morning, Jim. You're up and about early.'

'Morning. Thank you for the drink last night.'

'No problem. Thank you for being so candid with me.'

Jim nodded. 'I hope I persuaded you to reconsider.'

'I did think about what you said. However, as we're not touching the standing stones, the wider good will be served by continuing with the dig.'

Jim pointed at his feet. 'What? Here?'

'Juliette has permission for a limited excavation. We're exploring something we picked up in the last scan.'

Jim thrust a hand out in front of him. 'But that's bedrock. What are you proposing to use? Dynamite?'

Gill moved closer and squatted on the bare rock, gesticulating for Jim to follow him. 'Look here. We found it full of dirt, but this is a drilled hole. It's a foot deep and opens into a cavity below. We've found two more just like it and a fissure around the edge. We believe this stone covers another which will carry a Chi Rho carving.'

Jim moved closer and studied the features Gill was indicating. 'But this is a protected area. It's never been excavated. And I understood it never would.'

Gill shrugged. 'Juliette made a case. The trust listened.'

Jim turned around and looked about at the plastic trackways. 'You're planning for heavy equipment?'

'Aye. We have a long lifter coming down from Kirkwall in about two hours.'

Jim was shaking his head. 'In the middle of the most precious stone circle. This isn't right.'

'We're taking precautions. No matter what we find, we won't take any risks with the standing stones.'

Jim glared at him. 'Our forebears, my ancestors, considered this a sacred place. You and the others. You're not welcome here.'

'Look Jim …'

'You say you have permission. I've not seen any papers up at Skara.' Something in Gill's hesitation made Jim's eyes light up. 'Why are you in such a tearing hurry to excavate this site?'

'Juliette will be here in a bit. I know you have concerns, and I'm sure she'll be happy to hear them.'

'Aye', Jim spat over his shoulder as he walked away. 'She'll hear alright.'

Two hours later, the site was bustling as volunteers arrived, and a colossal crane began a slow reverse down the temporary trackway. It was a multi-wheeled, all-terrain vehicle, seconded from the Stromness port, where it had been laying rock armour around the new pier. Above this metal beast, a high blue sky had chased away the mist, bathing the island in a crystalline light. When Juliette arrived, she seemed touched by its beauty.

'You look better', said Gill, leaning over her to give her a light hug.

Her face cracked into a wicked smile. 'Don't think you can smooze me into a green light. And there's no need. I've made up my mind to go ahead.'

Gill nodded, biting back a smile. 'Before we leap in, we might have another problem.'

'Technical or personal?' she asked, drawing her coat tighter against the cool morning air.

'I was down here not long after first light. Jim was standing where you are now with a face like thunder.'

Juliette raised a hand. 'Yes, he harangued me all the way from my car to the Comet stone. Then the crane arrived, which became a bigger threat to his precious stones than me.'

'Is he going to cause us a problem?'

'Maybe.' She paused. 'I've told him he's welcome inside the tape as an observer. Maybe the intrigue of it all will lure him in.'

Juliette and Gill watched from a distance as two volunteers used soft brushes to clean the edges of the rock apron. Then Gill stepped in to study the drilled holes. Utilising a camera tipped onto the end of a metal proboscis, he spent half an hour surveying the three holes and the stone's underside. As he withdrew to talk to Juliette, the crane team started to uncoil strands of metal rope.

'The rock seems sound, but we're not going to know for sure until we lift it', he reported.

Juliette looked concerned. 'How can we be certain we've got a good grip on it?'

'The rock around each of the holes shows no cracking or flaking, but I can't see a lot of room below. I would say the capstone is lying pretty snug on top of whatever's underneath.'

Juliette let out a slow breath. 'Incredible craftsmanship.'

'I imagine the ropes would have had knots to stop them slipping through the holes. Once the capstone was in place, they'd just cut the ropes and leave the knots in the holes.'

They called the crane driver over and talked the problem over with him. After some back and forth, they agreed they would use metal splints driven into the holes, then sprung into the horizontal to allow the cables to grip the stone. The risk of dropping the capstone on whatever lay beneath was substantial, so they agreed they would only raise the capstone high enough to slide it to one side onto a raft of fence posts. With everyone aligned on the plan, they made final preparations to begin.

'It's obvious you're just going to sheer the rock', Jim barked at Gill. It was almost lunchtime, and the crane was ready to lift the capstone.

'We're going to inch along', Gill replied. 'Any sign of crumbling, we'll put the whole thing in reverse.'

'This is ridiculous, McArdle. I demand you stop this until we recruit more appropriate expertise.'

'Jim, I've got this', Juliette shouted over the noise of the crane engine.

'I'm not happy', Jim called back. 'I'm going to speak to Edinburgh. See who signed off on this.'

Warning shouts went out as the crane took up the slack, and the three metal cables rose to form a high pyramid above the capstone. When everything was ready, the driver looked at Gill, and Gill looked at Juliette. She nodded and said, 'All ahead. Dead slow.'

The crane engine roared, and gradually the stone started to rise out of the ground. Pulling on protective eyewear, Gill lay with his head close to the ground. As soon as he saw daylight underneath, he signalled that the first of the rollers should go in. The stone kept rising until a raft of posts cradled it from below. Gill signalled with his hand, and the driver stopped the ascent and initiated the lateral transfer. Gradually the stone swung westwards, the posts being lifted and laid to provide a continuous cushion beneath it. Then slowly, the stone eased down, with some of the fence posts splintering as they took the uneven weight distribution. The cables dipped as the tension released, and after what seemed like an age, the crane engine fell silent.

Gill and Juliette stood at the lip of the mud-filled impression where the stone had rested for four thousand years. Carefully Gill crouched and probed the surface with a small trowel,. 'It's all rock, just as the scan showed.' He gently ran his tool over a section on the south wall of the pit. He revealed a straight edge in just a few strokes, followed by a corner section.

'This angle is consistent with a hexagon', he said.

'What about the other thing?' Juliette asked quietly.

Gill stepped into the centre of the pit and started to brush the surface with his hand, quickly at first, then more slowly as he found what he was looking for.

'Mrs Morrison', Gill whispered back. 'I do believe we've made a discovery.'

As the light began to pale into the late afternoon, Juliette watched as Gill and two volunteers removed the remaining loose dirt from the excavated area. A carefully cut hexagonal shape of grey sandstone emerged with a Chi Rho symbol etched at its centre. Surrounding it was a manufactured channel barely thick enough for Gill to insert his hand. The hexagonal cavity had been chiselled from the indigenous bedrock and the Chi Rho stone laid into the resulting recess.

‘What do you think it is?’ Juliette asked.

‘Best bet is still a grave’, said Gill, striding around the pit, measuring the gap between the bedrock chamber and the hexagonal cover. ‘It’s big enough.’

‘But the Neoliths didn’t do that kind of thing. They used ossuaries like Maeshowe.’

Gill shrugged. ‘We’ll know soon enough when we lift the stone.’

‘I beg your pardon?’ Jim was sitting beside them on the capstone and hadn’t spoken for hours.

‘It’s the obvious next step’, said Gill.

‘But you said it could be someone’s grave.’ Jim stood up, his face flushing red. ‘They deserve to be left in peace.’

‘Jim. We’re archaeologists’, Juliette said quietly. ‘It’s what we do. Besides, it might be covering access to a chamber.’

Gill shook his head. ‘I doubt it. The scans would have detected any large cavity. Besides, given the pre-iron age tools they were working with, I think they’ve outdone themselves already.’

Jim looked ready for another outburst, but his phone rang, and after a brief hesitation, he stepped away to answer it.

‘I’ve spoken to the crane company’, said Juliette. ‘They can leave their gear overnight but need to have it back in Kirkwall end of tomorrow. Snagging works on the new jetty.’

Gill glanced at the dig and nodded. ‘Okay. Let’s see if we can fit a rope cradle around the hexagon. Then we can go for the lift first thing tomorrow morning.’

‘I don’t think so’, said Jim, stepping in between them. ‘I’m just off the phone with Charles Downshire. He’d like Mrs Morrison to call him immediately.’

‘Shit’, muttered Juliette, walking away to a place where she could talk in private.

Jim glared at Gill. ‘I’ve lived amongst these stones all my life. And generations before me did the same. Then folk like you come in here to destroy something that has existed for millennia. Frankly, you disgust me.’

‘We’re not destroying anything, Jim.’

‘All archaeology destroys something. You dig, you sort, you disassemble and finally, you remove.’

‘It’s just science. I don’t need to defend humanity’s need to explore and explain.’

Jim drew his jacket around him. ‘Maybe it’s not humanity you should be worried about.’

The two men held an uneasy silence for fifteen minutes until Juliette returned. When she did, she was scowling.

‘Trouble?’ asked Gill.

She looked down at the stone. ‘With the Trust’s thanks for my many years’ service and its collective regret at my deteriorating health, he proceeded to fire me.’ She fixed Jim with a hard stare. ‘Thanks a bunch, Mr Robertson.’

Jim pulled his cap onto his head. ‘We need to respect due process. I’m sorry it came to this, but these monuments are too precious. If you’ll excuse me.’

Gill watched Jim stride towards the car park, then stepped towards Juliette. ‘I’m so sorry. We should have been more patient.’

‘I told you. I don’t feel like being patient anymore. I don’t have the sodding time.’

‘What are you going to do?’

‘I explained the situation to Downshire and the stone we’ve uncovered. Then I asked for a couple more days to put the monument back on a visitor footing again.’

‘Sure. We can backfill tomorrow. We’ll need the crane to put the capstone back.’

Juliette’s eyes glinted. ‘Aye, but first, we’re going to recover the hexagonal stone. Put it with its twin at Tormiston Mill.’

Gill’s mouth fell open in silent protest.

‘Charles and I go way back’, she smiled through free-flowing tears. ‘He had to sack me, but I’ve got three days to clear my desk, so to speak.’

Gill blinked at her.

Her face cracked into a smile. ‘He’s letting me lift the stone. I’ve to recover it to Tormiston, including anything I find underneath.’

He did embrace her now. Faster and firmer than he meant to, then recoiling as if he’d hurt her. She gave him a pained smile. ‘Now, away home. We’ll see what tomorrow brings.’

Chapter 29

'Charles Downshire, please', Jim shouted into his phone. A technician was repositioning the crane to lift the Chi Rho stone. 'I know it's a Sunday, but do you know where I can reach him?' Another pause. 'All day? But I need to get an urgent message to him?' He sighed. 'Certainly. Yes … I'll call back later.'

'Thinking about lying in front of the bulldozers, Jim?' said Juliette. She pulled on a cigarette while she sat on the capstone they'd lifted the day before.

'Shouldn't you give that up?' said Gill nodding at the smouldering tobacco.

'Bit late for that.'

'On behalf of the Trust, I demand you stop this dereliction immediately', Jim spat.

Juliette snuffed the remainder of her cigarette on the side of the pack and popped the butt inside. 'Quoting Charles Downshire, I have the Trust's reluctant permission to recover any artefacts revealed by our unauthorised excavation before making good the site', she said curtly. 'And I'm genuinely sorry if you find any of this upsetting. But I'd say it about makes us even.'

Jim stared at her for a few moments. 'Well, I'll not stand here to watch this vandalism any longer. And there are bigger fish in this pond than Charles Downshire. You mark me.'

Juliette opened her mouth to respond, but Jim stormed out of the stone circle towards the car park.

'Clock's ticking, Mrs', said the crane drive, also finishing his smoke by casting the butt onto the heather and grinding it with his heel.

Juliette nodded. 'Let's fit the rope cradle, and then we're good to go.'

Gill and the volunteers worked around the stone for twenty minutes, pushing the thin nylon rope deep into the crevice between the hexagonal stone and the bedrock. The crane company had designed it to grip tightly, like a drawstring bag, once the crane started to lift. They wouldn't know for sure it would work until they began. Everyone stood back as the crane took tension on the metal cables, and the cradle drew tight. As the ropes gripped the stone, Gill stepped in to grasp the edge of the cradle to stop it from swinging. Slowly the stone began to rise. The engine pitch roared far above the day before, and Gill glanced back at the driver.

'What's up?' he called. 'It shouldn't be as heavy as yesterday.'

The driver shook his head without speaking, while gradually, the stone kept rising. The upward motion stopped when it was a little above the surrounding rock apron. Gill stood ready as they prepared to swing it sideways three metres to where a neat stack of logs awaited. But the lateral motion didn't come. Instead, the whole apparatus shuddered, and the engine pitch suddenly dropped before dying entirely. Gill waited, the stone swaying slightly in the light wind, as the crane driver threw his control pad back into the cab and walked over to them.

‘Not sure what’s up. She doesn’t have any oomph this morning.’

‘Can’t you at least swing it around?’ Juliette asked.

‘Sorry, love. She’s stuck for the moment. I’ll phone my boss and see if he has any suggestions.’

Gill and Juliette looked at each other. They were tantalisingly close to seeing underneath, but the stone still hung suspended above the cavity. Gill’s senses were buzzing now. He needed to see under that stone so badly it almost hurt. ‘I’m going to have a peek underneath’, he said. ‘Coming?’

Juliette glanced at the steel cable and the bulk of the hexagonal block hanging just above the surrounding rock edge. ‘Knock yourself out’, she said. ‘I’ll wait for reinforcements.’

Gill smiled as he dived into his kit bag for a torch. ‘I’ll give you a running commentary’.

He knelt into the gully and shone his light across the underside of the stone. ‘Not quite as smooth as the top side, and no further inscriptions.’

‘What is it covering?’ Juliette asked.

‘Some form of pit hewn into the rock. I can’t see inside. Hang on a sec.’ He wriggled down into the gap between the suspended stone and the surrounding bedrock. Then he pulled himself under the gently swinging slab, easing his chest over the pit's edge to see inside. Casting his torchlight around the cavity, he took in the scene. He didn’t have room to turn his head, but Juliette’s upside-down face appeared in the gap on the other side. Peering at her across the underside of the hanging rock made her seem a long way away. ‘I see human remains. They look poorly preserved but still absolutely remarkable for a Neolithic site of this age. The skeleton looks complete and is lying on a raised platform with another gully around it. It looks like the entire construct was to keep the remains as free of groundwater as possible.'

'Any grave goods?' Juliette called.

'Not that I've seen so far. Hang on. Let me see if I can check the other side.' He leaned further into the pit, and as he did so, he thought he felt the stone above him sink a little, perhaps as it moved in the wind.

'Mind yourself, Gill. I'm detecting movement', said Juliette urgently.

He distinctly felt it this time. The stone sank lower, compressing his rib cage and forcing air out of his lungs.

Juliette screamed. 'Gill. Get out of there!'

He fought to retreat, but with a perceptible lurch, the stone sank another centimetre. With his rib cage trapped inside the chamber, he started to panic. Forcing his elbows against the rock, he propelled himself forward and slithered his legs into the gully. Feeling pressure, he yanked his left foot after him as the Chi Rho stone slowly rumbled down into its original position. The voices outside sounded muffled. Lots of shouting; Juliette screaming. He lay still, catching his breath in the stale atmosphere, and listening to his heart pounding in his chest. After a few minutes, his adrenalin subsided. Cramped as he was in the gully below the corpse, he fumbled for his phone. Remarkably, he still had one bar of reception. He called Juliette.

She sounded shaken to the core as she answered his call. 'Hello?'

At first, it was all he could do just to breathe into the phone. As he recovered, he couldn't help but make light of the situation. 'Gill McArdle here. Calling from beyond the grave.'

He pulled his phone back as Juliette unleashed a volley of swearing. When she'd finished, he asked, 'What's going on out there?'

'I think the crane driver just shat himself. Suffice to say, we have technical problems. One of the hydraulic lines has split. A mess of oil all over the heather. Are you okay? Do you have air?'

'Lemme check.' He switched off his torch and glanced around the chamber. 'Yeah, I can see some chinks of daylight where the rope cradle is forcing a gap between the upper and lower stones. If I don't exert myself, I should be fine for a few hours.'

'Okay. Save your phone battery. We'll be in touch as soon as we have a plan.'

They rang off, and Gill slumped fully onto his back. For fifteen minutes, he lay like that, allowing the trauma to ease out of his body. But his mind began to wander, and soon he was thinking about what would have happened if the stone had come down on him. As claustrophobia surged in his chest again, he decided to distract himself by getting back to work.

Flicking his torch back on, he cast it around the chamber to search for grave goods. It was difficult to turn his head without grazing his face on the underside of the Chi Ro stone. But wasn't it logical that someone of importance, buried in this hidden tomb, would take something with him for the afterlife? He had allowed himself to expect a trove of finds. But after twenty minutes of fumbling, he saw nothing. Not even the mist of garment fabric.

Disappointed, he diverted his attention to the human remains. The skeleton was male; the shape of the pelvis told Gill that. The thin bones and swollen joint ends told him his roommate had been very old when he died. The bones were dark with age, and when he leaned out and gently squeezed the detached femur lying next to him, it was soft to the touch.

'Okay, buddy. Who were you to end up buried like this?'

Gill examined the body again and noticed the teeth were in remarkably good shape despite the man's advanced age. He shone his torch on them, and the beam caught the glint of something bright. He edged as close to the skull as possible, hoping to twist his arm to shine his torch down through the corpse's open jaw. There wasn't room to manoeuvre the torch, so he tried from below, directing the beam up through the arch of the jawbone. Again, he saw a metallic glint. With rising curiosity, he slid his fingers up through the jaw and into the mouth cavity. Gently probing, his fingertips touched something hard. Gripping it between two fingertips, he carefully slid it out of the skull and into his hand. Holding it up to the torchlight, he saw it was a gold ring. Stained a little by the putrefaction of its former owner, Gill took a few seconds to rub it clean. The style was straightforward, a band of hammered gold, thick enough to last a lifetime of wear.

'Another mystery', he said aloud to himself. He couldn't think he'd ever seen a piece of Neolithic jewellery quite like it. He rubbed the ring again, his fingertip catching the faintest impression of a pattern on the inside of the band. He held it close to his face and repositioned his torch. He could make out the faintest inscription and focused the beam on the text. What he saw caused him to gasp violently.

The ring slipped from his fingers and trickled across the exposed skin of his neck. Shaking, he reached for it again, groping in the dark to where it had tumbled beneath him. His hands were trembling, so he steadied them by leaning his wrists on the rock above his head. Focusing his torch beam, he read again the words, in English, 'The Heavens Declare.'

Chapter 30

Three hours later, his phone rang. Juliette sounded stressed. 'Gill. You doing okay?'

'Aye', he said. The muffled noises from outside his tomb had become intense over the last hour.

'Hydraulics have been patched. We're going for a lift. Keep well back from the edges if you can, and don't roll out until we give you the all-clear.'

'Got it.'

He braced himself as a circle of silver light exploded into his vision. Slowly the stone rose in the air until it was grasped on three sides by gloved hands.

'Okay, Gill. Shift it.'

He sprang up from his resting spot and onto the ledge between the gullies. Moments later he was free. Grasping Juliette's outstretched hand, he nodded his thanks as he passed her. Without stopping, he strode out to the very edge of the stone circle, where he leaned against an upright slab and filled his lungs with fresh air. Behind him, the crane engine roared as the slab travelled sideways before being eased down onto the nest of wooden posts. Jim Robertson leaned against another stone a little way off, eyeing Gill with suspicion.

Gill waited for the crane noise to die away before rounding on him. 'What do you know about the man buried here?' he shouted.

Jim's eyes opened wide in alarm. He pushed off the stone and then stepped backwards as Gill strode towards him.

'I don't know how you did it, but if this is your idea of a sick joke?'

'Gill, go easy', said Juliette coming up behind him and touching his arm. 'You're probably in shock.'

Gill gave a hollow laugh. 'That's an understatement.' He turned to face her. 'I recovered something from the grave. But you're not going to believe me because you weren't present to corroborate its discovery.' He dug into his jacket pocket and thrust the ring into her palm.

Her mouth opened wide in joy. 'Gill, that's wonderful!'

Gill shook his head. 'Get it back to the Mill. You'll see there's an inscription on the inside. Have a read of that and tell me if you still think it's wonderful.'

'Gill. What's the problem?'

'Someone is messing with my head, Juliette. I'll be back later when I've had a shower.' He ignored her protests and walked off in the direction of his car.

It was almost 7 pm before he could drag himself back to the dig site. He'd gone for a run to relieve his stress and got satisfactorily lost in country lanes between Stromness and the lochs. A shower and a meal had finally exorcised the trauma of his confinement. As he got out of his car, he could immediately see the crane had gone. In the dimming twilight, contractors were lifting the trackway, and the last volunteers were packing their stuff. He found Juliette down where the pit had been, the capstone back in place, its peat carpet systematically restored.

'You didn't hang about', said Gill drawing up alongside her.

Juliette blew a lungful of smoke up into the blue-black sky. 'We're a couple of idiots, Gill. I thought it best to cover our embarrassment.'

'But I take it you recorded the site before reinstating the ground?'

'Aye, photos, drawings. The works. The skeleton and the hexagon are safely back at the Mill. Along with as many bags of dust as we could gather up.'

'Any idea how it was done?'

'You mean, get a contemporary gold ring into the mouth of a four-thousand-year-old corpse beneath two sheets of bedrock that haven't been disturbed in two hundred generations? No. Not a clue.'

He sighed and said nothing.

'But it's pretty bloody clear to me that this whole thing is a set-up. The ring, the Chi Rho, your theory about the Orcadian clock.' She waved a finger in his general direction. 'You and I, my friend, have been led a merry dance. It's ruined my reputation, and unless you're very careful, it could ruin yours too.'

'Sorry I dragged you into this', said Gill.

'I called you. Remember?'

'Have you shown the ring to anyone else?'

Juliette shook her head. 'But I had to confess to Charlie Downshire that our site is most likely compromised. He'll record the whole damn project as "unexplained".'

'I'd still like to go through the material you gathered.'

'Sure. For the remainder of my tenure, you have the full run of my lab. Which ends on Tuesday, I'm told.'

'And I'd like to run a full examination of the bones. DNA test and everything.'

'The trust will do a DNA as part of their standard analysis over the next few months.'

'No, more urgent. I want to get a sample off to a lab, ASAP.'

Juliette glanced sideways at him. 'Why the rush?'

Gill shrugged. 'Due diligence.'

'Okay, unicorn man. As you wish.' She turned for her car. 'I'll take you up to Tormiston.'

Gill nodded and followed her. His head still needed data, but his heart had already anticipated a dreadful possibility.

A few minutes later, Gill stood looking at the bones. After recovering them from Brodgar, Juliette had hastily laid them out on a workbench spread with a clean white sheet. A bag of smaller bones lay beside the skull, waiting for more expert hands later in the week.

'Wasn't a big lad, was he?' said Juliette.

'Just old', Gill replied. He leaned over the table, collecting the skull and jawbone in his gloved hands and carefully peering at the teeth.

'What are you looking for?'

'Any sign of dentistry. If the ring was a plant, the skull could be as well.'

'Already checked. The teeth are in good nick; what's left of them.'

'Aye, I see the molars are gone. They would have helped.' He gently set the bones down again. Then he prepared a small bag and tweezers before lifting a small strip of bone from a split femur into the bag. 'You're sure I can't help you with this test?'

Juliette shook her head. 'The Trust wouldn't want me to outsource this. But I'll put a rush on it.'

He passed her the bag and sighed. 'Given him a name yet?'

'Brodgar Man', said Juliette. 'I wanted to call him "The Joker", but I'm in enough trouble as it is.'

Gill managed a thin smile. 'Aye, well, let's see what we can find out about him. Maybe we'll recover something from this fiasco.'

Juliette leaned against the table while a prolonged cough battered her body. When she recovered, she looked him in the eye.

'I'll say this about Gill McArdle. He puts his heart and soul into a dig. You coulda' died today.'

He nodded. 'I have that reputation. And talking of reputation, there's something you should know about me.'

'Oh, yes?'

'As a PhD student, I cheated on a sample. My career staggered for a couple of years. The long and short of it is, my future in academia ended with that mistake.'

She leaned back from him as if he'd walked a dog turd into the room. 'I see.'

'And if we ever go public with this ring, I wanted you to hear that from me first. Before somebody else rubs your nose in my mess.'

Juliette laid down the sample bag and gripped the back of a chair. 'And did you, Gill? Cheat this time?'

He shook his head.

'Okay then,' Juliette turned and switched off the lights. 'That's enough for one day. I'm going home to get pissed. Coming?'

Gill glanced at her before looking away. 'I need a clear head for something. Look, I'll catch you in the morning.'

Alice answered the door after his second attempt at gentle taps.

'Gill! Come in.'

'You sure? Kids in Bed?'

'Aye. My mum is here doing some tidying up. Come and say hello.'

They stood in the kitchen making small talk while Alice made hot drinks. Leaving Mum in the kitchen with the ironing, they made their way to the lounge. The TV news was playing, and Alice flicked it off before settling down.

'Sorry I've not been in touch', said Alice, pressing her hand against her forehead before dropping it in her lap. 'But it's been a stressful couple of days.'

Gill sipped his drink and set it on the floor beside him. 'What's up?'

'A policewoman was here. Asking more questions about David.'

'What kind of stuff?'

'Where he has worked, places he liked to visit. Whether he had overseas contacts outside of his local colleagues.'

'Did she say why?'

Alice sighed. 'The coroner is unwilling to release a death certificate for David while there's still a chance he just ran away.'

'I presume they've got his banking details?'

Alice nodded. 'Not that it will help them. I've checked again. Nothing has moved on David's accounts since he died.' She shuddered for a few moments, and Gill thought she might cry. But recovering, she pressed on. 'I check every day. Do you think that's wrong of me?'

'No', said Gill as forcefully as he dared. 'This thing with David's car; you should be alert for anything unusual.'

She wiped her left eye, composing herself again.

'Listen, at the risk of upsetting you further, I'd like to ask a favour.'

'Sure.'

'I'd like to get a DNA sample for David.'

Alice took a long sip of the coffee she had nestled in her lap. 'Why? Has someone found something?'

'I'd just like to be prepared', Gill said, stumbling. 'The police should have asked already.'

Alice nodded. 'Alright. What do you need?'

'Hair would be best. Maybe from a comb or brush.'

Alice thought for a moment, then nodded and left the room. When she returned, she was carrying a child's drawing. 'Noah did this at school last year. He was doing a project on hair and eye colour for his immediate family tree. It was David's idea that we all cut off a lock of hair so Noah could paste them onto his poster.'

Gill took the sheet and allowed Alice to point out David's sample of dark brown hair. 'David's people were Cornish, I recall. Do you know if his folks were born there, or did they move around a bit?'

Alice smiled. 'Oh, they were locals. Accents as thick as butter. David's dad worked in the china clay industry. His dad before that, apart from a spell in the army.'

'Thanks', said Gill. 'I'll take the whole sheet if that's okay. I'll get it back to you in a few days.'

Alice suddenly looked pained. 'You will tell me if they find him, even a tiny part of him. It doesn't matter how awful. I just need to know.'

Gill held her gaze for a long moment. 'I promise.'

Chapter 31

Gill spoke to Cassy first thing on Monday morning. 'I've sent you hair samples for David and his immediate family. The courier had them on a flight this morning, so they should be with you by lunchtime. I need a DNA profile for David, ASAP.'

'Got that.' He heard Cassy flick the pages on her desk diary. 'Hoping to book some team-time with you this afternoon. I know we're well organised, but the clock is ticking.'

'Aye. Let's start at 2 pm. We can run through everything in a couple of hours. Oh, and I need to bring you up to speed on the results of the Brodgar dig.'

'Already! But you just started.'

'A few crossed wires on the paperwork meant we couldn't hang around.'

'And …'

'The Chi Rho was where we thought it would be. And underneath that stone, we found human remains.' He paused and considered trying to explain the compromised nature of the site. 'Listen, it's complicated. I'll fill you in this afternoon.'

'You sound stressed.'

'Aye, lots going on.'

Gill was interrupted by a knock at his bedroom door. He asked Cassy to wait while he opened the door to his landlady.

'Sorry to disturb you, Mr McArdle, but there's a police officer here to see you.'

'Okay. I'll be right down.'

'I've shown him into the TV lounge. I'll make sure the other guests don't disturb you.'

He could hear Cassy barking down the line. 'Police, Gill? What's going on?'

'Speak to you later. Promise to tell you everything.'

Detective Sergeant Douglas Ayles was a broad, fit-looking man, not far from retirement. He pointed to a sofa and suggested they both sit.

'What's this about?' Gill asked.

'I'm following up on yesterday's incident at Brodgar. I gather you were almost crushed.'

'Within a whisker. I could almost believe someone was watching out for me.'

'Have you made any enemies since you've been on the island, Mr McArdle?'

Gill was startled. 'Why?'

'We've discovered someone tampered with the crane's hydraulics. They'd slit the cables so they gradually tore when the machine took the load of the stone.'

'You're certain?'

'My forensics people showed me the damage to the pipe. Hence my question.'

Gill puffed out his cheeks and leaned back in his chair. 'I can rub people up the wrong way. But to make someone want to kill me? I'm just not sure.'

Sergeant Ayles flicked through his notebook. 'Juliette Morrison mentioned Jim Robertson was making a bit of a fuss around your archaeological dig.'

Gill nodded. 'He was offended by it. But that's okay. His point of view is the site's too precious to excavate. But I doubt he would stretch to murder.'

'I know Jim from a way back', said Ayles carefully. 'I'll have a word with him.' He turned to a fresh page in his book. 'Can you tell me who else you've encountered since arriving on Orkney?'

'Well, this is my second trip in as many months. You'll be aware of David Trevelyan's death up at ScoCion?'

Ayles nodded as he wrote. 'My DI has that case. We're treating it as a disappearance for now.' He held his hands out in a calming gesture. 'At least for now, as death isn't proven.'

'David was a friend of mine. We only recently linked up again. I'm helping his widow liaise with the accident enquiry at ScoCion. So I've had dealings with their reception and security staff as well as senior managers.'

'And how's that all going?'

'Fine. Professor Harley seems quicker to believe that David might have absconded with state secrets rather than being microwaved to death in that huge machine of his. But on balance, I'd say our conversations have been professional.'

'And you're involved with this dig, of course.'

'Juliette Morrison is running that. It went quite well, despite Jim's discordant voice at the margins.'

'Only quite well?'

Gill turned to look out of a window for a second. 'It's been a complicated dig. We spotted evidence suggesting the site may have been interfered with.'

Ayles paused from writing and looked up at him. 'What kind of evidence'

'It's just things don't add up.' He shrugged. 'You get this kind of thing in archaeology from time to time. You open up a one-thousand-year-old crypt and find a bottle top inside.'

'Maybe somebody got sloppy.'

'Maybe', said Gill.

Ayles nodded. 'I'll come back to you if it becomes important.'

'Can I ask you a question?'

'By all means.'

'I'm sure you are aware of the Euan Mearns case?'

'Aye. Another missing person. What about it?'

'It's just that Euan lent me a notebook before he disappeared. I've never met him. He passed it to me via Juliette Morrison.'

'And what was in this book?'

Gill was suddenly unsure how much to tell the officer. 'Numbers and dense calculations. We were able to decipher some of it. It influenced where we carried out our dig.'

'And do you think Euan might have made this attempt on your life?'

'I think that's unlikely, given he was trying to help me. I mention it in case it becomes relevant.'

Before looking up at Gill, Sergeant Ayles quietly made some more notes. 'You're wondering if the person that tried to kill you may have succeeded in killing Euan?'

Gill shrugged. 'The possibility has occurred to me. The one thing I established about Euan is that the Brodgar monuments are very important to him. Maybe someone took offence at what he was doing.'

'And what was he doing, to the best of your knowledge?'

'Taking measurements around the stones. Probably doing what the rest of us have been doing these past weeks; trying to work out the significance of them all.'

Ayles let out a long sigh. 'You weave a tangled web, Mr McArdle.'

Gill smiled. 'So I've been told.'

The officer excused himself, promising to be back in touch. Gill glanced at his watch. No time for a run now. Breakfast first, then it was time to write up the Brodgar dig. He grimaced to himself. What on earth was he going to say?

He found Juliette at Tormiston Mill, sorting through paperwork. She seemed lost in thought, and to catch her attention, he tapped her open door. She turned to face him and smiled.

'Good morning', she said.

'I came to apologise. I wasn't feeling very sociable when we parted yesterday.'

She beckoned him in and pointed at a chair. 'Don't worry about it. Quite understandable after the day you'd had.'

He grunted. 'Lying trapped in someone else's grave under a couple of tonnes of sandstone always tips my temper.'

She laughed, and then turned serious. 'Have you heard the police think the crane malfunction was sabotage?'

'Sergeant Ayles came to see me this morning. Among other things, he was asking about Jim.'

'I don't think Jim would do something like that, do you?'

Gill shrugged. 'Our work upset him. I dunno. You know the guy better.' He picked at a mark on his trousers for a few moments. 'Listen, I was trying to write up the dig this morning, and I keep hitting a wall. I was thinking about Euan and wondering if somehow he could have stashed the ring?'

'Maybe. Any idea how? And why?'

Gill shook his head. 'I gather he was a bright enough lad. Do you mind if I get a copy of all the site photos? See if I can figure out how he might have done it?'

'Be my guest. I'll put them on a pen drive for you', said Juliette hunching over her PC. 'Tell me, do you think finding a contemporary ring puts all our discoveries this week in doubt?'

Gill sighed. 'Fraid so. If the ring is a plant, the rest is probably just window dressing. We might be the victim of a stunt. Something planned back in Wilson's era. Maybe one of the locals saw the increasing curiosity for archaeology among the Victorian middle class and decided to leave something worth finding. Maybe Wilson himself planted something that might vindicate his stories.'

'All the same; a ring with an English inscription! Not very subtle.'

'I know', said Gill, staring out at the isthmus through the office window.

'I left the ring with a jeweller friend for the morning', Juliette continued. 'She's brill; been working with gold for forty years. She'll try to identify the tools used to manufacture it. Might give us an insight into when the ring was made.'

'Yeah, that's a good idea. Let me know what she comes up with', said Gill, accepting Juliette's pen drive. 'What's next for you?'

'Big hospital appointment next week in Inverness. Got to decide whether to go for another round of chemo or hang up my gloves and enjoy whatever time I've left.' She tapped the cigarette packet on her desk. 'I'll probably do the latter.'

Gill nodded once and wasn't sure what to say.

'Oh, before I forget. I pulled my last remaining favour and got Brodgar Man's bone fragment off to Aberdeen for testing. I've been promised an initial DNA result early tomorrow, although I don't see what good it will do us.'

'Thanks. Appreciate that. Listen, I'm here a couple more days, then back to Dundee on Thursday evening.'

Juliette stood and gave him a brief hug. 'I'll see you tomorrow then.' She nodded out the window at the sky. 'That's assuming you get away at all. That decent weather forecast has disappeared in a puff of smoke. Looks like we're going to get a squall.'

Cassy and the rest of the team listened in silence as Gill detailed the previous day's adventures. He omitted the ring's textual inscription, plus the possibility the crane was sabotaged.

'Grief', said Cassy. 'You take your work far too seriously. I wouldn't take a paper cut for this job.'

'I'm always in the service of our readers', joked Gill. 'Craig. Can you run us through the final edits?'

The meeting ran at a pace, with the running order of this month's features being debated and confirmed. Gill had decided to lead issue sixteen with the Glasgow discovery. It was a macabre story, but the anomaly of finding ancient Egyptian mummies in a Glasgow basement was too mind-bending to ignore. And the story would lay the groundwork for an article Gill was building around the Persian links to ancient Orcadia.

As the call wrapped up, Gill asked to speak to Mhairi.

'Our friend Wilson is coming under a bit of scrutiny' he said. 'The possibility exists that as far back as 1850, he may have polluted our dig site. I need to decide if he's credible or not.'

'We're talking about his Persian research, right?'

'Yes', said Gill.

‘Sure. Ancient Persia isn’t my area of expertise, so I’ve reached out to an old university contact. I hope that’s okay?’

‘Of course. Anybody I’d know?’

‘Adina Mofaz. She’s head of International Culture at the National Museum. And she does some lecturing which is how I came to meet her. She’s Iranian by birth and Persian history is her specialism.’

‘Good contact.’

‘Let me remind myself what we talked about.’

Gill waited while Mhairi opened various documents on her computer.

‘The good news is that Wilson quotes a trusted historian called Dionysius of Miletus as his principal source’, Mhairi began. ‘Dionysius was Greek but was interested in the history of Persia. One of his reputed books was called, *Description of the Inhabited World*.’

‘Reputed?’

‘We’re talking 5th Century BC. The book itself no longer exists. Unfortunately, we have to rely on another respected Greek writer, Herodotus, to tell us a little of what was in Dionysius' book.’

‘Why’s that a problem?’

‘Because Herodotus was slagging him off. He accuses Dionysius of literally making up stories and quotes Dionysius’s *Temple of the Stars* myth as an example.’

‘Right. How does that story run?’

Mhairi cleared her throat. ‘The histories mention someone; a “King of the North”, who could predict the movements of the stars. He led an advanced and peaceful society to great prosperity, and when he died, his people built a temple to the sun and all the heavenly bodies to remember the king's dying promise that he would be born again. Dionysius records that this was from a Sumerian source. That's in Wilson's favour, at least. Sumeria had trade and cultural links around the known world and was contemporary to Brodgar's construction around 2000 BC.'

'Somewhere along the line, Sumeria gets gobbled by the Babylonian empire', said Gill.

'Yes, and later becomes part of Persia, in a conquest also recorded in the Bible. In Babylonian and later Persian culture, they venerated Sumerian history and language. What caught Dionysius's eye was that the histories contained astronomical data of a thoroughly scientific character. In a nutshell, our friend Wilson credits this northern kingdom as kick-starting the Persian's grasp of astronomy.'

'But Herodotus thought it was all garbage?'

'Yes, but it doesn't sound like he got in a boat and checked for himself.'

'What do you think, Mhairi?'

'I see three things that might be significant. Firstly, this northern king has a messianic echo. This idea sounds authentic as it predates Christianity, so it isn't a copycat. Secondly, when you look at the British Isles back in the Neolithic era, you have to remember the cultural poles were flipped. Southerners building Stone Henge were copying an earlier, more advanced kingdom we now suspect was Orcadian. We don't have documents to prove this, but it's generally accepted there was a flow of ideas from north to south around this period. Those influences are in the archaeological record.'

'And the final thing?'

'Soon after the Neolithic period, the Babylonians make a giant leap forward in astronomy. Again, that's in the archaeological record. However, we've no evidence they had the tools or the grasp of incremental science to explain this breakthrough. Basically, it seems to drop in their lap.'

Gill was silent for a moment, absorbing the information. 'What's your take on Wilson? Did he honestly believe in the northern kingdom?'

'He was scrupulous, Gill. You see that in his hand-drawn plates and his attention to detail. I think he honestly believed an advanced civilization existed on Orkney, and it influenced the rest of the known world.'

Gill spent the rest of his day recuperating. Wet and windy weather asserted itself, and he was grateful he wasn't lying under a stone slab, waiting for rescue. Instead, he curled up in the guest lounge at his B&B with a large pot of tea and his laptop. He inserted Juliette's pen drive and reviewed all the site photos before, during and after his entrapment. Using these, plus his memory of the site, he tried to imagine how a fraudster could have inserted the ring without leaving any clues. After an hour, he took a final slug of tepid tea and gave up.

Frustrated, he decided to look for clues elsewhere. He tabbed to his digital copy of Wilson's *Temple of the Stars* and began to read.

In Wilson's writing, he found the same copious detail he'd read in the first book. The man had a habit of inserting long apologetic paragraphs where he was unsure about facts and needed to speculate. Gradually, as he listened to the evidence, Gill caught Wilson's conviction in the authenticity of the northern kingdom.

He'd been impressed by Mhairi's analysis. He found her narrative compelling, even if he never found evidence to verify her hypothesis. Gill became more excited as he read the final chapter of Wilson's book. Here he claimed to unlock the cypher to the astronomical map inherent in the Orcadian monuments. But reading on, he found Wilson did a bizarre thing. Rather than lay out his mathematical findings in the way Craig had done one hundred and seventy years later, Wilson bailed out. Reporting that he had recorded data points his analysis could not explain, he hedged his bets and listed further potential research. He explained that his explorations would be ongoing and assisted by local amateur enthusiasts without mentioning their names. They would continue to study the stones and publish their findings when the time was right. In honour of the mythical king who claimed he would be born again, he christened this group, "The Vigil".

Gill was absorbing the implications of this sharp left turn in Wilson's writing when his phone pinged. He read the text, then glanced outside at the darkening, rain-drenched sky.

'Tonight of all nights, she wants to talk', he muttered before dragging himself to his feet.

Chapter 32

He found Jenny's car in a tourist layby close to the Ring of Brodgar. He pulled up behind her and dimmed his lights. Even as the engine switched off, he had the strangest feeling of momentum as the wind rocked his car. All afternoon, heavy clouds had built up behind a freshening breeze, and now they released a torrent of rain. He tugged his jacket tight around him before stepping out of his car. The five steps to Jenny's passenger door were like a dash through a car wash.

She sat silently watching him as he wiped rain out of his face. She didn't wear her usual professional smile, and he thought she looked sad.

'So', he said, pausing while he composed himself. 'This is a wee bit cloak and dagger. What's on your mind?'

She turned away from him, and with her elbow resting against the window, she slumped her face against her open palm. 'I'm having second thoughts about this. I could get in serious trouble.'

'Your text said you needed to talk.'

'I think you'll find it hard to take this seriously.' She looked out into the darkness. 'Sorry for dragging you out. Let's not do this.'

Gill could see her expression reflected at him in the glass. He sighed. 'We've both come out on a stinking evening. At least tell me what's bothering you. Maybe I can help. If I can't, then I'll stay out of it, whatever "it" is.'

She faced him again and stared at him for a long moment. 'David's accident. The company hasn't been honest with all the facts.'

'Okay. But there was a full accident enquiry. Are you saying the company lied?'

Jenny shrugged. 'What's a lie these days? They omitted some data; didn't disclose certain facts.'

Gill nodded slowly. 'Like what?'

'For a start, it wasn't the first accident.'

'I'm not following you.'

'Over the last six weeks, dozens of small faults have slowed our research. Sensor problems, equipment malfunctions, endless dodgy cameras. Poor David was at his wit's end.'

'Did David make a mistake under pressure?'

'No', Jenny sniffed.

'Might he have had a breakdown? Run away?'

'No.'

'Could he have harmed himself?'

'Pity's sake, Gill. No!'

Gill dropped his voice to calm her. 'Jenny. Tell me what you think happened.'

'The accident enquiry found that the control room team all thought someone else had checked David was safely out of the chamber before the beam fired. That's definitely not true. We lied. We all lied about that one.'

Anger rose in Gill's chest. He pushed it back so he could hear her out.

'The truth is we were all distracted. Something happened in the control room moments before the accident throwing everyone into a panic. In all the fuss, no one checked David was safe.'

Gill's hand came swiftly to his forehead, smearing wet hair against his skull as he drew it over his head. 'What on earth would cause the whole team to take their eyes off the one guy working to keep the test on track?'

'You're not going to believe me.'

'Jenny!'

She swiftly raised her hands in front of her, holding them in that position until he calmed down and let his body slump back into the seat.

'The experiment was primed to send three targeting pulses before the main blast that did for David. The schedule had them firing three seconds apart before the main discharge. Because the battery arrays keep charging until the ion beam fires, each targeting pulse has a distinct energy signature. We'd just passed T minus four minutes when the first scheduled pulse appeared on the detector array.'

Gill shook his head. 'I'm not following you. How could it show up before the machine fired?'

'That's what Harley said. He started yelling down the comms to the guys at Sleet Moss, saying they had an equipment error. Then it got worse.'

Gill raised an eyebrow as he looked at her but said nothing.

'Everyone was rushing around running diagnostics. Someone quickly realised the second of the pulses had registered on the detectors twelve hours before.'

'Twelve hours', Gill repeated. 'Are you telling me the experiment sent two pulses back in time?'

'The place went ballistic. Everyone was yelling out ideas.' She glanced at him. 'But no one thought to put the countdown on hold. I'm so sorry, but we just let it run. No one thought to check on David.'

'And the final pulse', said Gill quietly. 'When did it show up?'

Jenny shook her head. 'No sign of it. It fired on schedule but never registered at the receiving station.'

'It disappeared?'

'The time effect seemed to rise exponentially as the countdown progressed. One of the team postulated it might have hit Sleet Moss long before we set up the receiver array.'

'And what about the main pulse that killed David?' said Gill.

Jenny dropped her face into her hands. 'Again, the time effect means we'll never know.'

He realised he had been holding his breath. He exhaled and looked at her. 'What is it, Jenny?'

'The lack of a body. Come on, Gill. Join the dots.'

'Even if David had been vapourised, you should have detected trace gases.'

Jenny pulled her left hand to her mouth, fighting to restrain the tears rolling down her cheeks. 'When they realised David was missing, they analysed the air in the particle cannon. I don't know what they were looking for, but I do remember Doug saying they found no trace of him.'

Gill felt his jaw drop. 'You think the final ion pulse went even further back in time?' He rubbed his chin. 'That somehow it carried David along with it?'

Jenny lifted her face and stared at him with moist eyes. 'The company has been looking for his body. They've been using dogs to search along the path the beam would have taken between discharge and receptor.'

'Do they have a theory?'

'Nothing solid. And none of this is official. But the best idea on the board is that David was carried along in some manner we don't understand. But the beam didn't have enough energy to carry him to the detector station.'

'Oh, Jenny', said Gill. 'The beam's path was through solid sandstone. Are you saying David was transported into rock?'

'Probably not the living David. But certainly his remains, his molecules. That's what they're trying to prove. They want evidence. Something they can use to calibrate future experiments.'

'More tests?' said Gill. 'This thing is dangerous. It has to stop.'

Jenny nodded. 'I agree. I've told them that.'

'Then why are they still working? There should be a big chunk of police tape right across the entrance.'

Jenny paused as a car passed them on the road, moving slowly as it worked its way down the narrow lane in the gale. 'Now the accident enquiry has almost wrapped up. They are looking at a hearing, probably a fine and maybe a little more regulation. But the guys at the top are excited. They've moved beyond real-time messaging over long distances and seem to be working on something else.'

'You're doing the right thing telling me about it. We'll go to the relevant authorities and get this stopped.'

Jenny suddenly grasped his arm. 'I'm scared, Gill. When I realised what had happened and the company was lying, I submitted my resignation. But Harley threw it back in my face. Said I'd stayed quiet too long. That I'm complicit.'

'At first, maybe. But you're a whistle-blower now, Jen. If you go to the police tonight, you'll absolve yourself of blame.'

Jenny pulled back from him and shook her head. 'I feel threatened. I've got family on the island.'

'They're scientists Jenny, not the mafia. I really doubt ...'

'But I've told you what happened.'

'So far, we've got nothing we can prove. It would only be our word against Harley's. And for the time being, we can't be sure exactly where David is.'

'That much is true', she sniffed.

Gill sat back and thought for a minute. 'Okay, I suggest you say nothing. In the meantime, I'll ask around. Ask some open questions. See if I can get them to show their hand.'

'And if the police get involved?'

'I'll vouch for you. Tell them you brought your suspicions to me. I agreed to help you find something solid you could take to the authorities. In the meantime, I have a date I need you to check. It fell in August this year. I'd like you to see if it has any significance at ScoCion.'

Jenny's shrug was fast and shallow. 'What date?'

'15th August.'

Jenny thought for a moment. 'Means nothing to me.'

'Can you make discreet enquiries? My instinct tells me it's important somehow.' He searched her eyes. 'Is that okay?'

She turned away from him and looked again out into the blackness. 'Okay', she said at last.

After another soaking on the way back to his car, Gill waited for Jenny to make a U-turn and move off. He sat in the darkness, imagining what it must have been like for David to get trapped in the beam. Then he thought about the old bones he'd found at Brodgar; the skull with a ring in its mouth. 'Oh, God', he whispered. 'Don't let it be true.'

Chapter 33

Sergeant Douglas Ayles took a deep breath and knocked on Jim Robertson's door. He glanced over his shoulder where a younger, fitter officer stood at the ready. But Jim wasn't going to make a run for it – where would he go? In the event, when Jim answered the door, he just nodded and said, 'Morning, Douglas. You're about bright and early.'

The PC followed Ayles inside but stood stiffly by the door while his Sergeant took the seat Jim offered him beside an unlit fire.

'Twice in one week, Sergeant. What do I owe the pleasure?'

'I'd like to offer you one last chance to be honest with me.'

Jim picked at a loose thread on the arm of his chair, then stroked it back into the fabric. 'I've not made a habit of living outside the law. Didn't I cooperate when you came with your search warrant earlier in the week?'

'And I was grateful. I'm checking you still haven't found your pocket knife?'

'Not yet, unfortunately. It's handy around the garden.'

'If we ever find it, I expect it will have your blood on it.'

'Sorry, Douglas. I'm not following.'

'Are you right-handed, Jim?'

'Yes.'

'Could you show me your left hand?'

Ayles noticed that Jim held his gaze a little longer than was natural before he complied. 'Nasty wee scratch that. You were unlucky to catch two fingers.'

Jim looked down at the thin red sores. 'Juliette Morrison's dig. Ripped my hand while moving some fence posts we were using as rollers.'

'Oh? Sorry to hear that.'

Jim folded his damaged hand out of sight. 'What's this about?'

'Forensics didn't find any prints on the sabotaged hydraulics, Jim. That had all been wiped clean. However, they did lift a little blood from the crane ladder. The left side handhold, to be exact.'

'Oh. I see.'

'I'm picturing the saboteur gripping the hydraulic pipe in his left hand while he sliced it lengthways with his right.'

Jim said nothing, so Douglas continued. 'Thank you again for the DNA sample. We've had time to compare with the blood taken off the crane.'

Jim sat back in his chair and closed his eyes, allowing his head to fall back against the rest for several long seconds. 'The damn thing was greasy. And I was nervous.'

'You're admitting it then?'

'Douglas. I'm trying to protect something significant.'

'Important enough to go to prison for?'

Jim nodded with his eyes closed. 'Yes.'

‘Well, I’m sorry. But I need to ask you to come to the station.’

‘Douglas. I want to ask you; when the time comes, what side will you be on?’

‘Jim. On your feet.’

Jim opened his eyes and fixed his gaze on Ayles. ‘Someone is coming. Someone more … wise … more powerful than you’ve ever known. When he comes, Sergeant, you’ll not want to take the wrong side against him.’

Ayles stood and paused where the officer stood by the door. ‘Read Mr Robertson his rights. I’ll sit in the back with him on the way to the station.’

During his morning call with Cassy, the DNA results from David’s sample arrived at the *Mys.Scot* office, so he emailed Juliette with a request to print a copy. The call finished at 10 am, and around the time he expected Juliette would be clearing her desk at Tormiston Mill.

‘Could be related’, said Juliette as he walked in. She was holding two sheets of numbers side by side. One was from “Brodgar Man”, while the other was David’s DNA.

Juliette pointed at a succession of data points. ‘The Brodgar bone fragments gave a poor sample, but we can pick out a dozen areas of high confidence. They’re quite distinct on Orkney, and not at all common across the rest of Scotland.’

‘What’s you’re analysis?’ probed Gill.

'There's a high probability David was descended from Brodgar Man.'

'How do we deal with the fact David was Cornish?' said Gill quietly. 'And all his people were Cornish.'

Juliette tapped her laptop a few times and brought up a new page. 'Must be a coincidence then. Migration and trade up and down the west coast.'

Gill nodded. 'Maybe. But I'm going to run something by you. I warn you, you're not going to like it.'

Juliette gave one quick jerk of her head.

'When I collected David's personal possessions at ScoCion for Alice, it included his wedding ring. Last time I visited Alice, I asked her for a photo of it.'

He passed her his phone and waited while she examined the image.

Juliette slumped back in her seat. 'No. Sodding. Way', she said at last.

Gill gripped the back of a chair. 'I need you to consider the possibility David Trevelyan *is* Brodgar Man.'

'How?'

Briefly, Gill explained how David had disappeared in the belly of the machine and that his current whereabouts, living or dead, was unknown.

Juliette held her head in her hands for a few moments. 'You can't prove that from the DNA sample alone. Brodgar Man is too old. And the most likely explanation for the ring is still sabotage.'

'I concede that. But it is a possibility. Did you ever hear back from your jeweller friend?'

'Yeah. I called in yesterday evening and picked it up.' Juliette reached into a drawer and pulled out a small clear plastic bag. She stared at it for a long moment before sliding it across to him. 'My friend says both the ring and the inscription were manually tooled. Someone went to a lot of trouble to make it appear authentic.'

'Maybe it is authentic.'

Juliette waved a finger at him. 'Come on, Gill. The likely explanation is some kind of subterfuge by ScoCion. Get to the bottom of that, and I suspect you'll prove this business with the ring is a cruel joke.'

Gill nodded. 'Maybe. I'm working on that.' His phone buzzed, and recognizing the number, he moved towards the window to get better reception. 'Jenny? What's happening?'

'Yes. I'm at the airport. Listen, I have something for you on David's car.'

'I know. It was abandoned in a car hire return bay a few hours after the accident.'

'I've got more on that. I've known one of the security guys since I was a kid. You remember the police said the CCTV tapes from that afternoon didn't show anything out of the ordinary?'

Gill thought for a moment. 'I didn't see any footage myself, but I know they told Alice the person who left the car hid their face.'

'That's correct. But my friend ran all the number plates of every car that came onto the airport grounds that day. They've got a plate recognition system.'

'Could be useful, but you can't tell who owns the vehicles unless you have access to DVLA systems.'

'I don't need to. Professor Harley's plate stuck out like a sore thumb.'

'You're certain?'

'Came on site twenty minutes after David's car was abandoned and left again eight minutes later.'

Gill exhaled a long slow breath as he considered the implications.

Jenny continued. 'And I've looked into the 15th of August and found we ran some kind of test that day. But it was after hours, with no shout-outs to the main sponsors.'

'What kind of test?'

'No idea. The logs don't record the details.'

'Thanks. That's useful. Listen, what are you doing now?'

'I've just done a drop-off. I'm heading back to ScoCion to work on a press release.'

'Jenny, you might want to lie low for a couple of hours. This information gives me leverage, so I'm going to confront Harley. He hasn't been straight with us. So, if you want to keep out of the way, you could call in sick or work from home.'

Jenny left a brief silence. 'I'm your eyes and ears, remember. You might still need me.'

'Okay. Just be careful. If Harley is a fox and we corner him, we don't know what he might do.'

Gill hung up and turned back to Juliette. Pointing at the ring he said. 'I'd get that over to Skara if I were you. We need someone to take a very close look at it.'

'And where exactly are you off to?'

‘You ever heard of “cleaking”? It’s an east coast expression.’

Juliette said she hadn’t.

‘It’s where you shove an iron bar under a damp rock at low tide. You rattle it around for a while and see if anything tasty grabs hold.’

Chapter 34

'No, I'm sorry, Mr McArdle. Professor Harley is tied up in meetings all day', said Prisha, frowning at him.

'I insist', said Gill. He leaned on the receptionist's desk and scribbled some notes on the back of his business card. 'Give him this. Then tell him he has as long as it takes me to drink a cup of tea to come out and see me. Otherwise, I'm taking this information to the authorities.'

He turned away from reception and walked purposefully to the kitchen area Jenny had shown him on the first day. He ran hot water in a mug and dropped in a tea bag. As he reached for a spoon and started to stir, he realised his hands were shaking.

'What is the meaning of this?' Although Harley spoke forcefully, the volume was barely higher than a whisper. Gill turned to face him.

'That is your car registration, Professor. Certainly, a car with that reg is parked out front.'

'What are these other numbers?'

'Those are the entry and exit times at Kirkwall Airport on the same afternoon as David Trevelyan died.'

Harley took a few moments to respond. 'What of it? I'm at the airport every week.'

'Indeed. But on the day these numbers were recorded by the local security cameras, you didn't leave Orkney. It was three hours after you'd endured a very perplexing incident in the ion chamber. And two hours after your airport excursion, you were giving a heart-warming interview to local media concerning the death of a valued colleague.'

'That's hardly a crime.'

'No, but I'm pretty sure lying to the police is called perjury.'

Harley opened his mouth, then said nothing.

Gill finished making his tea, stood up and walked over to Harley, placing his mouth close to the man's ear. 'At the moment, the evidence is pretty circumstantial. But if the police make further enquiries, they'll be able to prove that you recruited a colleague to drive David's car to the airport. To keep those in the know to an absolute minimum, you collected your associate from the airport in your own car.' Gill paused as the colour started to drain from Harley's face. 'A few days later, you dared to suggest to my face that David hadn't died. That he'd run off for some reason or another. Or killed himself. And frankly, you should be ashamed of that.'

Harley withdrew two steps. 'Let's not talk here. Follow me, please.'

Gill picked up his drink and slowly followed Harley to his office door. Harley stood aside to let him in, gently closing the door behind him.

'You're right, of course', he said. 'And I very much regret it. It was a huge lapse of judgement.'

'And an incredibly callous attack on David's reputation.'

Harley looked haggard as he sank into a seat, waving his hand at Gill to find a chair. 'I was under immense pressure because of the failed tests. We've mistakenly stoked the expectations of our sponsors in recent months. The death of a key employee was another massive blow.'

'And you've experienced more than one accident. Haven't you?'

Harley cocked his head and looked at Gill sideways. 'Why do you say that?'

'Little clues in what people have said. Suggestions of niggles. I was challenged by your security people a few days ago on Rusky Hill. They implied David's accident wasn't the only one.'

Harley nodded, saying nothing.

'Sabotage or incompetence, Professor?'

'Or espionage, Gill?' Harley threw his hands out in front of him. 'I believe someone is interfering with our systems.'

'Who?'

'I don't know.'

'So why complicate things by moving David's car?'

Harley shrugged. 'To deflect. Buy a little more time. I'm a scientist, for pity's sake. Not some mercenary industrialist.'

'You achieved that alright, all the time knowing you would be tainting the reputation of someone you called a friend.'

Harley met Gill's gaze. 'Can I ask what you plan to do with this information?'

'The police need to address this particular line of enquiry. I think it would play better coming from you than me', said Gill.

Harley gave a deferential nod. 'Thank you. I'll do that straight away.'

Gill held up a hand. 'Not so fast. I'm going to ask you two questions, and in return for me giving you this second chance, you're going to answer them.'

Harley twisted in his chair slightly and nodded once.

'Okay. I know from two reliable sources, late on the 15th August, you conducted a test. I also know from another source it was significant in some way. I'd like you to tell me about it.'

'I don't see how …'

'Professor, all of this is linked, and when it all boils down, I'm a journalist. So if you want me to give you space to make your confession, then please, talk to me about that test.'

Harley sighed and got out of his chair. Slowly he walked over to a map of the solar system laid out on a log scale. 'We were running a real-time shout-out into deep space. The team fired a test message to a distant spacecraft, which sent back the data packet and a timestamp. The experiment was successful and validated our basic theories.'

'Hang on a second. You talked just a few weeks ago about a future test using a deep space probe, but you gave the impression that was years away.'

'It's smoke and mirrors, Gill. The Chinese are breathing down our necks on this. We need them to think we're way behind where we actually are.'

'But you said it would take years to commission and deploy a spacecraft?'

Harley walked over to a document cabinet and punched in a security code. He rummaged for a second, then pulled out a technical schematic. 'The European Space Agency has a probe called the LISA Pathfinder. It was launched on 3rd December 2015 and was put in orbit around the sun, one and a half million kilometres from Earth. It was a short-term exploratory mission to lay the groundwork for a larger project designed to detect gravitational waves. After the LISA probe completed its initial mission, ESA planned to shut it down. But as we hope to bring them on board as a sponsor, we persuaded them to give it to us.'

'And you're telling me, you ran a test on the 15th August and achieved real-time, that is, faster-than-light communication with this probe?'

Harley nodded, sitting down again. 'The relay came back by conventional means, which is why we worked so late that night. But the outward beam …,' Harley paused and allowed himself a self-satisfied smile, '… the outward data packet had zero delays, so we achieved our primary objective.'

'Congratulations', said Gill with absolutely no emotion. 'That leads me to my second question.'

'I'm assuming you're treating this information in confidence. We can't afford to let this slip to our competitors.'

'You've broken the law, Professor. This information exchange is part of your debt to society.' He took another swig of tea, then leaned forward in his chair. 'If the 15th August was such a raving success, what were you doing the day David died?'

Harley stared at the floor and spoke quietly. 'The 15th August data package was tiny. We realised much higher energies would be required to carry audio and video.' He took a long pause. 'And even more to transport solid objects.'

'Is this the speculative 3D printing idea? Sending data out into space to a mission ship so it can print its own parts?'

Harley shook his head. 'It was our first experiment with a far more radical application of our new technology.'

Gill frowned at Harley. 'Okay, talk to me.'

Harley got up slowly and cleared a space on a large whiteboard. 'This is Earth', he said, drawing a globe in the bottom left-hand corner, followed by a small square box some distance away to the right. 'What we've demonstrated so far is ship-to-ship data transfer, using the subatomic particles to carry the message. The next stage we're working on is aiming the particles at a point in space while simultaneously vaporising the host object. The physics is tricky. We use our new technology to toss subatomic particles towards target coordinates deep in space. We theorise that with sufficient energy input, the host object will reform around the subatomic particles we ejected.' He stopped, lifted his gaze and clasped his palms together. 'In essence, we hope to transmit entire objects into distant space.'

Gill scowled at Harley's illustration, suppressing the eddy of questions that swirled around his brain. 'You are kidding me', he said.

Harley slowly shook his head. 'It's quantum physics, Gill. Faraday harnessed electricity. Edison learnt how to tame light. At ScoCion, we're simply taking subatomic particles and moving on to the next level.'

'You can beam objects anywhere in the galaxy?'

‘That’s beyond even our theoretical capability just now. Our targeting beam holds its definition only as far as Jupiter.’

‘Is that where you sent David?’

Harley seemed taken aback. ‘No. No! He wasn’t beamed anywhere. The fatal error that took his life was his proximity to a massive energy discharge.’

‘And I imagine you’d have detected some residue of his body, even if it was just vapours?’

Harley winced. ‘We’d just lost a friend, Mr McArdle. It wasn’t a great moment for theoretical reasoning.’ He got up and wiped his sketch off the board. ‘Our research had been going so well. On the day of the accident we faced a host of technical malfunctions we haven’t got to the bottom of.’

‘What was the running order on the day David died?’

‘Do you mean the mechanics of the test?’

‘Exactly.’

Harley leaned back in his chair and studied Gill’s face for a second. ‘We’d set up a four pulse test. We designed the final pulse; that’s the main discharge, to transmit an object.’

‘What kind of object?’

‘A titanium orb, about the size of a tennis ball. We planned to vaporise it in the particle cannon and direct it to materialise in a target area at Sleet Moss.’

‘And the other three pulses?’

‘They tested the targeting array at three critical points in the electromagnetic spectrum.’

‘And this orb. Just a metal ball, or was it carrying instrumentation?’

‘Just a GPS locator and a small transmitter. If it went astray, we wanted the ability to find it again.’

‘And what happened to it?’

‘No sign of it. We theorise if we find David’s remains, the orb won’t be far-away.’ Harley glanced away. ‘And vice versa.’

‘I’m confused. You’re saying the orb transmitted successfully while all the metal on David’s person stayed in the ion chamber?’

‘Look, it was our first test transmission of a physical object. We’ve got a great deal to work out.’

Harley was starting to sound angry now, and Gill realised he wouldn’t extract much more from the man. But he was beginning to understand what had puzzled Arnold Broadbent. Reluctantly, the professor had revealed why he’d built a cannon rather than a rifle.

‘Last question’, he said, fighting to keep incredulity from creeping into his voice. ‘In the course of your experiments, have you ever observed any temporal effects?’

‘Come again?’

‘Well, you’ve been talking about space and subatomic particles and mixing in enough energy to light a small city. I’m just thinking E=MC squared and all that. You’re talking about faster-than-light travel, which sounds to me like you could potentially distort time.’

Harley suppressed a mocking smile. ‘You can’t change time, McArdle. You can’t go forward; you can’t go back. You are where you are.’

Gill shrugged. 'When I walked into this office ten minutes ago, you couldn't beam objects into space. Now it appears you can. It seems everything is possible. But I'm sure the safety inspectors will make up their minds when they look at your logs.'

Harley's eyes narrowed. 'Why are you asking about this?'

Gill stood to leave. 'The day David died, you had a room full of scientists. Maybe not all of them are as comfortable as you, writing off the death of a colleague as the price of progress.'

Harley sprang from his seat and stepped in front of the closed door. 'Who's been talking?'

Gill cocked his head to one side. 'You and I have been talking, Professor. Is there anything you'd like to add?'

Harley's posture deflated again, and he shook his head. 'What happens next?'

Gill glanced upwards and gathered his thoughts. 'First, you call the police and reveal your interference with David's car. That way, an hour from now, when they get a tip-off to check number plates at the airport on the morning David died, it won't come as much of a surprise.'

'Thank you. I think. Apart from the police, are we keeping this between ourselves?'

Gill shook his head. 'Right now, I'm going back to my B&B to write an article that will appear in my magazine in just under a week. Before I do, I don't know who you need to call, but take my advice and get your repentance in early.'

Gill stepped around Harley and grasped the door. After a few seconds of standing face to face, Harley slowly moved aside, leaving Gill free to stride across the foyer and out into the car park.

He took a few deep breaths and paused to look out over central Orkney, gazing over the lochs and the isthmus that divided them. From this elevated position, he could pick out the most prominent monuments, with traffic parked close to Brodgar and pedestrians making their way between the cars and the stones. He knew what it felt like when his mind crystallised uncertainty into conviction. And this was one of those moments. He stood and surveyed each dial on the Orcadian clock and experienced a sudden burst of pride. 'If you've done what I think you've done, you're a clever bugger, David Trevelyan. A clever, clever bugger.'

Chapter 35

Gill gave Harley some breathing space before he spoke to the police. One hour after leaving Harley's office, he sat in his car at Stromness and phoned the station in Kirkwall. The inspector posted to the ScoCion accident enquiry wasn't available, so Gill gave an oral statement about Harley's actions over the phone and arranged to appear in person later in the day. Gill expected to feel a sense of relief, of an endpoint, but instead, he had the growing sense that something was wrong. Badly wrong. Either Harley still wasn't being straight with him, or there was another force outside of his control. On impulse, Gill jumped in his car and drove to the other side of the village, where he banged on the door of the David Street Hostel. It took almost a minute for the manager to come to the door.

'Terry, I'm not sure if you remember me. I called a few weeks ago.'

Terry nodded. 'The magazine guy. Aye. Come in.'

Two teenage lads were picking at a late lunch as Terry showed Gill into the kitchen. They glanced up, nodded curtly and turned back to their phones. Terry didn't ask this time but just popped tea bags into two mugs and put the kettle on.

'Don't suppose you've come across our Euan on your travels?' said Terry without looking up.

Gill shook his head. 'No. Not a peep. He hasn't been back?'

'No one around here's seen him.'

‘I did make some progress with his book. It’s a long story, but it looks like Euan was trying to solve a very complex puzzle.’

Terry grunted. ‘That’s Euan. Always working at something. When he first came here, it was Sudoku, and eventually, it became ... well, I don’t understand enough of it even to explain it.’

‘Did he ever talk about ScoCion?’

Terry laughed. ‘You still don’t understand our Euan. He only talked when absolutely necessary.’

‘In what sense?’ said Gill, accepting the mug of tea.

‘Mealtimes, duty rosters, the weather forecast. Euan only spoke to exchange information. No small talk with that guy.’

‘Feckin’ weirdo’, said one of the lads at the table without looking up.

‘As I’ve explained’, said Terry elevating his voice but still looking at Gill. ‘It’s the lad’s condition. A bit like you and your recurring bouts of kleptomania.’

‘Least I’m a thief with a social life’, said the lad, turning his back on Terry.

‘But to properly answer your question’, said Terry, perhaps you should come with me. Gill picked up his tea and followed Terry out of the kitchen and up a grubby staircase to the first floor. Terry flicked on some lights, and Gill followed him down a dingy corridor until they stopped outside a bedroom door. ‘A cop called by the other day to say they’d suspended Euan’s case. I’m free to re-let the room, so I’ll be packing up his stuff this week.’

Gill sensed a whisper of disappointment in Terry’s voice. ‘You do your best for these kids, don’t you?’ he said.

Terry shrugged. 'A little bit social worker, a little bit jailer.' He smiled. 'Mainly, I'm their mum. Cuff them around the ears when they misbehave. Anyway, now the cops have finished, I thought you'd like a look around. Might yet do Euan some good.'

Gill smiled and nodded as he watched Terry unlock the door.

'He's alright, isn't he?' said Terry. 'Euan, I mean. Just taken himself off somewhere?'

Gill glanced at his feet. 'Honestly. I don't know.'

'I'll leave you to it', said Terry after a pause. 'Just let me know when you're done.'

Gill waited as Terry walked back down the corridor, keys swinging from the clip on his waist, then gently pushed the door and walked in.

Euan's room was like any teenager's room, and then it wasn't. Posters covered the walls in neat rows. Instead of musicians or football teams, the genre was Sci-fi scenes; spaceships real and imagined, a map of the solar system, schematics of non-existent starship engines. Immediately to Gill's right as he walked into the room, three old laptops sat side by side on an improvised workbench. Gill flipped up their lids and left them to boot up while he searched the rest of the room. A single bed filled the darkest corner of the room; the faded duvet cover bought long ago for a child. Next to this was a small bookcase filled with puzzle books. Gill plucked a few at random. They had all been filled in neatly with Euan's distinctive handwriting. Many were years old. Below these were computer journals of more recent vintage. Gill flicked through a couple, but they were technical beyond his comprehension. Goodness knows how Euan had obtained these on Orkney.

In the corner opposite the bed was a large but ancient wardrobe. Gill pulled it open. Euan had laid out one half with clothes in small neat piles. The other was given over to equipment Gill recognised. A lightweight theodolite and coils upon coils of cord, and an industrial tape measure amongst other tools. Half a dozen cardboard poster tubes nestled in one corner, bound together by a frayed piece of string. Gill left the door ajar and turned back to the machines.

To his surprise, the computers booted up without needing passwords. He opened the documents explorer on each in turn and searched for anything interesting. Instead, he found each machine clogged with old gaming software: worldbuilding, destiny adventures, multi-level task-based programs. The stuff was all quite dated, as Gill recognised several games from his youth. He opened a few and found their adventures were complete. Nodding with respect, Gill concluded Euan had a singular gift for problem-solving.

Nothing in the room suggested why Euan might have departed so suddenly. And at the back of his mind, Gill began to wonder if Harley, in his poor treatment of David Trevelyan, might be capable of even worse foul play if the guileless Euan had strayed across his path. Thinking about ScoCion, his eyes landed on a technical drawing on the wall above the PCs. Looking more closely, he saw it was a colour animation of the layout of the ion cannon and its supporting laboratories. Held to the wall by blue tack, Gill eased the brochure loose until he held it in his hands. Dated two years before, it was a publicity sheet for a series of community open days held after the completion of the site. The glossy material reflected light from the room's single window, and as Gill tilted the paper slightly he saw someone had traced around the drawing, perhaps more than once.

On instinct, he turned back to the bookcase, looking for folders or single sheets Euan might have sketched on. The neatness of the shelves made it a short and fruitless search. He turned to the wardrobe and pulled out the poster tubes. He opened each in turn, and from three, he pulled out arm's length strips of cream-coloured wallpaper. Gill spread them out on the floor. Reams of Euan's tiny writing packed the unprinted side of the sheets. At the centre of the first, Gill found a sketch of ScoCion, stencilled from the wall-hung version. From this anchor point, lines and boxes sprang out where Euan had interpreted the facility's capabilities. Gill screwed up his eyes and read a few of the boxes. He laid aside the first sheet with growing alarm and examined the second. He tossed this aside, too and scanned the third.

There was a chair in the room, a cast off from some office. Gill sank into it and urged his brain to fuse the ScoCion schematics with Euan's conclusions in the book of numbers. Then he grabbed the second sheet off the floor and searched for a paragraph he'd read earlier.

'Oh no', Gill spoke out aloud.

After a hasty thanks and goodbye to Terry, Gill was in his car and hurrying back to ScoCion. He parked in one of the visitor's spaces alongside a police car. As he ran into the building, he hoped this was because Harley had made the call. Prisha, the receptionist, advanced from being frosty to downright hostile.

'What the hell do you want now?' she said. 'Professor Harley is in a meeting and cannot be disturbed.'

'Actually, I've got something he needs to see.'

The receptionist turned away from him and leaned into an intercom. 'Security to the front desk, please.'

Fumbling for his phone, Gill searched for a number and tried to connect.

The answering voice was forcibly bright, 'Jenny Struan.'

'Jen. Are you in the building?'

'Yes, but …'

'I need you in reception right away.'

Jenny hung up without speaking and appeared moments later from a corridor at the far end of the atrium, just as two uniformed guards ran down a passage from the opposite side of the building. They all reached Gill simultaneously. In a flurry of shouting and arm-waving, he waited until Jenny calmed the situation enough to extract him towards the coffee area.

She sat down and put her hand up to speak first. 'Professor Harley has the police in with him right now. Did you help with that?'

Gill nodded. 'Without mentioning your name, I confronted Harley about planting David's car at the airport.' Jenny looked uncomfortable while Gill carried on. 'Then I pushed him about the system test on the 15th August. I'm glad to say he revealed the mission objectives.'

She leaned towards him. 'What did they do?'

'Hooked up with a distant spacecraft. Got a message out in real-time, with confirmation of that coming back via a conventional transmitter. That gave Harley proof of concept. But then they rushed ahead. They should have had a clue something was up when the showpiece test I attended in September went wrong. Still, Harley pressed forward with an experiment to teleport a small object between here and Sleet Moss.'

'Wait a second. Teleport?'

Gill shrugged. 'Until I know Harley's term for it, that's what I'm calling it. But the experiment failed and David was vapourised in the machine. Harley should have called a halt, but didn't. He buried his head and planned even more tests, even though something was wrong.'

Jenny sat wide-eyed. 'Go on.'

Gill laid three cardboard tubes in front of her. 'I think I've discovered the problem with Professor Harley's machine.'

'What are these?' asked Jenny, pulling one of the maps out of a tube.

'They are floor plans for this place', Gill replied. 'They're crude, but all the annotations suggest that their author has been inside the ScoCion building on multiple occasions.'

She flattened the paper on a nearby table. 'That's impossible. You've seen the security here.'

Gill pointed at the plan. 'I see potential ingress points marked here, here and here. By the looks of things, our map-maker watched this place being built.'

'Who is he?'

'Euan Mearns. He's been missing for weeks. I believe he's hidden in here all that time.'

'Parts of this operation are 24-7. He'd be spotted.'

Gill ran a forefinger over parts of the map. 'Think about it, Jenny. Every cupboard, every crawl space. This guy knows them all. But that's not everything. Look here.' Gill watched the colour drain out of Jenny's face. 'I'm not an expert, but these look like system passwords. And these sheets of paper are just the ones he didn't take with him.'

Jenny looked into his face for a second. 'Follow me.'

She walked back across the concourse and brushed aside Prisha's protestations as she marched towards Harley's office. She followed an authoritative rap on Harley's door by walking in. Two uniformed officers were taking a statement from Harley, who looked ashen-faced.

'Sorry, miss', said one of the officers. 'We need the professor's undivided for a few more minutes.'

'No problem', said Jenny. 'It's urgent, so I'll wait. It's just that Gill McArdle is here. He's discovered a bug in our system. ScoCion has been hacked.'

Chapter 36

The two policemen taking Harley's statement quickly realised they were out of their depth. After reaching out to the most senior officers on the island, Gill stepped in to suggest another detective they might call. Meanwhile, Harley sat at his desk with his head in his hands. The suggestion that an embedded intruder had compromised critical systems had crushed the remaining fight out of him.

'We need to organise a search', said Jenny. 'Can we use the annotated drawings you found in Euan's room?'

Gill nodded. 'That should give you some of his hiding places, his food sources and junctions where he might interface with ScoCion systems.'

'ScoCion has six floors, seven kilometres of corridor and one hundred and fifty-two rooms', mumbled Harley, his hands still cupped against his face. 'If he has access to all systems, he'll realise what we're doing as soon as we start looking for him.'

Gill nodded at the officers. 'I've got an idea that might help track him down.'

To avoid alerting Euan to their plans, it took Harley three hours to organise a detailed GPS sweep of the ScoCion building and ping a signal to the missing titanium orb. Harley detailed Euan's possible escape routes from the location detected three floors below, and gradually they formed a plan.

Under the control of the police officers, a cohort of ScoCion staff descended on Euan's likely position. It was another two hours before they found him, crouching in a distant storeroom, surrounded by laptops and neat stacks of mouldy food containers. They placed him in protective custody in a conference room and debated what to do next. The first instinct of the officers was to remove Euan to the local police station, but Harley's agitation convinced them to keep him close by. Someone needed to question him about what systems he had affected, but it wasn't clear who had the competence. After a heated debate, Gill persuaded the police to refrain from questioning Euan. 'His mental state is quite fragile. I suspect he thinks this is all a big game. If we change his context too much, I think he'll clam up.' He was mid-way explaining this to Harley for the third time when the receptionist came over and hovered until she got his attention.

Prisha's tone was apologetic. 'Sorry to interrupt, Mr McArdle, but the inspector has arrived.'

Gill thought she looked exhausted. He murmured a few words of thanks before striding out to the atrium, where a burly man with sagging facial features and a prominent bald spot was in animated conversation with the first officers on the scene. He turned to face Gill, leaving it to the younger man to close the distance between them.

'It's almost bloody midnight. What now, McArdle?'

'Inspector Wiley. Good to see you too.'

Wiley pulled an ugly, indignant face. 'So, we're the X-Files now. You and me. Plucky warriors against the sodding Celtic paranormal!'

Gill held up his hands. 'Honestly, I didn't know who else to call.' He dropped his voice so only Wiley could hear him. 'Look, you and I are not exactly pals. Put it this way; I'm not about to start sending you birthday cards. But you've got an open mind, and on a good day, you're quick to catch on.' He watched Wiley's face for a few seconds while the inspector tried to determine if he was catching a compliment or an insult. Then he continued. 'If you'll let me explain, I'm hoping we solve a very perplexing crime.'

Wiley looked at the floor for a few seconds, then focused on a distant point and nodded. 'Okay, McArdle. Find me a room where we can talk, and get someone to bring me a continuous supply of coffee. Let me have a word with the local plod and then let's get on with it.'

'Don't like Professor Harley', said Wiley while biting down on another sandwich. 'Slippery as shite. What makes you so sure the kid caused the accident and not the dodgy professor?'

'Harley takes his share of the blame', said Gill.

'Moving Trevelyan's car. Making up stories for the Safety Inspectorate. I don't know if the bugger has nine lives, but this will cost him two or three.'

'I see two issues at stake', said Gill, reaching uninvited for one of Wiley's biscuits. 'ScoCion has taken a pretty cavalier attitude to health & safety. Their senior management tried to cover up a fatal accident. And then we have Euan. Did he intentionally manipulate ScoCion mechanisms knowing it would cause David's death, or did his interference with the system unintentionally trigger the accident?'

'The arresting officers seem to think Euan is a bit slow', said Wiley, pulling the plate out of Gill's reach.

'I think the word is "autistic". In Euan's head, it's all a big game. He may not have realised the consequences of his actions.'

'Let's have a chat with him.'

Gill rubbed his face. 'Are you sure? It's the middle of the night.'

'He's awake, isn't he? You start him talking. It'll give me a minute to get the measure of him.'

'Doesn't he need a solicitor?'

'Not been charged yet. Just a chat for now. And only if the wee minger consents.'

Euan sat, arms folded, with a cup of tea and some biscuits untouched on the table in front of him. Gill tapped the window and walked in.

'Euan. I'm Gillan McArdle. You left me your book. Do you remember?'

Euan's twisted his neck to see Gill. Despite the late hour, the lad didn't look tired. 'You're from the magazine.'

'This other man is George. He's a police officer. Is it okay if we talk to you?'

Euan stared at Gill for a moment, then shrugged.

'I wanted to thank you. You gave me your book and helped me with the first part of the puzzle.' Gill smiled. 'I wouldn't have got past that level without you.'

Euan transferred his gaze to Wiley, then back to the opposite wall, but said nothing.

Gill moved a little closer. 'Euan, why did you give me the book of numbers? Why not someone else?'

Euan thought for a second. 'I like your magazine. You're good at solving things.'

'How did you know I'd be at Tormiston Mill the day I first met Juliette?'

Euan glanced up and right. 'Jenny Struan sent you emails. She promised you a car because you were working with Mrs Morrison.'

'And you could read those emails?' said Wiley.

'In ScoCion, I can read all the emails.'

'But why send me your book? What did that achieve?'

'In case I died.'

Wiley shot a glance at Gill. 'Why might you die, son?'

Euan studied Wiley's face for a moment while he considered his answer. 'This puzzle isn't like the others I've done. It's more real. If I can die in a computer game, then I could die in real life.'

'If you had died, why was it important I had your book?'

Euan blinked and gave a tiny shake of his head. Then he looked at Gill as if his question was the most insane thing he'd ever heard. 'This puzzle is awesome. It's like the biggest, hardest quest I'll ever do. If I didn't finish, then someone else had to.'

'Why the secrecy? Was someone scaring you? Is that why you are hiding in this laboratory?' said Wiley.

'I'm not a child', Euan replied. 'I don't do things because I'm scared.'

'Then why are you hiding inside ScoCion?' asked Gill. 'Instead of outside among the stones?'

Euan regarded Gill impassively. 'I'd done that part of the puzzle. The solution to that part points in here.'

'Why do you think that?'

Euan physically pulled back a little. 'Aren't you doing the puzzle?'

Gill pulled out a chair and slowly sat down. 'Yes, I'm doing it alright. I'm just approaching it from a slightly different angle.' He dropped his gaze towards the table while considering what to say next. 'I know ScoCion was a landmark on the Brodgar map. I'm guessing you found the significant date in the middle of August?'

Euan nodded. 'Jim thought that would be the end of it. That the man he was waiting for would come back. When that didn't happen, I knew the puzzle had another level.'

'Are you talking about Jim Robertson?'

'Yes. I met him among the stones. I saw him measuring and thinking, so I knew he was working on a puzzle. He wouldn't tell me what it was. He invited me to join his group and promised to tell me about the puzzle later. He started to tell me about a man who was coming, but I didn't care about that. When I found out what the puzzle was, I left the group. I wanted to work on it alone.'

'You and Jim', interrupted Wiley. 'Are you friends?'

Euan stared blankly back at him. 'No.'

'Are you enemies?'

'No.'

'What about parents? Where are your mum and dad?'

'My mother is dead, and my father doesn't love me. I was in the foster system, but now I live at Terry's house, and it's nice because I don't have to speak to people, much.'

'What did you do after you left Jim's group?' asked Gill.

Euan turned to him. 'I did lots of things.'

'Can you tell me about the things you did that relate to the puzzle?'

Euan glanced up and right. 'I kept working. When the day came, the 15th August, for that is what the puzzle was really about, I stood at a distance and watched Jim's group to see what would happen.'

'Go on', said Wiley.

'The whole day passed, and some people started to leave, which was strange because someone had done a lot of work to set the puzzle, and that meant something important should happen. Then right at the end of the day, I saw headlights up at ScoCion. I already knew ScoCion was part of the puzzle because it's on the map. I'd been researching it for a long time, before I realised the next stage of the puzzle was going to happen here. I waited that day until the cars were gone, and then I came up. The gates were locked, but I walked around because it's never properly dark at that time of year. I found a back entrance and got inside. After that, I moved around.'

'You hid well', said Gill. 'They never knew you were here.'

'You did. The men who found me said you knew exactly where to look.'

'That's because you kept the titanium orb.'

Euan glanced away and briefly looked cross. 'I shouldn't have kept it. But I thought it might be part of the puzzle.'

'Why did you remove it from the chamber?'

'It takes lots of energy to transmit elements with high atomic weights. I removed it because I needed the energy to transmit something else.'

'But you kept it with you?'

'I didn't realise it had a GPS beacon.'

Wiley sat down and opened his mouth to speak, but Gill glared at him and shook his head. 'Tell me. Once you came here, did you ever leave?'

'Only once. To leave my book for you at Tormiston.'

'What were you doing inside ScoCion for all that time?'

Euan's gaze slipped from Gill's face to the floor. 'This building is massive inside. I found places to hide and food to eat. I read their notes and discovered the machine's purpose. I knew from the stones that whoever had set the puzzle had gone back in time. To make the puzzle work, someone would have to go back in time to initiate it. It's a continuous loop, you see. For us to find the puzzle today, someone had to go back to yesterday. I changed the machine, so the puzzle worked.'

Wiley leaned deep into Gill's personal space and made a gentle clucking sound. Gill ignored him. 'How exactly did you change the machine, Euan?'

For the first time, Euan shifted slightly in his seat. 'I waited for the right experiment and then I trapped a man in the chamber.'

'The engineer?' asked Gill.

'Yes. I wanted to go myself, but that would have created a circular reference.'

Wiley cleared his throat. 'A what, son?'

'It's a formula that cannot calculate because it references itself. The person who solves a puzzle cannot be the one who sets it.'

'Let me be clear', said Gill. 'You're saying that over the space of just a few weeks; you learnt how to manipulate ScoCion's systems?'

'I had all their documentation. I didn't need to write any code. Just edit what was there.'

Wiley laid his hands on the table. 'Euan, are you saying you killed a man?'

Euan shook his head. 'I didn't kill him. I sent him back.'

A silence hung in the air for a moment until Wiley leaned into Gill again, motioning towards the door. But Gill pressed on. 'Where did you send him, Euan?'

'You mean, *when* I did I send him. To before the stones, I think. Otherwise, we would have no puzzle.'

'Did you not think about the consequences for the man trapped in the chamber?'

Euan screwed up his face. 'Consequences?'

'Yes. If what you say is true, you took a man out of the life he was living here and now. A life with friends and family. And you sent him somewhere that was alien to him.'

Euan placed his hands on the table and held them, palms up. 'The puzzle was already set. It just needed farming to make it work.'

'Farming, son?' snorted Wiley.

'It's gaming slang', said Gill. 'Euan used resources within the context of his game to strengthen his capabilities.'

'It's not my game', Euan snapped back. 'It was already here.'

Gill struggled to keep emotion out of his voice. 'I'll ask you again, Euan. Did you consider the consequences for the man you sent back?'

Euan was starting to get flustered now and couldn't keep exasperation out of his voice. 'His life's work was already written in the stones.'

A long pause drew the conversation to a close. Eventually, Gill nodded and glanced at Wiley. 'Okay. Thank you, Euan.'

Wiley wearily got to his feet, pausing as Euan turned forcefully towards him. 'Can I go back to Terry's now? I think this puzzle is finished.'

Gill could see Wiley was working to contain his anger.

The inspector joined Gill at the door. 'We're going to have to see about that, son.'

'Fat lot of good that was', spat Wiley. 'If the kid is guilty of anything, he'd get off on the grounds of diminished responsibility.'

Gill sighed and leaned his weight against the office wall. 'I know it sounds like nonsense, but I suggest you confront Harley with some of Euan's claims. If you push him, I suspect he'll show you test data proving Euan's ideas are plausible.'

Wiley broke into a braying laugh. 'Time travel! You need a holiday, pal.'

Chapter 37

Sergeant Ayles opened the interview room door and held it open as Wiley brushed past him. The Inspector glanced around the unfamiliar room before pulling up a chair in front of a man charged with attempted murder. Wiley looked as if he was in a foul mood. Perhaps it was the loss of a night's sleep, or maybe he was always this way. He made a bit of a show, organising his paperwork and finding a pen that was to his satisfaction. Meanwhile, Ayles set up the recorder and introduced those attending the interview.

'Jim Robertson', began Wiley. 'Can I call you Jim?

In response, Jim nodded.

'Please repeat for the tape that you have declined to have legal representation at this meeting.'

Jim shook his head. 'I don't need a lawyer.'

Wiley nodded. 'And you're not retracting you're earlier confession that you tried to kill Gillan McArdle?'

'I'm not, no.'

'Can you help me understand your motives, Jim?'

'Motives?'

'Well, I have to confess, there've been a few times when I could have crushed Gill McArdle's head under a four-tonne block of sandstone, but I've never acted on that impulse. Why did you?'

Jim rocked in his chair a few times before answering. 'I believed it was my duty.'

'Duty. Why?'

'He was attempting to desecrate a grave.'

Wiley looked up from his notes and pushed back his glasses. 'But he's an archaeologist. They dig stuff up, don't they? And I gather he had the partial consent of the trust.'

'Hardly. The dig permit wasn't until next May.'

'If they had delayed the dig, would you have tried to kill him then?'

Jim looked away and thought for a moment. 'It depends. But yes, probably.'

Wiley tilted his palms towards Jim. 'What's so special about this grave?'

'With respect, Mr Wiley, as a secularist like Douglas here, you wouldn't understand.'

Wiley switched his expression to mock offence. 'Try me.'

Jim put his hands on the table and exhaled a long slow breath. 'I'm the custodian of a group called "The Vigil". We have a sacred duty to protect the stones and prepare for the king who said he would be born again.'

'Fascinating', said Wiley, although his face didn't seem to agree. 'And who is this king?'

'My group believes he will open the way for the second coming of our Lord.'

'I had a wander around Kirkwall in the early hours', said Wiley. 'Looked a bit grim in the dark but didn't look like the apocalypse to me.'

Jim raised a hand. 'Please don't insult me, Inspector. Whatever you think of my beliefs, I think I'm due a little tolerance.'

'Oh, you'll find I'm very tolerant, Jim. Go on then. What makes the stones so important?'

Jim sighed and made a show of mustering up his patience. 'A singular intelligence constructed the Orcadian monuments. That's not up for dispute. It's all in the maths.'

'Fine', said Wiley, making a note. 'McArdle mentioned that, so I'll run with it for the moment. This higher intelligence; where's it from?'

'Not an *it*. A *he*.'

Wiley dismissively waved a hand. 'Sorry, I was busy finding my tolerant face. Where is "he" from?'

Jim offered up empty palms. 'He was a highly enlightened individual. Just possibly, he was a supernatural being.' He saw the incredulous expression on Wiley's face and shouted down the officer's next question. 'He was a king who brought peace after a time of war. Abundant food after a long famine. And technological advance beyond the wildest dreams of his contemporaries. Goodness knows, when you look at our world, we could use a man like that.' Jim raised a forefinger to head height. 'Which is why I believe him when he said he would be born again.'

Wiley nodded and reached for a biscuit. He stared at Jim while he chewed. 'Like, reincarnated?'

Jim suppressed a sarcastic smile. 'Reincarnation, no. To the best of our knowledge, this king has been dead for four thousand years.'

Wiley clipped his pen shut and then used it to scratch the back of his head. 'He's dead, but you expect him to come back to life one day?'

'Yes', said Jim. 'He said he would be born again one day and he gave us a date.'

'A date! That sounds specific', said Wiley. 'What is this date?'

Jim screwed up his face and looked away.

'Mr Robertson, the date?'

Jim sighed. '15th August this year.'

'Okay. How do you know that?'

Jim gave his head a brief shake. 'It's complicated. Suffice to say the date is recorded in the stones.' He watched Wiley's face cloud again and tried to clarify his remark. 'The Brodgar stone circle, and the other Neolithic monuments. Someone built them to confer that particular date.'

'15th August', repeated Wiley.

'Yes. Look, if you're desperate to know the detail, ask McArdle. He seems to have worked it out.'

Wiley nodded and made another note. 'This, "Vigil", you mention; what exactly is that?'

Jim's gaze lifted upwards and right. 'We're a group of people devoted to waiting for the reappearance of the born-again king.'

'Yeah, we were discussing him a second ago. You reckon he's, what, Jesus?'

Jim shrugged. 'More probably a forerunner. Someone like John the Baptist.'

Wiley smiled and nodded. 'I remember him. The voice of "one crying in the wilderness". Sounds like you and old John would have had quite a bit in common. Lemme know if you fancy a plate of locusts.'

Jim pushed off the jibe by sneering and looking away.

'This group you lead. It seems you're all so devoted, you'd be prepared to kill to advance your aims. I'm going to need their names.'

Jim stared back at him but said nothing.

'Come on! Let's have a list of your Orcadian jihadists', goaded Wiley.

'Are you mocking us?'

Wiley ignored the question. 'Where is he? This king. I checked the calendar before I came in. Shouldn't he have popped up by now?'

'Well, he hasn't.' Jim hesitated, then glared at Wiley. 'Probably because of McArdle's interference. McArdle digging in his grave!'

Wiley lifted defensive hands. 'Just trying to get my head around why a good citizen like yourself, with not as much as a parking ticket to blemish his record, is suddenly prepared to become a killer.'

Jim lurched onto his elbows and stared at the table. 'Okay, let me try and explain this. When 15th August came, we gathered at the stones before dawn. You have to understand; I've devoted my adult life preparing for the king's return. I've no doubt about the date – I've checked it a dozen times. But we stood all day, and no one came.' Jim paused, his gaze drifting down.

'Go on', said Wiley.

'Some members of the group got frustrated and fell away. The rest of us kept waiting. A bit discouraged but hanging on. Then, just before midnight, we saw lights on Rusky Hill. It's one of the map points indicated by the stone cypher and matches ScoCion's location. We noticed a man watching us from the edge of Stenness. We called out to him, but he disappeared. The group chased after him but didn't catch him. After that, the group gave up and dispersed.' He sighed. 'But we'd recognised him.'

'Who was he?' interrupted Wiley.

'Euan Mearns. A lad who'd briefly been a member of the group. The thought occurred to me that Euan might be the man we were waiting for, although knowing his interest in the stones, I suspected he was just another foreteller like me. After that night, I didn't see him again, and it was like he had slipped off the face of the earth.'

'Eventually, someone reported him missing', offered Wiley.

'Not until quite recently', Jim continued. 'And then Gillan McArdle came sniffing about "The Vigil" with the sceptical air of the resolute unbeliever. He was hanging around the stones and trying to desecrate the circle's centre. By now, the group had shrunk to a core of truly faithful. We concluded that the king was delaying his return because of the desecration of his original resting place. Some in the group resolved to kill McArdle, and reluctantly, I agreed this was the only way forward.'

'You make it sound so reasonable', muttered Wiley. 'And was your group responsible for sabotaging ScoCion equipment?'

'No. We treated it with the respect that's due to any of the revered places identified by the stones.'

Wiley made some notes, and a period of silence opened up between the two men. Eventually, Wiley clicked his pen closed and looked up. 'I suppose that's the thing about religion.'

'Not sure what you mean …' Jim trailed off.

'You don't get what you want, so you decide it's okay to kill someone. You think if you do that in the name of God, or some long-dead king, or whatever, you can suddenly justify murder.'

Jim face hardened, and he looked away. 'We're done here.'

Wiley leaned back in his chair. 'I assure you, Mr Robertson. We most certainly are not.'

Gill stood outside the cell door and asked himself again if he wanted to face Jim Robertson. Sergeant Ayles jangled the keys again, impatient for Gill to make up his mind. At the officer's subliminal prompt, Gill nodded and watched Ayles unlock the door and walk into the cell.

As Gill followed, he thought Jim Robertson looked diminished, sitting on a low bed, wearing a bland tracksuit the station had provided for him. The sergeant asked him to stand up and present his wrists to receive handcuffs. He gave Jim a dry stare and said, 'I'll be right outside. Any problems here, we'll see what we can add to your charge sheet.'

'There won't be any problem, Douglas', said Jim, sitting back on the bed as Ayles turned and walked out, leaving the cell door ajar.

He returned moments later with a chair for Gill, which he placed near the door. 'Ten minutes, gents', he said, pulling the door.

Gill grasped the seat and sat down. 'Inspector Wiley said you wanted a word with me.'

Jim nodded. 'Up until a few weeks ago, I'd never heard of you, Mr McArdle. I wanted to understand the reason for your persecution of my group and my cause?'

Gill crossed his legs. 'I don't know what you mean.'

'Well, ever since Morrison recruited you to come and inspect the Chi Rho stone, you've done nothing but rake the precious ground my people hold dear.'

Gill was puzzled. 'You identified the midden. I'm not sure what you thought would happen. I'm an archaeologist, Jim. I dig things up.'

Jim forced out a smile. 'Dig things up! You stepped in the way of my destiny. Deflected it. And I need to understand why it became your personal mission to destroy us. Tell me that, and I'll be happy.'

'It did become personal, Jim. But I was never against you. I was just trying to help a friend.'

'That self-serving brat, Euan Mearns?'

'No. Not him. My friend David Trevelyan.'

'The chap who died at ScoCion? I was sorry to hear that, but at the end of the day, isn't he just a clumsy scientist who died at the hands of his own machine?'

Gill wasn't sure whether to answer *yes* or *no*, so he countered with his own question. 'Do you know the significance of 15th August this year?'

Jim sat back a little. 'I do.'

'Humour me. So that I know we're on the same page.'

Jim glanced away. 'It's all in the stones. The representation of the planets, the simple mechanics of their positioning points to a date.' He turned to face Gill again. 'But you know that. You've got Euan Mearns' book.'

'The one you wanted to relieve me of.'

Jim grunted. 'Twitch built his work on mine. And I built my work on the shoulders of those in "The Vigil" who went before me. It should never have fallen into your hands.'

'Euan left it with me for safekeeping.'

'If I'd known how close he was to solving the cypher ...' Jim's voice trailed off.

'What? Tried to kill him like you tried to kill me?'

Jim shook his head. 'He could have been a believer. I should have drawn him back in. It was a mistake to let him go off on his own, but we were so close to the date I put Euan out of my mind. And then he disappeared. I assumed he'd left the island.'

'Okay', said Gill. 'The date was recorded in the stones, but I'll ask you again, do you know its significance?'

'The king from ancient times. He was to be born again. The date must be his birth, or perhaps the start of his new earthly kingdom.'

Gill's head bobbed from side to side a few times. 'That's one point of view. Are you aware it was also the date of humanity's first test of faster-than-light communication with a far-off space object? It's not in the news yet, but in the future, this date will be as famous as Alexander Graham Bell's first transatlantic telephone call.'

This time Jim blinked but said nothing.

'Anyway, it now appears that my friend didn't die at ScoCion. A few weeks after the 15th August, they ran a follow-up experiment designed to test their theory about teleportation. Instead, Euan Mearns sabotaged the machine, which threw David back in time to the Neolithic era.'

Jim laughed. 'That's preposterous!'

'On that we're very much agreed', said Gill. 'But I do have several lines of proof that I'll be outlining in my magazine. But, "The Vigil" set me thinking. I started wondering if my friend David could be this king you've been talking about.'

Jim's head tilted a little to one side. 'I don't follow you.'

'Think about it. The core of your belief talks about a king who will be born again. The evidence suggests David Trevelyan died a very long time ago. But the David who became my friend wasn't born until thirty-five years ago. I'm suggesting this king of yours was born again, in 1988, then cast back four and a half thousand years, and is now naturally deceased.'

Jim shook his head. 'That's nonsense. And nothing you've said ties with the 15th August.'

'But it does. David was the chief engineer on the faster-than-light test. Knowing the exact position of the planets on that particular day was critical to the success of his mission. And that's why they're recorded so accurately in the stones.'

Jim shook his head more vigorously. 'You can't prove that.'

Gill smiled. 'I couldn't, at first.' He paused, then added, 'Until I realised we've already recovered his body.'

'What body?'

'The one we found in the Brodgar circle. The one you worked so hard to prevent us from uncovering. You seem to think that if we disturbed the bones of this messiah of yours, he'd take the huff and not come back. Whether he's your ancient king or not, those bones are all that remains of David Trevelyan. And I can prove it.'

'How?'

'The skull held a ring in its mouth, bearing the same inscription as one worn by David as his wedding band.'

Jim looked momentarily dazed.

For the first time, Gill could see what this man was losing. 'I'm sorry, Jim. This king of yours? He's been, he's gone, and he's not coming back. But he has left three sensational children and his unique contribution to human knowledge in the faster-than-light experiments.'

Jim said nothing but scowled and closed his eyes.

'I need to go. But just to let you know that David, this "king" as you know him, will always be with you in a small and important way.'

Jim opened his eyes but said nothing.

'We got enough DNA from the Brodgar skeleton to make a ninety-five per cent match with David. The thing is, David was from Cornwall, not Orkney.'

'What of it?'

'I looked into the Scottish DNA database, and it's likely that "Brodgar Man", as the body is now being called, was the first local inhabitant with the distinctive Cornish DNA pattern.'

Jim shrugged, and Gill got up to leave. 'In a little slip of police protocols, I managed to get a keek at the DNA test the police took from you after your arrest.' He paused, making sure he had Jim's attention. 'Your profile carries the same distinctive Cornish gene.'

'Sergeant Ayles', Jim called. 'This man is taking liberties with my personal data!'

Gill picked up the chair and pushed it out into the corridor. 'We'll never know for certain if David was the historical figure you were waiting for. One thing we do know, Jim. You're descended from him.'

Chapter 38

Gill drove through Kirkwall on what would probably be his last house call at the Trevelyan's for quite some time. He'd felt a measure of peace these last few days, but when Alice texted him earlier, asking for a visit, he wasn't sure what he would find.

He found Alice's door slightly ajar, so he pushed on into the porch. The warm sound of small children enjoying food greeted his arrival. Alice must have heard the door because her head appeared, and she beckoned him to join her in the family lounge. She gave him a fleeting hug, and they settled into separate sofas.

'Mum's feeding the kids', she said.

'They sound happy.'

She gave a sad smile. 'It's Grannie's gig. What David would call, "Dinner and a show".'

'Don't resent their fun', he found himself saying. 'They need to recover from this too.'

Her lips pursed, and gradually her frown softened. 'You know, that's quite insightful.'

He shrugged. 'Coming up in your rear-view mirrors, emotionally.'

A proper smile finally crept onto her face. 'About. Bloody. Time.'

'How are you doing?'

She looked away. 'Yesterday, I accepted Juliette Morrison's offer to view the bones.'

'Oh.'

'It was so weird. She explained that "Brodgar Man" had been a good old age when he died.' The back of her left hand came to her mouth, and she took a few moments to steady herself. 'It's him, Gill. Just being there beside him, I could feel it.'

He tried to keep uncertainty off his face. 'I believe that too.'

'And she showed me the Chi Rho stone.' Alice smiled at him and shook her head. 'The Chi Rho symbol. You should have mentioned it! David used it in all his personal messages. Look. I'll show you.' She reached over to a shelf, plucking a greeting card from its resting place and passed it to Gill. It was David's last hand-written message to her, apologising for messing up their anniversary meal and promising to make it up to her. He had signed it off with a single kiss and a Chi Rho, swiftly scratched in black biro.

Gill swallowed. 'What did the symbol mean to David?' he asked.

Alice took the card and cherished it for a few moments. 'Alpha and Omega. His promise to love me for ever and ever. And for us both to move forward in God's strength.'

Gill let out a long, slow breath. The answer to his puzzle had been under his nose since his first visit. And slowly, it dawned on him what David had tried to express, four-thousand years ago. 'When you see the effort, the gigantic human effort he invested to tell you that, one last time? Alice, you need to know, he loved you so much.'

Alice teared up at that and Gill had to wait a full minute until she could speak again. 'Dear God, I'm so glad you were here, Gill.'

'In … In a terrible sense, I feel guilty for what's happened to you.'

'Goodness sakes, Gill. Why?'

His shoulders jumped up and down. 'I dunno. One day I pitch up in your lives after all these years, and a few weeks later, David is gone.'

'It wasn't your fault. It couldn't be your fault!'

'If I'd been quicker connecting Euan Mearns to ScoCion…'

She waved a hand at him. 'You found David's body. It was no coincidence you were here this week.'

'You can't be saying …' He paused to clear his throat. 'That God sent me into this sorry mess?'

Now, she leaned across the room and grabbed his nearest wrist. 'I believe God knew what was coming. And he sent you to make it easier for me. To find David and explain what happened. Even if I grieve every day of my life until I see David again, I'll always be grateful you were here.'

Gill looked across at her. He felt wretched and wasn't sure why. Eventually, he found a form of words. 'This faith of yours, Alice, I don't want it.'

Her thin smile didn't judge him as she released her grip. 'Why not?'

He looked away, feigning distraction by some passing teenagers walking home from school. 'Because if I do, I'll have to make a choice. To either spurn a higher power I've come to believe in or find myself compelled to dig deeper and do something about it.'

Alice slowly shook her head. 'I think it's a bit late for you to worry about what you want.'

'I still have free will, right?'

'Sure. But what's the choice on offer? Ignore all the evidence there's a divine hand at work in your life? Or press forward and find forgiveness for your mistakes, and a source of hope for your future with Salina? Dare I say; you might even conceive of an eternity where you might see your old family again.'

He twisted his neck and shoulders as if evading pain. 'I think I like God better when he's a myth.'

Alice laughed. 'And I thought you loved to bury yourself in a big mystery.'

'I do!'

'Then, why dodge the biggest mystery of them all?'

Gill had no answer to that.

She stood up on her way to the kitchen and patted his hand as she passed. 'Look on the bright side. You were never the fastest learner. It will probably take you years.'

He could hear her in the kitchen. She was chatting to her mum while the kettle boiled, forcing herself to be bright for her children. He found himself thinking about Jim Robertson and his futile wait for his returning "king". Gill didn't want to be like that. Nor did he want to kneel by a manger in a stable. Or go to church. Or drink tea with old ladies, or sing the hallelujah chorus, or mumble hymns that made him want to scream with boredom. He didn't want to hang out with Christians or give money to the poor, to feel any compulsion to campaign for justice, or join in some half-hearted attempt to keep Sundays special. He seethed about all the things he didn't want and the people he didn't want to become, until at last, he was sure he could hear somebody laughing in the background. His mind flitted to that last day on Harris two years before, when Ailsa touched the surviving Waterhorse. What had she said? A king was coming, and this was his horse?

He covered his face with his hands. 'Oh, dear God', he whispered. 'Please don't be real.'

More laughing. Another batch of teenagers, walking past the house.

A minute later, Alice returned. 'I'd like you to help me with two things', she said, placing a mug of coffee beside him.

He pulled his hands from his face, and his eyes stung. 'Anything.'

'Tomorrow, I'd like to hold a small gathering at Brodgar. David lay there for all those years, and I think that's where we should go to say goodbye to him.'

'Sure. I'll speak to Juliette. Then Mack. I'll ask him to say a few words.'

'Thank you.'

'And the second thing?'

'The second thing', she said, her voice cracking and her forearms pulled tight around her face to suppress whatever was boiling inside her. 'You've been through a trauma and made it out the other side. Now I'd like you to pray that same healing for me.'

Chapter 39

The next morning came in cold and blustery. Gill stood back from Alice as she lingered in the centre of the Brodgar stone circle. David's remains were in a laboratory now, but this spot had been his grave for four thousand years. The small family gathering was a sober affair, with everyone dislocated by the obscurity of what had happened. Pastor Mack had done an excellent job, reminding everyone who David had been to them all. And whether dead in this century or one long passed, his eternal destiny was the thing that gave them hope.

Alice looked tired, but Gill found warmth in her smile as she walked over to him and took his hand. 'Thank you', she said. 'Thank you for finding him.'

Gill stared down at his feet for a few moments before looking back at her. 'You realise very few people will ever accept this version of events. Even the scientist in me screams that the bones we found were just the remains of another traveller from Cornwall. It's not unreasonable, you know.'

'I know', said Alice. 'But the ring, Gill. No one else can explain away the ring.'

'To believe the ring is genuine, you have to trust the person who found it.'

Alice smiled her thin, tired smile. 'I remember a time when you would have crawled over broken glass to make me happy. And the Gill McArdle I knew was never very good at lying.'

Gill blushed. 'That's why they caught me the one time I tried.'

Alice turned and looked down at the place where David lay. 'Sounds like he had quite a family the second time around.'

'Does it bother you? That he started again.'

After the shortest of pauses, Alice shook her head. 'You knew him. He enjoyed his work, but he loved being a family man.'

She looked over to where the rest of the group murmured amongst themselves. A few had started walking back to the cars.

'Come back and see us, Gill. I'd love to meet Salina.' Her hand slid away from him, and she walked slowly to where her mother was standing with the twins.

He watched them leave, threading back across the moor, their backs to him, heads hung low. Little Noah lingered the longest. He stood in front of Gill, staring up at him as if he had something to say. Eventually, Gill stooped close to the boy and beckoned him closer.

'A few years ago, I lost my mother to a horrible disease. A little while after that, my brother died in an accident', said Gill.

Noah's perplexed face stared back at him, wondering perhaps why this pep talk wasn't more cheerful.

'What I'm saying', Gill continued, 'You need to stay strong. There's always a little sadness in life but don't let it spoil the wonderful years you have ahead of you because the truth is, my sadness almost spoiled mine. You've been braver than I ever knew how to be. And you need to know your dad would be so proud of you.'

Noah rubbed his nose with the back of his hand. 'Will I ever see him again?'

'Your mother …'

'What do you think?'

Gill smiled and looked at the boy's feet for a few seconds. 'Do you know, I've come to believe you will. And meanwhile, every day you look in the mirror, you'll see a reminder of him.'

Noah nodded thoughtfully for a moment. Then without warning, he sprang forward and hugged Gill. When he stepped back, Gill was suppressing a lump in his throat. 'Now, you need to go and catch your mother. She'll be wondering where you are.'

Gill watched Noah turn and run, slowing to a walk as he closed the gap on his mum. Gill kept his attention on the boy for a minute. Then his eyes drifted, to the stones, perplexed by all that David had achieved. After daydreaming for a few moments, he checked to see if the child was safe. He stood up to better see across the hillocks and hollows of the moor. He could see Noah at the back of the group. But now, his hand was held tenderly by a large olive-skinned man in black leather, twin swords strapped to his back. As they walked along, the man tilted his body to talk privately to the boy. Gill watched as the pair stopped; Raphael squatting and drawing the boy to face him. Gill's heart raced as Raphael reached behind his left shoulder and slowly drew a sword. He held it for the boy, hilt first, bearing the weight of it as Noah traced his finger over complex etchings in the surface of the blade. Gill's eyes filled unexpectedly with tears, and he turned away from the scene.

It took him a minute to recover, and when he next looked up, Noah was running to catch up with his mother.

Raphael, and the sword he'd shown to the boy had disappeared.

The crunch of heather and bracken brought him back to his senses, and he became aware Raphael was approaching him from a completely different direction. Gill watched and waited until Raphael was close enough to talk.

'Is he all right?' Gill asked.

Raphael's broad shoulders indicated the slightest of shrugs as he gazed into the far distance. 'I've been watching Noah for a while now. He misses his father, but he will prosper.'

Gill stared at the man, boring his gaze into Raphael's inscrutable eyes. 'And were you watching over David?'

'Not me. Another', said Raphael, looking across to where the stones stood stark against the sky.

Gill shook his head to clear the fog. 'Why didn't you save him? Saved him the way you've saved me?'

Raphael's shoulders sagged a little, and he drew a hand across his chin. 'We did. Many times.'

'But you didn't bring him home.'

'That wasn't our assignment.'

Gill stared at him. 'But you could have. You could have stopped a decent family man from being separated from his wife and children. Instead, he plunged into some kind of Neolithic hell.'

Raphael turned sharply. 'It might have been strange for him, but it certainly wasn't hell. He grew to love this place. And he loved its people, and they loved him. That's why they raised the stones in his honour.'

Gill couldn't prevent a look of disbelief from spreading across his face. 'But how? He was one man. One man dislocated in time.'

'It's simple. David was a young man with knowledge far above his peers. In due course, he rose to become the preeminent man of his people. As king, he unified the northern tribes, pushed away famine and led a culture so advanced its influence would reach the Mediterranean. And when he finished all that, he allowed himself one indulgence. To plan these monuments so he could tell his first family he was safe with God.'

'David was ambushed by a delinquent young man playing an elevated video game. And you're telling me he was safe with God?'

'You've got a lot to learn, Gill', Raphael said, holding up a hand to stop Gill's protests. For a moment, they both stood silent. 'Which reminds me. You really need to take this.' Raphael drew the same sword he'd offered to Noah minutes before and offered it to Gill across his outstretched palms.

Gill studied the intricate Celtic engraving that ran the length of the blade. 'It's beautiful, but I'm not the sword-fighting kind of guy.'

'A time is coming soon when you might want to learn.'

'You make it sound like I'll need to defend myself.'

'Darkness has smothered the land.' Raphael sighed. 'Until the Light returns, we must stand. Will you stand with me?'

'What good is a sword in a twenty-first-century conflict?'

Raphael laughed gently. 'Gosh! Maybe the sword is symbolic of some other kind of power.'

'I don't know what it stands for.'

'Actually, I think you do.'

Raphael flipped up the weapon, catching the sword blade mid-flight and thrusting the hilt towards Gill. 'In the conflict still to come, who do you want to be, Gillan McArdle? A casualty or a general?'

Angrily, Gill studied the weapon in Raphael's outstretched hand. The man should have cut himself in that last manoeuvre, and yet his grip was firm and unbloodied. Making up his mind, Gill grasped the hilt and felt the weight of the blade. Slowly, he swung it from side to side, finding it far heavier than he'd expected and yet, beautifully balanced. As he did so, he had a flashback to the night in the B&B when he'd studied the words on David's ring.

'How do I know any of this is true?' asked Gill.

'You mean God and the Bible?'

'Yes.'

Raphael's hands fell to his sides. 'All of this and you still need more proof?'

'Yes', Gill spat.

Raphael laughed and turned to leave. Sniffing the air, he scanned the horizon. 'You and David were playing a chess game, do you remember?'

'It's still on my phone.'

'Then, on David's behalf, from his deathbed, I offer you his last move. He moves Rook to D8.'

Gill switched the sword to his left hand while he fumbled for his phone and entered his security code. 'As I recall, I had him on the rack.' He launched the app and looked up, but Raphael had already disappeared. Gill walked to the nearest sandstone slab and leaned against it. He brought up the game and punched in David's move. Staring at the screen for a few more moments, Gill double-checked the app before acknowledging he'd been outmanoeuvred.

'Checkmate', he whispered to himself.

Chapter 40

Gill shook the tension out of his limbs as the Thursday evening flight to Dundee cleared the airfield and started to climb out over the sea. The island of Shapinsay loomed in the window, then quickly fell away to the left. He was sitting alone in a sparsely populated cabin. Looking across the aisle, he watched the Orcadian islands for as long as he could, the rolling landscape punctuated by streaks of silver sunlight reflecting off countless sea lochs. He thought about Juliette Morrison and whispered aloud to himself in what amounted to a prayer for her well-being. She'd greeted him warmly that afternoon when he'd called as arranged at her home on the way to the airport. It troubled him that she still wasn't sure in her own mind what had transpired amongst the Brodgar stones. 'I guess we're not allowed the luxury of absolute certainty', he'd said, and she'd agreed with him. She'd looked diminished from the women he'd met only a few weeks before, but her last words to him as he turned to leave were as good a mantra as any. 'In future, McArdle. Just bloody go for it.'

But today, at least, Dundee lay ahead. The next publisher's meeting was tomorrow, and he wasn't expecting an easy ride. Afterwards, along with Cassy and the team, he would put another magazine issue to bed. Then he would be back in Montrose to see Gordon, and finally, by Saturday afternoon, he'd be alone with Salina. She planned to join him to visit his father, and then he would steer them towards her favourite east coast beach at St Cyrus. Somewhere along the miles of golden sand, backed by cliffs haunted by peregrines, he would address the best relationship in his life. He'd only known her a few months, but he was ready to offer Salina the deepest commitment in his power to give.

He dipped his hand in his pocket and pulled out the ring he'd bought from Juliette's jeweller friend. An eternity ring of sea-blue sapphires, interspersed with small diamonds. Salina had been engaged before and had been reluctant to wear the large diamond stud that tended to snag on everything. 'Too damn big to wear on a boat', she'd complained. He hoped the compact lines of the eternity ring would be more practical. He closed the box and put it back in his pocket. Gazing over the empty sea, he could see patches of dazzling water where sunlight was reflected, interspersed with dark patches beneath the clouds. The whole scene standing as a metaphor for the life he was challenged and, at the same time, blessed to live.

Chapter 41

Gill, we've got to be careful here', said Tony.

Gill glanced at Cassy, then at the other faces around the table at the publisher's meeting.

He'd never seen his boss looking so anxious. 'Do you want me to go through the evidence again? It's technical, but I'll make it as simple as I can.'

'It's okay. I get it. The problem is that time travel will not sit easily with people, no matter how many words you use.' Tony leaned back in his chair and peered back at Gill. 'I've always given you a long leash. But this is a massive risk to our credibility.'

Gill spread his hands out in front of him. 'Review the data, Tony. If you can find a way to tell the story but treat the time travel element as unproven, I'm all ears.'

'The data just isn't conclusive. What we've got is a theory. One that could make us a laughing stock.'

'I think we should take that risk. If only to put the spotlight on ScoCion's dangerous experiments.'

Tony got up and walked slowly to the conference room window. The outlook onto the back of the old post office building was unspectacular. 'I'll back you, Gill. Just try not to blow up a bomb under our best brand.'

Cassy cleared her throat. 'Can we take a middle way here?'

'Like what?' Tony asked.

'Spread this over a couple of issues. Put the mag to bed tonight, just focusing on the Orcadian Clock and other facts as we know them. Then ahead of the next issue, use our web content to be more speculative. Kick around some of the theories Gill is working on.'

'I could live with that', said Tony. 'We could pose some of these big questions in this issue, then lay it all out in the next mag and leave it to the readers to make up their own minds.'

All eyes turned to Gill while he considered Cassy's proposal. 'As long as we address the issue of public safety. We need to expose what's going on at ScoCion. Straight away. In the mag we close tonight.'

The room fell silent for a few moments. 'And what if ultimately you're proved wrong?' said Tony. 'What if the configuration of the Orcadian stones turns out to be a random pattern? What if your friend David simply died in a tragic accident?'

Gill shrugged. 'It'll be on me, and I'll take the fall.'

While everyone in the room held their breath, Tony's stern expression fixed on Gill. '*Mys.Scot* is a company asset. We'll go with Cassy's suggestion, but if this goes belly up, all three of us are on the hook for it.'

Gill reached out across the desk and grasped Tony's outstretched hand. 'Agreed.'

Tony glanced at this watch. 'Almost the weekend. Gill, Cassy, I think you have a magazine to finish.'

Chapter 42

Dundee - one month later

When issue sixteen went to press, early data suggested it would be the highest-selling issue ever. Tony was delighted, as the Orkney stories pulled in rafts of readers who'd never tried the magazine before. But for everyone working on *Mys.Scot*, it was a humbling experience. Mainstream media mocked their reports, and some regular readers cancelled their subscriptions. Most humiliating of all, one major retail chain removed the magazine from its *Special Interests* section and repositioned it in *Comic books*. Gill watched the credibility he'd built up during the Waterhorse discovery evaporate in a few short weeks. ScoCion threatened to sue, but withdrew when the Health & Safety Inspectorate published a damning report. Testing in the ion beam chamber halted, pending a thorough inquiry scheduled for later in the year.

Public criticism was only one part of Gill's troubles. For four weeks, he had lived with the consequences of accepting Raphael's gift. He'd known the sword was symbolic of a holy book, several thousand years old and laced with meaning, explicit and obscure. Learning how to bear the sword meant understanding the book. So he read its histories, its stories, songs and letters. It should be simple, he told himself. He'd tackle it a piece at a time and see where it took him. Then, three weeks after his return from Orkney, the thing exploded. It started when he saw a theme emerging during his reading that linked to something he'd seen elsewhere. He dug deeper, and many more related passages presented themselves, spinning off in multiple directions, but piece by piece, building to the same end narrative in a cypher more complex than Brodgar. Reeling, Gill realised he could read this book for a thousand years and only scratch at the surface of its meaning. And yet, what he did comprehend now changed his world. A day came when he confronted three interlinked stories; a ram in a thicket, a prophet tossed into the sea, a rabbi nailed to a cross. He laughed at the irony. Cried at the implications. And he sat, reading, in a bar, until the weary staff asked him to go home. Rather than get a taxi back to his flat in Broughty Ferry, he took himself back to the *Mys.Scot* office and let himself in. He sat at his desk and read all night.

Early the following morning, he was standing in line for a breakfast takeaway. He realised he was shaking, and he wondered if it was exhaustion. He bought his food and started to walk across the city centre, having a rhetorical conversation in his head. When he'd been walking for an hour, he discerned the other half of the discussion was a gentler, more intelligent and far-seeing mind than his. Convinced he was having some kind of breakdown, he sat on a wall. And as he closed his eyes, the voice continued. It told him a story of a time, still in the future. A story of personal suffering, defeats, and an ultimate victory he could reach for. And it spoke of Gill and Salina's role in what was to come.

'Why us?' Gill shouted in his mind. 'Why me? Why Salina?'

'Because', said the voice. 'You are willing to be rescued.'

'Are ye gaun'ae eat tha', pal', said a different voice beside him.

Gill returned to himself and remembered the cold, sticky package in his hands. He looked up to find Barcode Charlie peering down at him.

'A'm on ma wey tae wirk. Wis gaun'ae buy a piece but looks like ye got tha' goin' spare.'

'It's cold now, Charlie, but you're welcome to it.'

'Cheers, pal', said Charlie, pocketing the pack and rubbing his hands on his jeans. 'Ye look like ye seen a ghaist.'

'Yeah', said Gill rubbing his face. 'Though, I'm not sure "ghost" is the word I'd pick.'

Charlie's smile was cheeky without being insulting. 'A wee bird says ye teuk the swuird.'

As Gill thought about the weapon Raphael had handed him, he could feel the full weight of it resting in his right hand. 'Aye. I did.'

Charlie's chin dropped to his chest as he nodded deeply. For a moment, Gill thought his tough-looking acquaintance looked faintly empathetic. 'Solomon wants tae meet ye.'

'And who is this enigmatic, Solomon?'

'Soly will tell you whan you're ready. Texted me the morn and telt me whaur tae find ye.'

Gill threw up a weary shrug. 'I've been wandering around the city. How could he know where I'd be?'

Charlie cocked his head and peered at Gill. 'Man, you're in way ower your heid.'

'Do you think I should meet this Solomon?'

'Aye, the suiner the better. Tell ye whit's really goin' on.'

Gill was too tired to argue. 'Okay. Let's do it.'

'Soon. Soly'll text ye.'

'See you then, Charlie.'

Charlie winked at Gill, then walked away.

Chapter 43

Editorial comment, Mysterious Scotland, Issue 16.

A few weeks ago, I found myself on Orkney attending a memorial for an old friend. Tragic, you say, but people die every day, and many good people go before their time. Someday we'll all go to our graves, never to be heard from again. But now I find myself asking, is that true?

I've had reason lately to reconsider Christianity's claim that a believer can achieve life after death. The experiences that led me to that are very personal and don't have a place on these pages. Suffice to say, if God does exist, he's probably speaking to each one of us right now in our own individual way.

For my friend David, his experience was so profound, so incredible; his story demands to be told. His body is dead now, and whether his soul is in heaven or not, that's between him and his maker. But believe me when I say that after his apparent death, David did live again.

A few weeks before his accident, I visited David at his work at ScoCion, an advanced research facility on Orkney. And I was grateful for the hospitality shown to me by that organisation. While I was there, I also found time for a local archaeological mystery. An artefact turned up that left the good folk of Historic Scotland scratching their heads. They showed me a symbol carved in stone, the use of which dates from a particular time in history. But they had discovered it in a place suggesting a much earlier date. I was just as foxed. But then someone slipped me a book full of mathematical puzzling. Its meaning was closed to me until I got it into the hands of one of the technical staff on Mys.Scot. Then, gradually, its clues started to emerge.

To understand where I'm going with this, you first need to grasp the context. Orkney-based ScoCion is a particle physics laboratory charged by its sponsors to develop faster-than-light communications technology. Their machinery is sophisticated, their people are among the brightest in their field and their goal is ambitious. But in a routine experiment, my friend David Trevelyan was vaporised. The authorities arrived and carried out an investigation. The first draft of their report identified the cause of the accident, and ScoCion has been appropriately chastised. But I believe ScoCion still has important questions to answer. Until then, I urge the authorities to suspend all work at ScoCion until they can fully assess the implications of this research.

In the pages that follow, I will explain my belief that David did not die on the day of the accident. Instead, I believe he was carried back in time, some four thousand years, where he found himself in ancient Orcadian society, and lived out the rest of his natural life in that place. Then, contrary to local culture, his people buried David's body at the centre of a Neolithic structure known as the Ring of Brodgar. That's a preposterous claim, and you'll demand evidence before you believe me. That evidence lies in a series of articles in this month's issue. Quite simply, it's all in the stones. We'll tell you the facts that we know for sure. And we'll tell where we're speculating. Some of this is pure science. The rest is so subjective, you'll only know if it's true by listening to your heart.

This is my sixteenth issue as editor of Mys.Scot, and its development has included the most challenging weeks of my life. I'm so grateful to have at my side one of the finest teams in investigative publishing and our readers who have become our volunteer army of clue finders, fact-checkers and code breakers; fans of the enigmatic, ambiguous and obscure. Best of all, we have Alba, dark and ancient. It's my belief she will continue to yield her secrets, for she is, Mysterious Scotland, and the best is yet to come.

The End

If you have enjoyed 'The Stone Cypher', I would be so grateful if you could leave a review on the site where you bought the book. And please stay in touch. This story is going to get a whole lot bigger in the months to come.

Tormod Cockburn

The next adventure is ...

This Jagged Way

Following the coronation of Charles III, Scotland's most revered artefact, 'The Stone of Destiny' arrives at its long term home in Perth Museum. Desperate to rebuild his shattered credibility, Gill McArdle is working hard on several stories along the Firth of Forth. But he's presented with a problem when the discovery of an ancient inscription revealed in a ruined church throws question marks against the authenticity of The Stone. On the trail of an old, old story, Gill finds himself opposed by someone prepared to kill to prevent the truth being revealed. Obstructed at every turn, Gill realises his discovery exposes a stark choice – for him, and all of Scotland.

Join the Reader's Syndicate at TormodCockburn.com
Or Click on any of the thumbnails

Mysterious Scotland Reader's Syndicate

Join our Readers Syndicate at TormodCockburn.com for new publication alerts and for free material. We'll shortly be adding more free material, exclusively available to members of the Syndicate.

Mys.Scot

Acknowledgements

Let's hear it for libraries! In my case, especially the Mitchell Library in Glasgow. A grand edifice full of astonishing detail you won't find anywhere on the internet. And the wonderful librarians who help us navigate it all. Also, to Michael Ward for his inspirational research of CS Lewis in his book, The Narnia Code.

My thanks to friends and family who read early drafts of this book. Especially to Audrey, proof-reader in chief, biscuit-bringer and most precious sounding-board. Finally, to the good people of Orkney, forever cheerful, even in the most dismal weather, with wry smiles on their faces because they know they live amongst legends.

Printed in Great Britain
by Amazon

25400465R00212